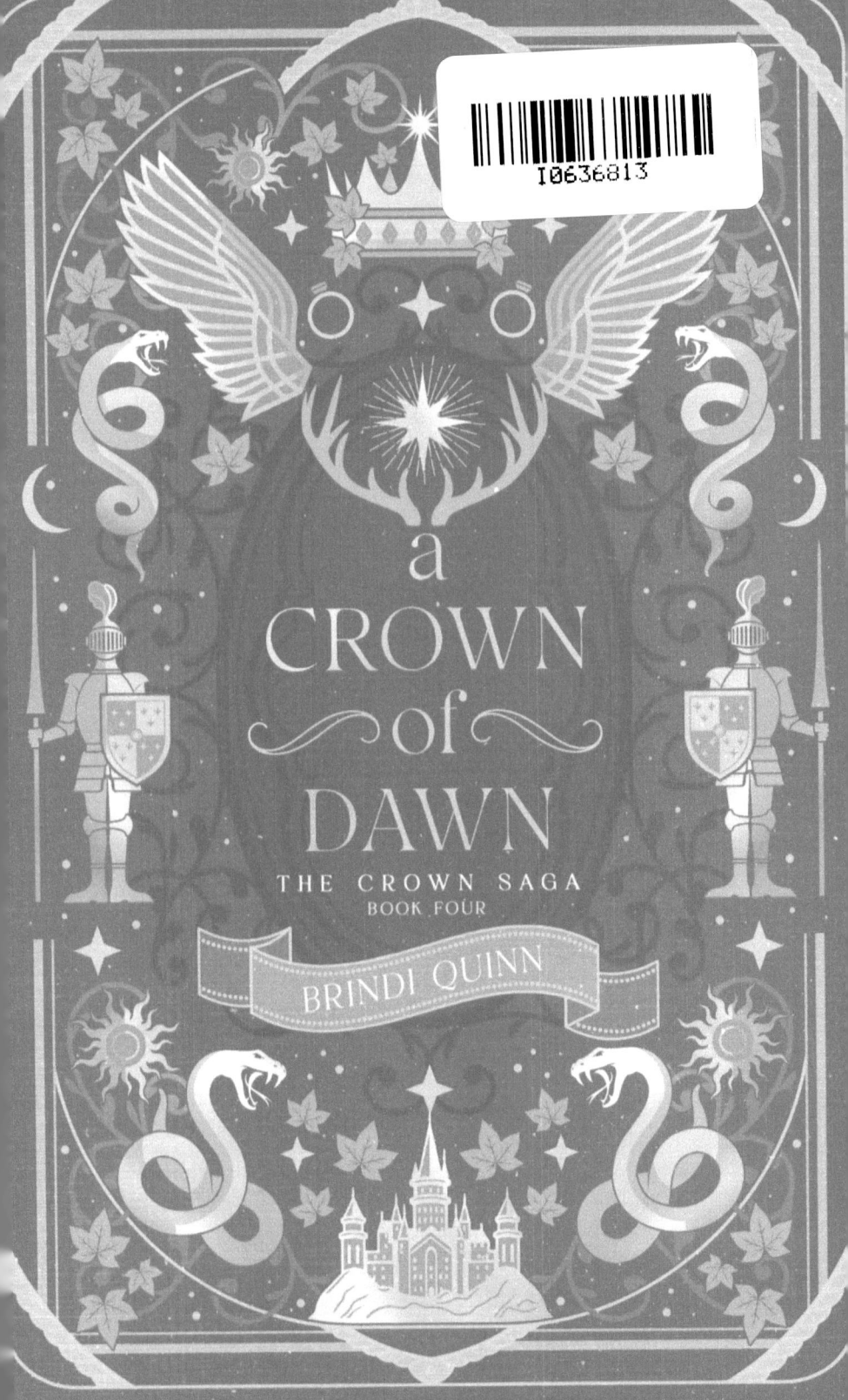

a
CROWN
of
DAWN

THE CROWN SAGA
BOOK FOUR

BRINDI QUINN

A Crown of Dawn
Copyright © 2021 by Brindi Quinn
Re-Crowned Edition, 2025

N & E

Published by Never & Ever Publishing | @neverandeverbooks
Edited by Meg Dailey | @thedaileyeditor
Cover and title by Saint Jupiter | @saintjupit3rgr4phic
Artwork by Natascia Mora | @moranatascia
Maps by Centaur Maps | @centaurmaps
Interior by Brindi Quinn via Vellum

ISBN (Paperback): 978-1-949222-98-2

A CROWN OF DAWN

Originally published April 30, 2021.
Lovingly revised, refreshed, and re-crowned in 2025.

SERIES READING ORDER

Book One: *A Crown of Echoes*
Book Two: *A Crown of Reveries*
Book Three: *A Crown of Felling*
Book Four: *A Crown of Dawn*

For all who wield their scars as crowns—your story matters.

CONTENT WARNING

The Crown Saga contains references to child abuse, child trafficking, and exploitation, which—though not depicted in graphic detail—may still be distressing for some readers. The series also features moderate to graphic violence, large-scale battles, and occasional body horror, including monstrous transformations. Romantic and sexual content ranges from mild innuendo to explicit scenes. Additional sensitive topics include coarse language, alcohol use, magical coercion, emotional manipulation, and pregnancy depicted under perilous circumstances.

DRAMATIS PERSONAE

THE QUEENS & THEIR COURTS

- **Merrin Iralore (22)** — Queen of **the Crag**. Compassionate, irreverent, devoted to putting an end to the cycle of destruction once and for all; wields both halves of the Nemophile's Crown and an alchemist's practiced hand. Hopelessly in love with her best friend's knight.
- **Beau Lysavere (23)** — Queen of **the Clearing** and Merrin's sister-in-crown. Regal, freckled, unfailingly composed. Expecting twins.
- **Sestilia of the Cove (26)** — Former bearer of Exitium and the Nemophile's Crown. Sea-queen with a mind that turns like riptides—lonely, lethal, fiercely devoted to Merrin, and only half-fond of Beau. Once dragged Merrin back from the brink of death.

KNIGHTS & ALLIES

- **Sir Windley of the South (25)** — Beau's infamous guard, grappling with resurfaced demons. Hair flickers through prismatic hues while shadow-sharp instincts strain their leash. He'd follow Merrin clear off the map—and keep walking.

- **Sir Rafe of the North (20)** — Dutiful blade at Merrin's side. Sword crackles with fire or frost—depending when you meet him. Torn between Soleil, Luna's shadow, and a very mortal queen.
- **Edius "Edi" (late-20s)** — Broad-shouldered Spirite mimic turned honorary knight; long hair, longer secrets. Will bargain, borrow faces, or break oaths—whatever it takes to pry an old friend from a looming curse.
- **Meraflora "Flora" (late-20s)** — Warm-hearted herbalist who hid Windley after his escape. Honey-voiced, braver than she seems. Merrin created her in another life to save Windley from an unfortunate fate.
- **Gwen (age unknown)** — The quiet mystery Edius calls his fiancée. Saving her is Edius's every motive—even when he cannot find the words to explain why.
- **Mother Poppy (ancient)** — Royal tome-keeper, former regent, grandmother in all but blood.
- **Sir Albie (deceased)** — Merrin's lifelong warden and heart-father. Though his watch has ended, the wisdom he forged in her spine still marches beside every step she takes.

FOES

- **Charmagne "Charm" (mid-20s)** — Rose-haired Spirite, her temper honed to shattered glass.

Humans are "pets," Merrin's crown is the prize, and her twisted games have escalated into open war.

- **Pip "Pipsqueak" (appears ~18)** — Moon-pale prodigy who occasionally appears older than he usually looks, as if something darker lurks inside. Responsible for the death of Merrin's beloved knight.
- **"Master" Ascian (deceased)** — Lavender-eyed puppeteer who once owned Windley. Met an untimely end at the hand of the Nemophilist.

OTHER POWERS & PRESENCES

- **The Widowbirds** — Long-tailed messengers bonded to royal blood; summoned by a filigreed whistle, each note attuned to one of the Ten Northern Queens.
- **The Echoes** — Shadow-hands that obey only the Nemophile's Crown, glimpsed behind closed eyes and heard at the mind's edge.
- **The Scarlet Wood** — Living forest of blood-red leaves.
- **The Emerald Wood** — Night-bright sister-forest.

THE FOUR GODDESSES

- **Luna** — Goddess of frost, tides, and the silver moon. Once bound to Sir Rafe by oath, she now circles above like a spurned satellite.

- **Soleil** — Goddess of sun-fire and relentless dawn. From her rainbow-sherbet sanctum she branded Rafe with her flame and now watches to see whether his heart can survive the blaze.
- **Exitium** — Goddess of Destruction formerly bound to Merrin's soul. Hungers for ruin, and tempts with power that always costs more than it gives. Re-shackled to Merrin—for now.
- **Vita** — Goddess of creation and Exitium's eternal counterbalance. Gentle does not mean harmless: where Exitium devours, Vita overgrows—both can bury kingdoms—one beneath shadow, the other beneath bloom.

BLOODLINES & BEASTS

- **Drakaina** — Primeval, wing-serpent "mothers of monsters." Hatched in the same void-dawn as the goddesses but refused to bow; after losing the First War they were banished to an unwaking realm.
- **Dracons** — The first children of the Drakaina— predators forged to devour. Taller, older, hungrier than modern Spirites. Thought wiped out by angelic crusades.
- **Angels** — Star-blooded wardens created to police the mortal realm. Featherless now; their divinity lingers as embers in certain bloodlines (magicians, mostly).
- **Royals** — The original humes Vita sculpted first— held so long in her palm that a thread of divinity soaked their blood.

- **Spirites** — The second offspring of the Drakaina —adopted and re-worked by the goddesses until fangs learned flirting and hunger learned restraint.

NEMOPHILIST

Noun. A wanderer drawn to the enchantment of forests; one who finds solace among trees and deep woods.

THE *Queendoms*

SNOWY
NORTH

QUEENDOM
OF THE
CLOUDFALL

QUEENDOM
OF THE
CANYON

QUEENDOM
OF THE
CACTI

DESERT

QUEENDOM
OF THE
CRATER

WILDERNESS

QUEENDOM
OF THE
CRYSTALLINE

THE CRYSTAL
SEA

QUEENDOM
OF THE
COTTONWOOD

QUEENDOM
OF THE
CURRANT

THE SCARLET
WOOD

FOREST
FORTRESS

QUEENDOM
OF THE
CLEARING

QUEENDOM
OF THE
CRAG

INN

QUEENDOM
OF THE
COVE

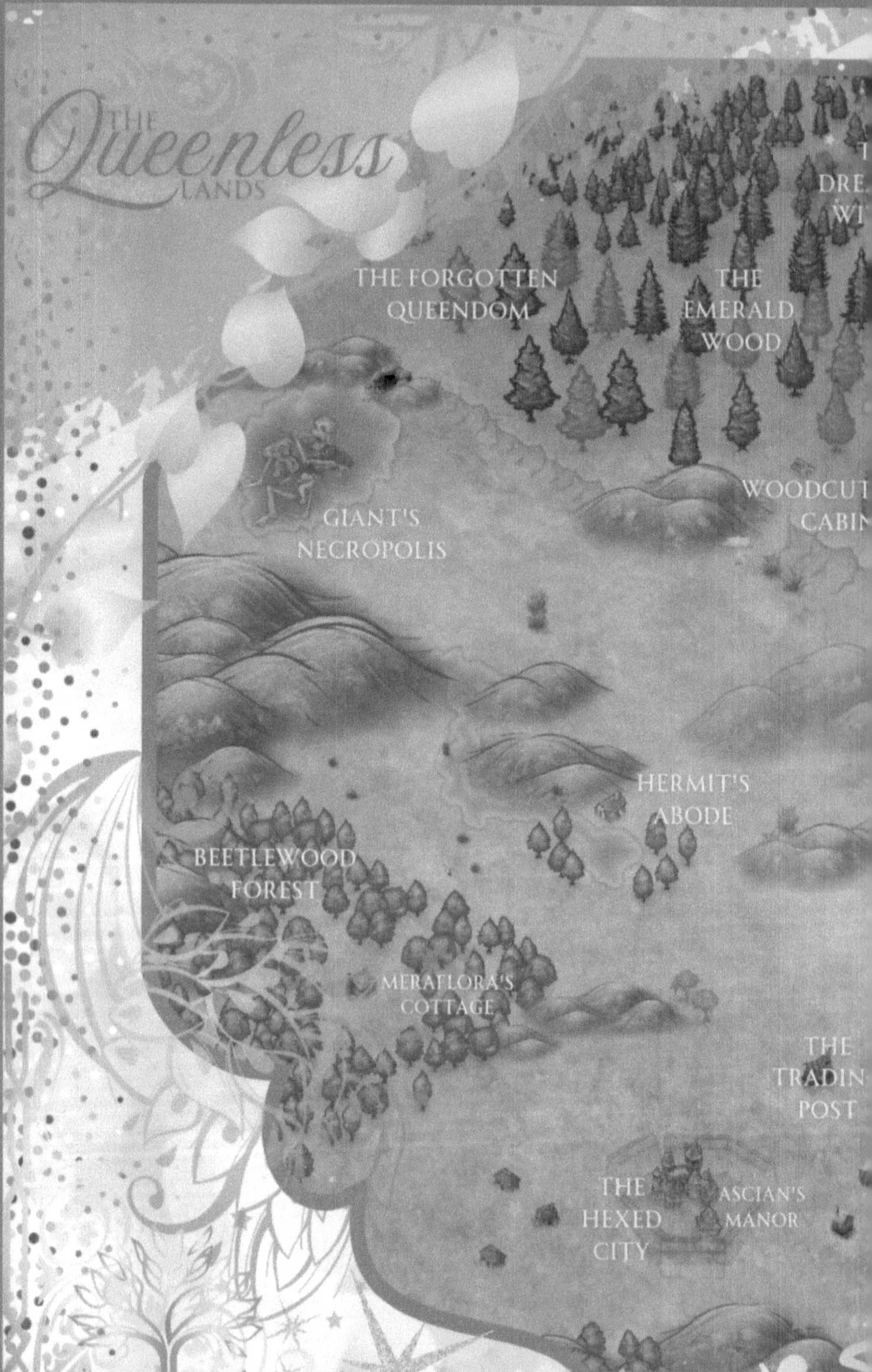

THE Queenless LANDS
THE FORGOTTEN QUEENDOM
THE EMERALD WOOD
GIANT'S NECROPOLIS
HERMIT'S ABODE
BEETLEWOOD FOREST
MERAFLORA'S COTTAGE
THE HEXED CITY
ASCIAN'S MANOR

THE
WILLOW
GROVE

THE GOLDEN
FIELDS

THE
EDGE OF
NOWHERE

THE BLUE
FLOWER
FIELDS

SOUTHERN
SPIRITE
CITIES

CONTENTS

PREVIOUSLY IN A CROWN OF FELLING...

After the events in the gem-studded cavern, bathed in dawn's light, Sestilia's castle descended into chaos. Windley carried me swiftly through halls in search of a healer, stepping over incapacitated guests now freed from their hexes. Along the way, he alerted Rafe and Beau, and though I protested their leaving the safety of their chambers, they followed.

Beau commanded her cavalry to secure Albie's body and initiate a search for Charm and Pip—two enemies notoriously elusive, able to change their appearances at will. And they weren't hiding their power. Windley tensed repeatedly as he carried me, eyes anxiously flicking over his shoulder.

He waited until I was safely settled in the castle's healing chambers, laid carefully in a bed near Sestilia.

She was alive but weak, exactly as I'd been after releasing Exitium. She would recover, and I would see her in a new light. Unstable or not, she had merit, as I'd told the echoes days ago. Even the darkest souls held the potential for redemption.

"I need to go after them, love," Windley murmured, voice soothing as a lullaby.

I knew it, yet couldn't voice it without breaking.

"I'll be back before you wake, I swear," he whispered, pressing his forehead to mine.

Be careful, Wind. I couldn't speak, but he saw it clearly in my eyes.

"I'm always careful." His usual confidence failed him; he couldn't even muster a faint grin. Instead, he lowered his lips to my ear, breath warm and reassuring. "I'll help you through this, as you've helped me. Whatever it takes." His kiss on my forehead lingered, imprinting his intentions, as if leaving protective armor to shield me from the dangers still lurking beyond these walls.

Then, he slipped away.

Beau stayed by my side—beautiful, regal, freckled Beau. "Oh, Merrin. I'm so sorry." She eased the stray locks away from my forehead, a comforting, motherly gesture. "Sir Albie loved you dearly. I can't imagine the ache in your heart."

Rafe stood quietly nearby, sword still simmering with faint fire, dark curls tipped in silver. He didn't speak but placed a steady hand atop my head, standing statuesque as Beau wept— for me, for us, for the great loss both our queendoms had suffered.

Albie had been dear to many.

Hidden in my pocket was a token taken from his body. Proof, perhaps, that I wasn't who I believed myself to be—that my ties to Albie ran deeper than I'd ever imagined.

I only loved poetry because Albie had read it to me, in his grizzled voice, on countless nights when sleep refused to come.

But whose poetry had he shared with me all those times?

Through all this, Vita tried to comfort me, but I pushed her away, too bruised to accept the comfort she offered. I knew it was for the best. I knew Albie would want me to survive—it would've been senseless for both of us to fall.

My heart was broken—but my spirit endured. Albie would want me to carry forward. And so, I would.

I had promises yet to fulfill—to deliver the destroyer to the end of days so this story might still reach a happy ending.

Yet peace felt out of reach, knowing I'd never again see my knight. My heart was broken, but my faith endured—scarred, yet standing.

I wasn't alone in my grief.

Edius carried guilt heavier than chains, desperate to atone, driven to fix the unfixable. He was both hero and villain, as so many of us were, tangled in the intricate web woven from the crossings of our stories. We were driven to choose lesser evils, forced again and again to reckon with our choices, our courage, and our faith.

And Edius—he was fighting desperately for something precious, fragile, and pure.

I

EDI

This story would be better if Gwen were the one telling it. Lovely, fluttery, magical Gwen.

But, as always, captive ones, you're stuck with me.

It's good to see your faces again—lovely faces that they are. I only hope we don't cause them too much strife before we're through.

Hmm? Too much to cover in one sitting? It seems there is.

Well then, we'll do our best.

My heart had never felt heavier.

Nor had velvet curtains ever weighed so much—the ones separating me from the hopeful promise of daylight beyond the royal medical chambers, where I now lay.

Windley had returned before I awoke, as promised, allowing Beau and Rafe a reprieve from my bedside. Yet he was worn himself, slumped in a chair, head resting against the cot in an exhausted slumber. He and Edius had failed to locate Pip and Charm; the rogue siblings had scattered their power across the grounds like an impenetrable fog, cloaking their whereabouts. Whether they remained in the castle, or even the city itself, was anyone's guess.

Two days had passed, and my body was healing—physically, at least. Spiritually, the wounds were too raw and too deep—impossible to touch.

At least Sestilia had gotten her wish: bed confinement for us both. Not that she knew—her vitality was nearly completely drained, sending her into a deep slumber while Captain Delagos assumed command of the castle. The Cove's queen-in-waiting, it seemed, had vanished some time ago.

And then there was Edius.

Edius, who had stolen the life of my most beloved knight.

Edius, who hadn't dared face me since.

Edius, who—according to Windley—had retreated to the tavern with paper doors and brightly colored umbrellas, wallowing in his failure, drowning himself in drink and townsfolk eager to lie with a Spirite.

Had I forgotten anyone?

Oh, yes. The goddesses.

Both now bound to my soul, both whispering from its farthest reaches, both vying for my attention.

"I know your heart aches, little royal, but you must mend the Crown of the Wood. It is dangerous to allow the destroyer to move unchecked within you."

I pushed Vita's warmth away again, her compassion unwelcome. I didn't want anything Nemophile-related.

I wanted only to forget everything that had happened in the spider queen's chambers.

"Merrin?" Windley stirred at the foot of the bed, running a weary hand over his face. His indigo hair was tousled, eyes heavy from sleep. "Fuck, sorry. You're supposed to be the one resting."

He dragged his chair closer, eyes softened with shared pain.

"Oh, love...I can't bear it, that look in your eyes." He brushed the barest whisper of a fingertip against my temple. "May I?"

He meant to dull me.

Whatever my response would have been, it dissolved under his touch, leaving only a quiet drift behind.

The room was dark when I next woke. Windley was gone, replaced by Rafe sitting silently at my bedside.

Moonlight threaded silver through his wavy hair, the faintest ember-glow seeping from his belt. When he noticed me awake, concern rippled beneath his stoic façade.

"Your Majesty! Er—" He cleared his throat, voice lowering into a hush. "Do you need anything?"

My mouth was sandpaper-dry. "Your papers."

He blinked in confusion. "What?"

"I wish to transfer you formally to the Queendom of the Clearing. And I wish to do it now. Fetch me your release papers, Rafe, so I can sign them."

"That can wait, Your Majesty—" He startled slightly. "Your Majesty!"

Poor Rafe. Always the least adept at handling emotion, and yet—I'd chosen him as my victim of release. Perhaps precisely because I knew it wouldn't wound him the way it would the others.

I clung to him, trembling, soaking his shirt with my grief.

Awkwardly, he placed a careful hand upon my head and turned his gaze respectfully aside, allowing me space to shatter.

His presence was calming. Solid. A lighthouse standing

resolute against stormy seas, or an ancient tree rooted deeply, unshakable even amidst the fiercest of winds.

And then, after some time had passed—

"A knight's greatest honor is to fall for his queen." Rafe's voice was subdued, thoughtful. "He said that often, you know. To every new recruit."

Such a painfully Albie thing to say.

Rafe's shirt patiently bore my tears, until at last my body could no longer endure the ache of bending.

The next time my eyes opened, they opened to something strange.

In the dimness of the chamber, a figure stood motionless at the foot of Sestilia's bed.

A striking man, broad-shouldered, hair long as a maiden's.

Edius.

He had finally come.

It was the creak that woke me—the creak of his hand pressing into the mattress as he lowered his mouth to the sleeping queen's forehead.

"E—Edius?" My voice cracked. "Are you marking Sestilia?"

At my words, he froze.

He turned slowly, glancing back behind him—where two of Sestilia's guards and one of Beau's lay incapacitated.

I shifted upright.

"You're...not Edius."

The figure straightened in one gradual stretch.

"Pip?" I ventured. "Is that you?"

The impostor retreated toward the door, coal-black eyes fixed to mine, glittering like cut obsidian in the gloom.

Holding his stare, I discreetly formed a fist beneath the

blankets, willing the tree in the corner's branches to harden to spear-points—

But the impostor fled before I could strike.

"Windley! Rafe!"

Windley answered first, bursting through an adjacent door. "Merrin! What's wrong? I stepped out to relieve mys—" His gaze caught the fallen guards. "*Damn!* Who was it?"

"I'm nearly certain it was Pip! He just ran out, disguised as Edius!"

"ARGH! I've had it with these games! It's impossible to feel them clearly in all this haze!"

He glanced rapidly from me to the door, debating whether to leave me unprotected.

In response, I willed the tree's sharpest branch to lance through the empty air—a deliberate display of strength.

"I'll be back," he vowed.

And he was gone, chasing a ghost through shadowed halls.

I remained behind, guarding Sestilia's sleeping form, wondering what Pip could possibly gain by marking her.

Two more castle guards soon stormed into the chamber, dispatched by Windley. They moved swiftly, tending their fallen comrades and checking the sleeping queen's safety.

Meanwhile, I stole cautious glances beneath my bandages at the wound in my chest—an ugly, raw thing, far too deep. A living person shouldn't bear such a mark, shouldn't lose so much blood and live.

"Do not squander this gift given to you by the elder knight—"

I silenced Vita immediately.

Windley returned shortly, breathless and frustrated. "Lost him—he vanished in the damned fog." He rushed to my side. "He didn't hurt you, did he?"

I shook my head, quickly recounting what I had witnessed.

"The fruitcake?" Windley cast a wary glance at Sestilia, as if she might leap from her sleep and strike. "Why?"

A question neither of us could answer.

"Argh! This is maddening! What's their goal? Blasting their power at all hours, clashing like angry waves. And it doesn't help that fucking Edmond refuses to come here and stand guard. I mean, I get his guilt, but you'd think he'd rather make amends than...whatever he's doing. The inn has a line out the damned door!"

"Send for him," I said quietly. "Tell him I wish to speak with him."

"Merr..." Windley frowned uncertainly. "Are you sure that's—"

"Send for him."

"Of course, my queen. But I doubt he'll come."

"Tell him I'm prepared to deliver his punishment."

Windley paused at that, lips twisting thoughtfully. "Yeah, that might do it." He lingered by my bedside, searching my face. "Rafe said you woke earlier, when I stepped away. Please know, love, my only desire is to stay at your side. But things are chaotic right now, and I'm the only one sensitive enough to feel their power—"

"I know," I murmured. "It's fine."

But the way he looked at me—it was as if he wanted to absorb my grief entirely through his gaze alone.

"Let me know, Merr...when you're ready."

He took my fingers like a lost relic, pressing tender kisses to each knuckle. "I'm here, understand? Right here. So tell me, whenever you're ready to heal."

But I wasn't ready.

"I'll get you help, so your focus won't be split," I said. "Send for Edius, and I'll convince him myself."

Windley's expression darkened, sadness etched deeply into every line of his face.

Still, he nodded. "Alright."

Then he left me in the care of strangers.

Strangers were easier.

Strangers didn't look at me like that.

"Queen Merrin?" One of the guards approached, offering the same concoction they'd been giving Sestilia to keep her sleeping, keep her healing.

I declined it.

Instead, I wrapped myself tightly in pain and grief, drifting once more into sleep—empty, dreamless, and dark.

"Merr?"

Windley's whisper pulled me from the abyss. From a world where I'd forgotten what happened. A world where Albie still existed—or perhaps never had.

"Windley."

His face hovered into focus, hair a dismal gray.

"Any news?"

"None," he said softly. "The ripples have gone still. But let me worry about that. How's your chest feel? The medic says you're healing."

It hurt.

"I feel fine."

He knew I was lying.

"Queen Beau stayed with you all day. She said you've been tossing."

"Did they say when I can get out of bed?" I diverted.

He pressed a cool hand to my forehead. "A lot of your vitality's going into sealing that wound." His opposite hand hovered carefully over my bandages. "A few more days, I'd guess."

I placed my hand over his. "And how do you feel, Wind?" It was a sticky question, one I only now felt strong enough to voice. "I know you're grieving too. The thing that happened... It's hard on all of us. How are you?"

"Oh, darling." He rested his forehead against mine, a quiet benediction. "Don't worry about me."

He stayed like that for a long while.

It was difficult.

Opening my eyes each time, knowing I'd wake to a world where my dearest knight no longer breathed.

But each time I did, I felt as if I were collecting pieces of my fractured heart.

Tiny fragments, scattered. Slowly reforming into something that might someday resemble a whole.

I wasn't the only one fractured.

Windley, Beau, Rafe—all bound by their love for Albie. They carried him in their hearts.

Yet there was one among us fractured for another reason entirely.

"There's something else," Windley intoned, forehead still pressed to mine. "He came. Edius. He's in the hall. Are you sure you want to see him?"

"I'm sure."

Windley hesitated. "I know that heart of yours, Merr. Don't...feel like you have to forgive him right away. Even knowing he did it to protect you, you still have every right to your feelings. If you need contempt, then feel contempt. Be selfish, queenie. Just this once. Whatever it takes to heal the wounds gauze can't fix, okay?"

Windley kissed me sweetly, then sent the other guards from the room, allowing Edius to enter.

Poor, broken Edius.

The thewy Spirite looked even worse than Windley—ragged, hollow-eyed, barely holding himself upright. He wouldn't meet my eyes as he shuffled into the room. And then there was—

"Edius! Your hair! It's...violet?"

Because he was making no effort to maintain it.

"Meh?" The dull word barely passed his lips; his gaze flickered toward me for just an instant.

I could feel it—the ache of his heart, deeper than Windley's, deeper than Beau's or Rafe's. His heart, once cold and dormant, throbbed heavily with unbearable regret. Shame. Guilt for what he had done to Albie. Sorrow for Gwen slipping through his fingers once again.

Edius was wounded. Just as I was wounded. Just as we all were.

As Windley sank wearily into a visitor's chair near Sestilia's bed, Edius approached—eyes everywhere but on me—before settling at the foot of my cot. He seized the bed frame, leaning forward with a deep exhale.

"Sorry I didn't come sooner. I was..." He faltered.

"Bedding everyone in the queendom?" I said under my breath.

His grip tightened, knuckles whitening. "Trying to draw out Charm and Pip." He released a slow, frustrated breath, loosening his hold. "They...didn't take the bait."

Ah. So that was it.

"Come here, Edius."

His eyes met mine fleetingly before he reluctantly pushed himself closer. "How you feeling?" he asked, glancing at my bandages.

"I'm all right."

"Sure you are." He struggled for words. "I've been thinking

about what to say, but I've got nothing. Keep thinking I could've pushed your grandad knight away. Could've forced him down instead of...what I did."

Yes. I'd considered all those scenarios too.

"If you had done that, I would have perished," I told him. "I'm only alive because I accepted Albie's remaining life into myself."

"I know...but..." His voice was hoarse. "I smelled hex in there. Thought it stuck to me from dealing with those party guests. If I'd realized sooner it was your knight, maybe..."

Ignoring the pain in my chest, I shifted carefully to the edge of the bed.

"Merrín?!" Edius yelped, casting a worried glance at Windley. "Shouldn't you stay put?"

Contempt? Selfishness? Perhaps they would help me forget, help me rebuild. But there were other ways to heal.

Hearts are fickle, uncontrollable things. Sometimes the key to healing your own heart is comforting the heart of another.

"Edi." I reached for him, grasping his shoulder, pulling him close until he pressed gently against my trussed chest, the fabric hiding crimson stains. "It hurts me to feel your heart so wounded. Please, divest it."

At first, he resisted, stiff as stone. Then, gradually—hesitantly—he melted into me, like someone carefully lowering a heavy anchor.

Edius was not a person who had been held often in his life. His breath trembled as he clutched the small of my back, fingers twitching against the fabric.

"Punish me," he rasped, too low for Windley to catch. "You're supposed to punish me."

"To punish you would do nothing for my grief," I replied, my words scarcely louder than a sigh. "Nor for your guilt."

His breath hitched, jagged in his throat.

I let Vita's light wash over me—the same light I had pushed away these past days. I opened myself to it now, allowed it to fill me, not for my sake, but for his.

As the light flowed from me into Edius, he gripped me tighter. "I'm so sorry, highness."

"I forgive you," I whispered. "And someday, I'll thank you, though I'm not strong enough yet."

He held me, and I held him, grief shared between breaths, until his heartbeat quieted like a calming sea.

Mine felt lighter too. Not whole, but closer to it than before.

When he finally pulled away, hand braced on the bed, face level with mine, something softer touched his gaze. "Sorry I've kept my distance," he admitted. "Didn't know how to face you. Struggling to accept they got away. Worried about Gwen."

I reached up, carefully tucking the amethyst strands of hair behind his scarred ear. "Will you rejoin my guard, Edius? Windley needs you. I need you. Together we'll find them. We'll free Gwen, and we'll have vengeance for Albie. Together, alright? You're not alone."

His expression wavered. Slowly, he nodded. Again, more firmly. Then, compelled by something beyond himself, he leaned forward and pressed his lips softly to my cheek.

"Yes...My Queen."

His first time calling me such.

And as he spoke, his heart did beat—for me—twice. This time I let it slide, and as he withdrew, his hair transitioned smoothly back to its usual color.

"Get cleaned up, yes? Then report to Windley." I offered a small, tired smile. "I'll heal as fast as I can, so we can pursue them."

He waited a breath, then left.

The moment the door clicked shut, I collapsed against the

sheets. Exerting Vita's power was a lot for someone with as little vitality as I had now.

Windley was beside me in an instant, springing toward the bed. "Lion queen!" He helped resettle me, disapproval etched clearly on his features. "Always for others, Merr. What about you?"

"I meant what I said," I hummed quietly. "Making him suffer wouldn't heal my grief. We needed him stable. To help you."

Windley sighed heavily, resignation softening his eyes. Then he took my hands sympathetically between his own. "Speaking of your grief..." His voice was low. "Unburden it, Merrin. Let it fall on me. Use me as you let others use you."

Not yet.

And I hated that my inability to do so caused him pain.

"Hold me, Windley," I whispered. "It'll help me more than you know."

Something he could do. Something that would make him feel useful. Something that would warm the abyss I saw whenever I closed my eyes.

Contact could be a remedy all its own.

Windley obliged. He set aside his hatchets, shed his guard's jacket and boots, and slipped into the cot beside me.

The warmth of his chest was steady against my cheek— solid, safe. For the first time in days, I felt grounded, grateful for his stalwart presence more than ever. I told him so, and he pulled me closer, his body's heat chasing away the cold grief had left behind.

Wrapped in him, I drifted into healing sleep.

I awoke to commotion.

2

THE LAST FAREWELL

"You must stay still, Queen Sestilia!"

"Merrin! I want to see Merrin! Unhand me, Cardory!"

A lovely little whirlwind tackled me before Beau or Windley could stop her.

I raised a calming hand. "It's all right."

The pair exchanged wary glances as Sestilia climbed eagerly onto my bed.

"Merrin! They said you got hurt! Can I see?" She poked at my bandages with wide, curious eyes. "Ooh, that's a juicy one. Were you stabbed? What sort of blade? How deep? By whom?"

By whom?

By someone I'd trusted most.

I swallowed the ache. "It's a long story," I said with care. "What do you remember, Sestilia?"

"I had entirely too much fun at my birthday, and I fell ill," she explained casually, her hair dripping into the surrounding sheets. "My digestion is dreadfully delicate—why else would I remain so tragically thin?"

"Wait, you don't remem—"

Windley cleared his throat loudly behind her, flashing me an empty vial before swiftly slipping it into his pocket.

A memory elixir.

Probably for the best.

"It was a grand party indeed, Sestilia," I smoothly amended. "And I must thank you. You were quite intoxicated, so you might not remember clearly, but you saved me from a terrible fate. I shall forever be grateful."

Her gemstone eyes shimmered brightly. "You're grateful to me?"

"Deeply."

She wrapped her arms tightly around my elbow. "Then you'll take holiday in my court!"

"I cannot just yet. There are pressing matters I must attend to first, but I promise—as surely as I returned for your birthday —I shall visit again."

She considered this, then seemed satisfied.

Of course, now that she was awake and able to command her formidable network of assassins, none of us could afford to linger.

I allowed her to stay curled up at my side that night, closely watched by Windley and Rafe, and vowed that by morning, I'd walk from this bed of my own accord—no matter how deeply the wound still ached.

"Are you certain about this, queenie?"

"Quite certain," I assured my favorite knave. "It's healed enough for me to manage. We've packed ample bandages and vera—I'll be fine."

Under a heavy gray sky, we stood in the courtyard, ready to part ways with Beau and Rafe.

Edius, sobered now, wore his once-wild hair gathered neatly into a knot—an outward sign of his renewed focus.

Windley hovered anxiously at my side.

As for me, I pushed away every thought that plagued me: the conflicting whispers at the edge of my mind, the persistent ache in my chest, the sting of loss buried deep in my heart.

We'd decided it was safest to leave in the early hours, before the spider queen awoke from her beauty rest—especially after an awkward dinner the night prior, rivaling only our first meal at the Cove.

Pip and Charm's ripples had begun again, west of the queendom this time—urgent and furious.

Luring us in.

We would oblige, putting an end to this tiresome chase once and for all.

Only then would I heed Vita's voice.

Only then would I unite the halves of the Nemophile's Crown.

Only then would I fulfill my promise to deliver the destroyer to the end of days.

"I wish I could join you," said Beau, pretty and freckled as ever, pressing her face against my neck. "I know I'm not a fighter, but I—"

"You're already doing me a great service by looking after my queendom, Beau. My cousin-regent Lekhana must be overwhelmed by now, and Saxon as well." I discreetly handed her an envelope, sealed with emerald wax. "Deliver this to Mother Poppy —it's a royal decree instructing her to aid you with your secret."

I placed a gentle hand over her belly, where magical twins grew.

"She will help you conceal it and arrange for someone in the Crag's kin to pose as their father."

Only one matter remained.

"Rafe's transfer papers," I prompted. "Where are they?"

"I nearly forgot!" Beau rummaged through her bag and produced a roll of parchment bearing her royal seal.

Instead of calling Rafe forward—

"Windley, come forth and kneel before me," she commanded softly.

Windley gave me a questioning glance, hesitation flickering briefly before he gracefully lowered himself to one knee before his queen.

It stirred strange emotions in me, seeing him genuflect before another, though he'd done so countless times before.

There he was—a demon disguised as a rogue—kneeling on the courtyard grass, his posture just shallow enough to tease propriety, those dark eyes a mix of wariness and wonder.

And then—

Magicians weren't the only ones who could invoke magic words.

"By order of the royal family of the Queendom of the Clearing, I, Queen Beau of the Clearing, hereby release you, Windley of the South, from all oath and fealty to the Queendom of the Clearing." Beau's voice resonated clearly and warmly. "From this day forth, let it be known that you are henceforth a citizen, loyal subject, and royal guard of the Queendom of the Crag and its sovereign ruler, Queen Merrin of the Crag."

Windley froze, visibly stunned.

Beau smiled fondly, giving Windley's head a playful tap with the parchment. "Here, Windley. I've already sent for it to be officially filed. Give this copy to your new queen, and take good care of her."

He accepted the document with unsteady fingers, unrolling it until the release lay clear before him.

A breath escaped; he dipped into a deep bow. Then—with quiet reverence—he lifted Beau's hand and brushed a kiss to the ring that bore her crest.

"Thank you, Your Highness," he said, voice hoarse. "Serving you has been an honor."

"An honor?" Beau laughed lightly, eyes sparkling. "Have you grown manners on your journeys, Windley?"

He raised his head then, eyes glistening and bright with mischief, the softness beneath unmistakable. Without warning, he leapt to his feet and charged toward me, scooping me gently around the waist—careful of my bandages—as laughter spilled from his lips. He spun me around, our joy lifting us both until the world blurred away.

When he finally set me down, he didn't stop there.

Windley sank deeply once more onto his knee, this time at my feet, his expression earnest, adoring.

"You'll never be rid of me again, my queen." His voice wavered, sincerity clear in every word.

Nor would I ever wish to be.

In that precious moment, everything else faded—the grief, the weight, the shadows of loss. Pure happiness blossomed within me, warmed by the sight of Windley before me, officially mine at last.

With tender devotion, he kissed my hand.

Then my lips, tenderly, lingering as though afraid the dream might fade.

And finally, with the utmost care, he pressed a kiss to my forehead, slipping the transfer papers securely into my pocket.

The Crag's newest knight, and forever mine.

Knight.

Knight.

I shoved that thought aside, turning a grateful smile to my dear friend.

"Thank you, Beau. But what about Rafe's papers?"

"Ah, yes. About that..."

Rafe stepped forward, composed. "Not yet, Your Majesty. Not until we return."

My gaze flicked uncertainly between them. "Return from where?"

"Rafe's going with you," Beau declared, her tone leaving no room for argument. "You'll need all the help you can get. If I cannot accompany you, allow me at least to send my heart."

Rafe grimaced as Windley and Edius exchanged amused glances.

"Hear that, angel boy?" Windley teased. "You're Queen Beau's heart now. Try not to flutter too hard."

Rafe's eyebrow twitched in annoyance.

Beau's laugh bubbled out, light and unrestrained, at their antics.

"Be safe, Merrin, my dearest friend," she whispered, holding me snugly once more. "I'll be waiting."

Windley's hand settled at my back as Beau and Rafe exchanged their final farewells, and Edius went to retrieve a certain troublesome stag from the Cove's stables.

"Queenie?" Windley said my nickname in a hush, as though sharing a secret.

I leaned my head against his shoulder. "Wind?"

"You're gripping so tightly, I can feel it." He meant my soul, no doubt. "We could delay our departure a few hours...talk it through?"

I had grieved with Rafe, and I had grieved with Edius. But

grieving with Windley would be different. Deeper. Something I wasn't ready for.

"I'm just glad you're officially mine, my gallant," I deflected.

Windley sighed, disappointment quietly threaded through his breath, though he masked it swiftly with his favorite teasing tone. "If we were alone, I'd show you exactly how glad I am."

I was fragile—my heart was a shattered thing held together by thin glue. I knew I'd share my grief with him eventually. Soon. But not today.

"Ugh! What's wrong with this thing?" Edius's voice interrupted as he struggled with an unruly stag. "No amount of charm works! It's like trying to beguile a gods-damned squirrel!"

"A rantipole stag for a rantipole queen," Windley mused, drumming his fingers lightly against the small of my back before releasing me.

"Ruckus!" I ran to my beloved beast, flinging my arms around his thick neck, grateful he would be joining us from here on out. "Have you been a good boy, Ruck? Of course, you have—but you look a bit plump. Have you been eating too much?" I poked playfully at his soft side.

Animals are comfort incarnate—souls quiet, affection honest. They listen even when there's nothing to say.

Ruckus accepted me as though no time had passed at all, as though he understood why I had left him and had simply waited patiently for my return.

I was just leaning into his warmth when I felt a firm hand slide around my waist.

"E-Edius?"

It wasn't a gesture of affection. Instead, he slipped his hand deftly into my pocket, retrieved Windley's transfer papers, and scanned them keenly before handing the parchment back without a word.

"Ed?"

He offered no explanation, merely turned away to collect his belongings.

And so it was, beneath the gray sky, that a queen, two Spirites, and a flame-wielding magician prepared for their departure—one final time.

3

SUN DAYS

Charm's bursts of power—and Pip's too—were radiating from a single location in the west, where the Cove's domain bled into the Queendom of the Crater.

The northlands housed ten queendoms: Clearing, Crag, Cacti, Cove, Canyon, Crystalline, Cloudfall, Cottonwood, Currant, and Crater. And the only person I knew who had visited all ten...

I touched my chest, where two coral pendants now dangled side by side, their chains tangled in ways they shouldn't have been.

Albie...and my mother?

Was I really the product of their hidden love? True, Albie had been older than my mother, though not impossibly so.

Vita would know. My divine-stained royal blood had allowed her to exist within me—surely she could tell me whether that blood was full or half.

But I wasn't ready to ask her yet.

The pendant felt heavier somehow, weighted down by

secrets I wasn't prepared to confront. I took a deep breath, straightening in my saddle. Now wasn't the time for family mysteries. Not when enemies waited.

Windley was watching me, his gaze never straying as we passed through country villages. His greatest wish was that I might finally share my grief with him, but that was a bottle I couldn't uncork just yet. So I let him pine quietly, pretending not to notice, and shifted my attention instead to the terrain ahead.

Gradually, the Queendom of the Crater spread out before us, grassy expanses yielding to dense columns of towering evergreens. The air cooled—crisp and bracing, tinged with pine. At its heart, an ancient crater cradled the castle and court, though we wouldn't be venturing that far. Spirite power thrummed from the outskirts, where scattered cabins—built from felled pines and sealed with resin—dotted the rugged terrain. Thin trails of smoke curled skyward, carrying the scent of warmth and char.

The smell of security.

"We aren't far," Windley announced as the sun dipped below the horizon. "Maybe an hour from the source of power. Wouldn't you say, Ed?"

Edius nodded in agreement.

"Then we move at night and ambush them under cover of darkness," I decided.

The Spirites readily agreed, eager to finally confront their nemeses. But one among us had reason to hesitate.

"Wait." Rafe's amber eyes dimmed. "A word, Your Majesty?"

It wasn't like him to request one-on-one time. While the others tended their borrowed stags, Rafe led me away, visibly battling inner turmoil.

"I'm sorry, Your Majesty. We can't do this tonight."

"We can't?" I asked, surprised. "Why not?"

"It's sun day."

It definitely wasn't Sunday. "No," I corrected soundly. "It's Thursday. And why should it matter what day it is?"

Rafe exhaled, bracing himself. "I mean *sun* day." His gaze flicked toward the darkening sky with obvious dread. "Remember back on the beach when Soleil...protected me?"

"You mean when she stole you and Windley away in my hour of need? Yes, vividly."

"Well, she released Windley because he irritated her, but once she realized what was happening with you and your shadows, she wasn't about to let me go. I had to...strike another deal to convince her."

My breath stilled. "What did she make you promise?"

He scowled down at the pine needle-strewn earth. "She calls me once a week at sundown—I have no choice but to answer."

"Really?" I frowned. "What could she possibly want with you?"

"Doesn't matter."

"Oh no, Rafe. We can't have that. Vita told me Luna and Soleil were never meant to possess those giant bodies. They were always meant to stay in the astral realm. Perhaps we could free you once and for all by destroying Soleil's physical form the way we did Luna's."

"No." His head shook adamantly. "I can't afford to lose my bond with her. If that happens, I'll be right back where I was with Luna, vulnerable to the wraiths again. I need Soleil's protection for..."

The twins.

I considered carefully. "I wonder if there's something I could offer her in your place..."

"NO, Your Majesty." His voice sharpened more than I'd

ever heard from him. "You have to stop. It's not your job to heal the entire world, alright? This one's mine. I've made peace with it." His shoulders relaxed slightly. "I'm sorry for the inconvenience. I would have mentioned it sooner, but I'd rather those two didn't know. If you truly want to help...cover for me."

I studied him closely, searching for any sign that he wished to be freed from this burden. There was none.

"I understand," I assured him softly. "Your secret is safe."

When we returned, I told the others that Rafe had concerns about the region and would be scouting through the night.

"We'll rest here and continue in the morning," I said.

"Sure." Windley knew there was more to the story but didn't press.

The campsite floor was yielding beneath layers of dried needles and plush earth, our fire brighter and warmer than most, sparked by Rafe's enchanted blade and sustained by the crackling pop of pinecones. These parts were rustic, the people fond of isolation and the wild beauty around them.

And there was something else I remembered about this region.

While Windley prepared dinner, I slipped away in search of thistle clusters native to the Queendom of the Crater. Envoys had once gifted them to me, and though they held no medicinal properties, they were well worth the dirtied knees and pricked fingers it took to collect them.

"There she is," Edius quipped as I returned to the tent. "Your boyfriend was getting anxious."

"Harder to spot you now, lion queen, without that enchanted glow," Windley's eyes brightened at my approach. "And what were you doing? Rooting around for truffles and grubs?"

I kissed his cheek and placed a prickly clump into his palm. "Make a wish."

He frowned down at the thistle. "What?"

"Make. A. Wish."

His brow arched. "Does wishing for something mean I can do it to you?"

"Whatever it is you're planning, you probably don't need to waste a wish," I replied cleverly.

Just what he wanted to hear. His smirk was instant, artful.

"You too, Edi." I handed him a cluster. "Make a wish. Only one, and you can't tell anyone. Got it?"

Edius rolled his eyes dramatically.

"Good. Now toss them into the fire."

The Spirites exchanged an amused glance, humoring me, thinking me grieving and perhaps unstable. That look didn't last.

"H-holy shit!"

That was Edius.

"What the fuck?"

That was Windley.

Both leapt back as the fire doubled in size, bursting into dazzling shades of pink, emerald, and violet—while above the flames, a miniature aurora shimmered like the northern sky had descended into our campsite.

"What was in those things?!" Windley gasped, eyes wide.

"Pixie spice," I said casually, gesturing to the painted fire. "It has no real use other than...this."

"Heh." Edius's grin was genuine this time, not just lighting his eyes.

"How long does it last?" Windley asked, pulling me down beside him.

"Mm, twenty minutes?"

He wrapped his arms around me from behind, keeping me

close as we watched the lights dance and swirl above the flames. The night sounds of the forest surrounded us, familiar yet distinct from the Scarlet and Emerald Woods. The firelight cast warmth across the campsite, breaking up the chill of autumn's eve.

For tonight, at least, there was comfort in the quiet.

As the colors over the fire began to fade, Windley whispered gently against my ear, "Do you want to know what I wished for?"

I had a feeling—words like *grief* and *unburden* likely lay at its core.

But I still wasn't ready.

He released a slow breath, catching my meaning without a word. "I know." His arms drew me closer. "I'll be here."

That night, I pressed against Windley harder than ever, drawn to his warmth and the sure, even drum of his heartbeat. He murmured comforts against my skin, trying—failing, yet still trying—to siphon my pain into himself.

I would grieve with him soon.

And when I did, it would mark the beginning of healing.

But not tonight.

I awoke to the sound of someone clearing their throat.

Rafe stood at the tent's entrance, arms stiffly folded.

Turning toward Windley—who'd been cradling me comfortably in his sleep—I found myself face-to-face with...

"E-Edius?!" My voice faltered. "What in goddess's name—?"

Edius stirred, flexing his arms around me as though waking tangled up together were perfectly ordinary. Blinking blearily, he peered at me with sleepy confusion.

"Er, Merrín?" His brow furrowed. "You, ah...come for a visit?"

Absolutely not!

Yet we were indeed on his side of the tent. I scrambled backward so quickly I nearly twisted myself in the bedding.

Rafe's expression remained an iron wall of judgment.

"Look, Your Majesty, I'll keep quiet about this, but—"

"Windley!" I shoved Rafe aside. "Windley, get in here!"

Windley shoved Rafe right back on his way in. "Oh goddess, if this is another spider—" He froze as soon as he saw us.

His gaze bounced from my guilty face to bleary-eyed Edius, then to Rafe's scathing stare. Windley released a long, long-suffering breath.

"Oh, were they cuddling again?"

Horror—pure and absolute—consumed me.

"AGAIN?" I screeched.

Windley's expression sobered, a reassuring calm settling over his features. "Relax, Merr. You've no idea how often people drifted into my bed back home—usually half-asleep, simply following the scent."

Edius, apparently unfazed, stretched casually, pulling his shirt lazily over his tank top as if we hadn't just awoken tangled together.

"It isn't fine, Windley!" I sputtered. "It isn't fine for me to love you and—and cuddle him! Doesn't that upset you?"

Windley's shrug was slow, deliberate. "You only reach for him when I'm gone, and you let go the instant I return," he said, rubbing his thumb over my knuckles. "The pull between us is stronger than any instinct in the world, Merr. As long as Ed isn't trying to mark you or spirit you off into the forest, sharing a little comfort won't undo what we are."

"But..." My eyes flicked involuntarily toward Edius's undeniably impressive physique. It was no secret he was well built; no secret his heart wriggled in ways it shouldn't; no secret I was particularly prone to the Spirite lure.

"Humans leave our hearts lying *open*, remember?" I whispered in a fierce rush.

Windley chewed at the inside of his cheek, arms leisurely folded. "Still tangled up in that whole lust-triangle dilemma, are we?"

Edius's head snapped up. "Pardon?"

Windley's grin bloomed, wicked and bright. "She's worried about a *lust* triangle," he clarified, as if discussing the weather.

"Windley!" I squeaked.

Edius arched a brow. "Because I'm keen to tumble her?"

"Because she's equally keen to tumble you back," Windley supplied, helpful as ever.

No. Absolutely not—

And with Rafe right there?

"It's fine, highness," Edius drawled, unruffled. "Most humans fancy a romp with me. Rafe might, too."

Oh my goddess.

Windley hummed thoughtfully, putting on an exaggerated show of moral calculus. "Well, there are elegant solutions. The three of us could simply—"

"NO."

"Or I could pull up a chair and enjoy the view while you two—"

"NO!" My voice cracked at a scandalized octave I'd never reached before.

Edius chuckled, splaying a hand over his chest where his defiant heart refused to beat. "Gonna decline, I'm afraid. Self-preservation and all that."

Windley, ever the incorrigible flirt, released a theatrical sigh. "Tragedy."

Meanwhile, Rafe—whose entire existence I'd momentarily forgotten—let out a deeply unimpressed, "Oh my goddess," before pivoting on his heel and exiting the tent.

"No, Rafe! Don't think of me like thaaaat!" My desperate plea trailed after him, fizzling weakly into silence.

Flustered beyond recovery, I hauled Windley aside by the sleeve. "It isn't harmless, Wind. Intimacy might be casual fun for Spirites, but for humans it tangles the heart. I can't keep cuddling Edius—kissing him, holding him—unless you actually care that I don't."

Windley's brows hit the stars. "You think I don't?" A low laugh escaped him—half-hurt, half-fond—as he smoothed a thumb across my cheek. "Of course I'd rather be the body in your arms, Merrin. But when I'm not, why wouldn't I want you warm and safe? I trust you. And Spirite or not, every part of me already knows you're mine."

Oh.

That was...incredibly sweet.

But I still wasn't budging.

"Edius, does waking up with me in your arms strengthen or diminish your instincts to feed off me?"

Reluctantly, Edius slid his gaze toward mine. "Makes 'em worse," he admitted quietly.

"Does it strengthen or diminish your instincts to steal me away?"

He sighed deeply. "Makes 'em worse."

"And marking me? Strengthen or diminish?"

A pause. "It...makes them worse."

A sudden shift rippled from the center of the tent.

Windley had seized me from behind, arms banded across my chest, his snarl low and territorial. Sharp canines caught the dim tent-light.

Ah.

This was precisely what I'd wanted.

"Windley," I kept my voice calm, deliberate. "I appreciate your trust. And I love that you want me comforted even in your absence. But because of our very natures, I must draw lines. Can you see them now?"

His answer rumbled out, raw and primal. "Yes." His arms cinched. "I won't let him have you."

"Er, highness?" Edius ventured, wary. "You might wanna be careful..."

I felt it too—the beast in Windley was prowling close to the surface.

"Edius is my friend," I continued in an even tone, "and neither of us wants more. But as you've said, your kind were made to tempt mine. The last thing I want is to fall to that temptation. My heart is unequivocally yours, Windley; I want my body to match. Edius and I won't share ground unless you're with us. Agreed?"

His embrace stayed vise-tight, breaths shuddering and uneven as he pulled me closer, possessive, while we waited for the hunger to ebb.

"Goddess above," he muttered after a silence that seemed to stretch on, arms easing. "Sorry."

I turned in his hold and wrapped him up in return. "And I'm sorry for pushing you that far. I didn't know how else to make the boundary clear."

He exhaled roughly, rubbing the back of his neck. "No. You're right. I've been treating you like a Spirite partner because I didn't want you feeling like a human pet. But you're neither. How do I claim you without claiming ownership of you?"

His genuine struggle over it was admittedly endearing.

"I am your partner, Windley, but I'm also human. Treat me

as you always have, and I'll help you navigate the parts that are new."

The tent flap rustled sharply.

"Oh, fuck, is this still going on?" grumbled Rafe. "At least move it outside so I can take down the tent. We have things to do."

Rafe was right; we certainly did.

I'd just moved toward the exit when—

"Wait!" Windley caught my wrist, tugging me back, planting a solid kiss on my forehead before moving warmly to my mouth. "I want to claim you so everyone knows you're mine —but also so that you know you're free."

I placed a loving hand on his chest, smiling. "I want that too."

Determination brightened his expression. "I'll figure it out." Turning abruptly, he called out, "Rafe! Oi, chap! Guard-talk with meeee!"

"Oh goddess, what now?" Rafe groaned.

I watched them fondly as I gathered our things, balancing grief with anticipation for the battle ahead.

"Highness."

Edius's hand found my shoulder.

"Hm?" I turned curiously.

"Keep his nature in mind, too, yeah? He'll bend himself into knots for you, but while he's seen plenty of your world, you've hardly glimpsed any of his. Just be careful you don't cage him in your effort to set boundaries. He's working hard to tame himself for you, but remember, in our world, sex isn't reserved for love."

I would soon discover just how true that was.

4

SERIOUSLY, ED?!

S igh. Human-Spirite pairings. There was a reason they
weren't common.

But we had more pressing business to attend to.
Namely, revenge.

Earlier in our journey, we might have approached it tacti-
cally—carefully planning, meticulously plotting—but considering how spectacularly our careful plans had failed us thus far,
we opted for a new approach:

Barrel in and hope for the best.

Charm and Pip hadn't let up their bursts of power—a clear
signal beckoning Windley and Edius to find them. A trap,
undoubtedly, but I had creation and destruction coursing
through my veins, Rafe wielded the sun's flames, and Windley
and Edius were unmatched in physical combat. Indeed, as we
approached the quaint cabin, Windley's hatchets gleamed
hungrily, eager for action after days of idleness.

In one palm, I summoned Vita's breath. In the other,
Exitium's—altered now without the echoes, lighter, airier, and
cool against my skin, though just as effective. I'd practiced on

several unfortunate bushes along the way, obliterating them with Exitium's force, then gently coaxing them back with Vita's healing.

"*Speak my name, Merrin, and your power will grow,*" Exitium whispered inside my mind.

No thanks. I was perfectly content with my current level of power.

The cabin that emitted the ripples stood isolated at the end of a narrow road. The dwelling itself was dilapidated, branches unruly and in desperate need of pruning, grass tall and tangled with weeds.

Rafe stepped forward, flaming sword drawn, but Windley and Edius quickly moved past him, creating a barrier between us humans and the cabin.

But truly, out of all of us—

I stepped confidently ahead of them, feeling power surge and swell in each hand. The circumstances were now vastly in our favor; we were no longer trapped in a barren cavern. Here in the wilds, life pulsed under my feet—limitless potential for crafting golems on a whim.

They were fools to call us here. I'd have expected Charmagne to have better judgment.

But as it turned out, judgment had nothing to do with it.

"Wait." Edius caught my arm before I got too close. "Why not just destroy the place with them inside?"

I shook my head firmly. "If they've been sending power bursts nonstop for two days, it's likely they have humans trapped in there."

"The kind of energy they're using, any humans inside are probably..." Edius exchanged a dark look with Windley.

Depleted.

Still, I refused to chance more innocent blood staining my hands.

"Windley, can you close your heart off? I'm going to see how many heartbeats I can sense, and yours is distracting. Rafe, move over there for a second? Ed, yours is fine."

"Heartbeats?" Rafe questioned, having missed a substantial stretch of our journey.

Closing my eyes, I concentrated, feeling for the pulse of the earth, the sigh of wind, the mild stir of leaves. "Two Spirite heartbeats. Two human heartbeats—one weaker than the other. And maybe a...cat or something?"

The cabin door swung slowly open, though nobody stepped outside.

An invitation.

Someone watched us silently from behind the shaded windows.

"Ugh, seriously?" Windley huffed impatiently, cupping a hand to his mouth. "You're going to have to come out here! Not keen on getting ambushed today!"

We waited a tense moment or two, but no response came.

Kneeling, I dug my fingers into the cool, spongy earth beneath layers of fallen needles, whispering the commands to form and grow. Moments later, two sturdy golems erupted from the ground with a sudden lurch, forcing Rafe to leap backward in alarm, flames flaring instinctively at his fingertips.

"Golems!" I called, my voice cutting through the hush. "Heed my voice. Enter the cabin and bring out everyone inside!"

They charged the cabin, bits of clay flaking away as they squeezed through the narrow doorway. From within came the thuds of toppling furniture and heavy objects being dragged.

When the golems emerged, each cradled the limp form of an adult. For a heartbeat I prayed they were merely unconscious—but slack limbs, hollowed cheeks, and chests frozen mid-breath said otherwise.

Not the heartbeats I'd sensed earlier.

A sick, twisting dread coiled in my gut. The golems dropped their grim cargo in a heap, and I turned away, pressing a trembling hand to my mouth. Windley rushed in, arms wrapping protectively around me.

"Goddess damn it," he growled, hurling a furious glare at the cabin. "Pip, what happened to you? You know better than this!"

Yet faint thuds still pulsed inside the walls—lives clinging on. Steadying my breath, I straightened.

"Golems," I commanded, voice wavering but firm, "retrieve the survivors."

They charged back inside, heavy footsteps echoing through the open doorway.

Seconds passed—then they emerged empty-handed, moving with a sudden, off-kilter urgency. One locked onto Rafe, lunging at him in a burst of clay and aggression. He retaliated instantly, fire arcing from his sword to sever its arm. The other barreled straight for Windley.

"STOP!" I shouted, my voice ringing with forced authority. Both golems jerked to a standstill mid-attack.

"Why is this happening?" I demanded, desperation edging my tone. Searching my companions' faces yielded no answers. Gritting my teeth, I tried once more:

"Golems! Heed my voice! Enter the cabin and retrieve whoever remains!"

They obeyed, clomping back inside. For an instant, hope flickered—but they returned yet again with no rescued bodies in sight, their focus snapped back to Windley, both charging at him as though newly reprogrammed.

"Lion queen?" he cried.

"STOP!" I barked again, freezing them mid-step. My heart pounded. "Why won't they obey me?"

"Oh, but they are," came a silky voice.

A voice I knew better than any other—

My own.

Yet it hadn't come from me.

"CHARM!" Windley roared as a flawless replica of me sauntered from the cabin. "How dare you wear the queen's face!"

The golems had obeyed commands spoken in my voice—but not by me. Charmagne wore an uncannily perfect Merrin disguise, complete with my wild mane, though she carried herself far more seductively than I ever would.

"Kill them," she purred in that stolen voice, lips curling into a loathsome smirk. "All but Edius."

I froze the golems mid-charge. "Return to the earth." With Vita's breath, I melted them back into the ground.

"Poo," Charm pouted. "I was hoping for a little fun. What else do you have?"

Here in the wild? My arsenal was vast. I bent low, coaxing pine needles up through the soil until they swirled around me, forming a deadly serpent poised to strike.

Charm lifted a hand, her tone mockingly playful. "Ah, ah, ah. Wouldn't want to harm an innocent, would you?"

"You are far from innocent!" I snapped, flicking my wrist and hurling the needles toward her.

"True," she acknowledged sweetly, patting her stomach. "But the little one isn't."

The barrage wavered midair, suspended by my sudden, involuntary hesitation.

"W...what?"

Windley lurched forward, spinning his hatchets impatiently. "Tch! You expect us to believe you're with child, Charm? How stupid do you think we are?"

"I don't know," she mused, tilting her head. "Why don't you ask Edi?"

Windley snorted dismissively. "Like it's his? Ha! To produce a child, that would require—"

"Oh, fuck," Edius muttered.

"E-Edius?" My needles fell, and Windley's smug look crashed along with them.

Windley recoiled as if physically struck. "Oh, *ew*, mate!" He grimaced, face twisting like he'd tasted something foul. "With Charm? Were there no other palatable options?"

Charm's eyes glittered wickedly through my stolen face. "Go on, Edi. Tell them how it happened," she purred sweetly. "Tell them—or I will."

Whatever threat hid in that promise contorted Edius's features into a tight, closed-off mask, his sphinx-like eyes flashing with a dread perilously close to panic.

He was hiding a secret.

One he'd hoped never to tell me.

And one I had no desire to hear.

"What? Scared her royal plumpness won't like you anymore?" Charm stuck out her lower lip in mock sympathy. "Afraid she'll kick you out of her precious harem? Your own fault for thinking you belonged there in the first place. Why on earth would she want a dirty thing like you hanging around?"

"Enough!" I commanded sharply. "You don't need a tongue to give birth, Charmagne. I won't hesitate to have it removed. Edius, don't listen to her. Whatever it is, we won't judge you."

"I really, really doubt that, highness."

I double-took, staring at him.

Charm studied her nails lazily, counting down theatrically. "Five, four, three, two—"

"I hate you, Charm." Edius's scowl deepened, and he exhaled with great reluctance, eyes fixed anywhere but on me.

"Don't...make a thing of it, okay?" He directed that mostly at Windley. "It was back at the manor, after I let this one go." He nodded toward me. "I was having...urges. And Charm, she... didn't look like herself."

The way he avoided my eyes said everything.

I already knew whose face she'd worn.

"Oh my goddess." That was Rafe—flat, disturbed, horrified.

"Oh my goddess!" That was me, echoing him exactly.

"You've got to be shitting me." And that was Windley.

"Fuck me, it was weeks ago!" Edius threw his hands up defensively. "I didn't know I was gonna become friends with you lot! I didn't even think I'd ever see you again. I was—I was gods-damned pissed, thinking of the beating I was gonna get when Ascian got home, and then she—" He dragged a hand roughly through his hair. "Look, when someone crawls into your bed with those virgin eyes and that soft skin..."

"Except it wasn't me!" I cried.

"Yeah, I knew that," he admitted, hesitating awkwardly. "But...it was the fondness I'd felt from you while pretending to be him. I'd never felt that before—not from someone like you. Charm knew it. She used it."

I clutched my arms to my chest, feeling suddenly exposed.

"That means you've seen me naked!" I cried. "I feel so violated!"

"Nah, there's no way she got that part right. Not like she's actually seen you bare. Just your face, mostly—and your, ah... shape."

"Oh my goddess," Rafe repeated, sounding as though he regretted every choice that had led him here.

"Oh my goddess!" I echoed, thoroughly skeeved.

"Mate! Not cool!" Windley chimed in again, clearly disgusted.

"I would never do it now! Not now that I've gotten to know

you. I was in a really bad place, alright? Besides, it was nothing like the real thing anyway. She was mean...and bitey."

"We'll talk about this later," I declared, shoving the unwanted imagery aside. "But there's something else we can't ignore. I do sense another heartbeat from her. I thought it was a cat."

"So Pip was right," Charm cooed, lips curling triumphantly. "You can feel heartbeats. Just. Like. Him. So—" She turned her false Merrin-face toward the Spirite men, eyes twinkling mockingly. "What'll it be? Kill me and Edius's unborn? Or agree to let me live in peace?"

"In peace?!" Windley snapped, nostrils flaring with rage. "After all the shit you've pulled? It's because of you that... that—"

That Albie was dead.

He couldn't bring himself to say it.

"What other choice do you have?" Charm crooned.

"Give me Ascian's ring," Windley growled dangerously.

"Hmm, how about no?"

"There are ways to keep you alive in misery until that psychopath you're brewing—"

"Hey," Edius cut in, voice flashing. "You don't know the thing's gonna be evil."

Windley snorted bitterly. "*Really?*"

Meanwhile, Rafe looked like he'd developed a sudden migraine.

Charm focused her taunts on Edius again. "Ed-ius," she lilted seductively. "Anything you wanna do to her, you can do to me, you know. I'll even keep on this thick costume for you." She slowly ran a hand along her side, speaking in my stolen voice. "Do you want me to tell you I love you, Edius? Want me to beg to be your pet? Please, Ed, come mark me. Suck the spirit right out of my oversized tits."

Edius wouldn't bite. He wouldn't. But I saw how his jaw clenched, his chest constricted.

His cocoon wriggled dangerously.

"Go to hell, Charm," he growled.

Windley's teeth flashed angrily. "What's wrong with you, Charm? Ascian's gone! You're free! You should be *thanking* Her Majesty, not tormenting her! *Why* do you insist on being such a cunt?"

"Because I loved Ascian, you cretin!" Charm's voice cracked with rage. "And then this human bitch waltzed into our life and blew him up!"

"Technically, we waltzed into hers," Edius noted.

"Shut up, *Ediot*! You lost the right to speak to me. I thought you were one of us! I thought you understood, but you think with your cock just like the rest of them!"

"Oh, come on, Charm," Edius rolled his eyes, as though dealing with a tantrum-throwing child. "You know that's not what this is about..."

But he glanced my way—

Checking to see if I forgave him.

A voice buzzed urgently in my head. *"Mer...rin...!"*

"Not now, Vita!"

"Listen...Me...rrin!"

"I can handle this myself!"

But the pressure grew, pressing insistently, until I had no choice but to drop the walls around my soul.

"The female beastling is not with child! It is illusion magic! She holds a feline against her to deceive you!"

No matter how hurt I'd been, I should've let her in sooner.

"Charm's pregnancy is a lie!" I shouted. "Vita says it's a trick!"

"Oh, thank Hades," Edius muttered, visibly relieved.

A sinister grin spread across Windley's face. "In that case —" He surged forward, hatchets thirsty and ready.

Deception foiled, Charm cursed loudly, releasing the terrified cat she'd concealed against her body. It scampered away gratefully as the rest of her illusion melted, her weak imitation dissolving into something fang-bared, crueler, more genuinely Charm.

Windley's hatchets whirled through the air toward her, but she sprang aside nimbly, summoning a massive axe from Ascian's ring.

The axe moved of its own accord, slicing menacingly toward Rafe.

He met it mid-strike, deflecting it with his flame-wreathed sword. Soleil watched from above, filling Rafe's skin with searing power until he blazed orange with celestial fire.

Windley's blade caught Charm's arm, eliciting a piercing shriek. In retaliation, she conjured a swarm of stinging insects and sent them hurtling toward him.

Clenching my fist, I stole the breath from the swarm, their lifeless husks dropping in a gruesome spray around Windley.

"Thanks, queenie!" he shouted, shaking dead insects from his hair in a quick flurry.

If only I could do the same to Charm. But her life force was dense, her power intricately woven within. If I wanted to weaken her, I'd have to get closer.

Edius lunged forward, grappling Charm as Windley moved to strike—but Charm was quicker than she appeared. I willed the ground beneath her to quake, throwing her off balance just enough to loosen her grip on the axe pursuing Rafe.

Edius toppled to the earth alongside her.

"Sorry, Ed!" I called hastily.

It worked in our favor—Edius now had Charm pinned, his

hands pressing her shoulders into the dirt as Windley raised his hatchet, poised to end this fight.

Until—

"No!" A desperate voice rang out through the chaos.

Windley faltered, giving Charm the opening she needed. She kicked his weapon aside and scrambled for leverage.

From the cabin emerged a wide-eyed youth with powder-blue hair, sprinting toward us. "No," he cried again. "Don't hurt her!"

Windley went rigid, his gaze locked onto the newcomer.

The very rogue responsible for the fall of his hometown.

The loss of his fellow soldiers.

The death of the knight who first welcomed him into the guard.

"...Pip?" Windley murmured, disbelief etched across his features.

"About time, you little monster!" Charm hissed from the ground.

But Pip wasn't alone.

He clutched a small human shield in front of him—a young girl, eyes wet with terror. The stronger of the two heartbeats I'd sensed earlier.

"Release that child at once!" My voice broke like a whip.

Pip edged forward, pushing the trembling girl before him.

"No! Let Charm go first!"

Rafe moved instinctively—ready to snatch the child—but Pip's eyes flared red in warning.

"I'll drain it before you reach me!"

Rafe skidded abruptly to a halt.

"Pip, why are you doing this?" Windley demanded, slowly lowering his weapons and stepping closer. "Ascian's gone. You don't have to live this way anymore."

Pip's vacant stare shifted uncertainly between Windley and Charm.

"Ascian...?"

"Don't listen, Pipsqueak! He's trying to confuse you. Quick, call one of your hexes!" Charm barked.

All around the yard, jagged spikes of earth burst upward, forming a protective barrier around Pip and his hostage. Charm cackled victoriously from her place on the ground.

"That's her, Pip," she purred venomously, gesturing at me. "The one with the bushy hair. See? She's already got two other Spirites under her control. Kill her—free them before she tries to enslave you, too!"

Pip's vacant eyes settled uncertainly on me, unreadable.

"O-okay, Charm."

"Aw, shit," muttered Edius.

"What?" Windley snapped, frustrated.

"Pip," Edius began carefully, "do you know who I am?"

Pip blinked at him.

"Do you know who that is?" Edius tilted his head toward Windley.

Pip blinked again.

Windley's fury simmered beneath a tightly restrained surface. "How strong of a potion did you feed him this time, Charm?"

"Strong enough to erase any dangerous ideas forming in that fractured head of his after he tried marking that crazy-eyed queen. He thought she was his wyrdbound one just because she got rid of his monster! Can you imagine?"

Windley's voice dropped, lethal and cold. "That's not why you made him drink it."

Charm's mocking smile faltered briefly.

"You gave it to him so Merrin would never have closure, didn't you?"

Charm was silent.

Windley's fists tightened at his sides. "If Pip can't remember what he did, there's no way for him to atone."

"Well, I suppose that's a nice bonus," Charm smirked.

Windley's voice sharpened dangerously. "This ends now, Charm. Right here."

In a swift, fluid motion, he pivoted and hurled his remaining hatchet.

It spun end over end through the air until—

It landed firmly in Charm's chest.

But it wasn't Charm who cried out.

Instead, Edius let out a strangled gasp, blood blooming vividly across his chest. He staggered and collapsed to his knees.

"What?! H-how?" Windley's voice cracked, horror flooding his expression as he stumbled backward. He'd intended to strike her—but now Edius lay on the ground, gasping for breath.

Charm lifted her hand, revealing two rings—one gleaming ominously: Ascian's. The larger of the two swirled with unnatural power, dark and pulsing as though alive.

"You'd be amazed at the spells Master's ring holds," Charm gloated, gripping the hatchet lodged harmlessly in her chest.

Windley's face contorted in horror as she casually pulled the blade free, entirely unscathed.

"I'm practically a god!"

The protective shimmer surrounding her faded, revealing a sleeve of deflection she'd concealed.

"Edi!" I lunged forward, catching him before he could fully collapse.

Charm towered above us, eyes burning with malicious triumph.

"You make this too easy, cupcake." She grabbed a fistful of

my hair, wrenching harshly as she bent low to whisper venomously into my ear. "Your compassion will always be your undoing. Every. Single. Time." Another sharp tug. She lifted her gaze to Windley and Rafe, sneering coldly, "Not one step closer, or I'll make her death hurt."

They'd both charged forward but froze, weapons raised, uncertain.

Little did Charm know, my tears were feigned.

She was no god.

But I had the power of goddesses on my side, and her distraction was all I needed.

Her ankle was within my reach. I seized it firmly with one hand, pressing my other palm to Edius's wounded chest, emerald light swiftly enveloping me.

This time, it wasn't involuntary.

This time, I intended every second.

As I had done with Albie, with Edius's blight, with the tadpole—I drew Charm's life force out through myself and into a trembling, gasping Edius.

"Hold on, Ed," I whispered as he reached weakly for me. "It'll be over soon."

"What...what is this?!" Charm shrieked, clawing at her rapidly wrinkling skin. Her lush, youthful glow faded, hair dulling and thinning as vitality drained rapidly from her body. She hunched, frail and brittle, aged beyond her years.

Edius gasped as his wounds began to mend, his strength returning, vigor knitting his body whole again even as Charm deteriorated.

"Ha—hahahaha!" The laughter that erupted from Charm's lips was no longer her own; it sounded rough, hoarse—an eerie death rattle from someone who no longer belonged in their own body.

Staggering and wheezing, her fingers curled defiantly around Ascian's ring. "Now I have no choice but to drain the last of your precious GWEN, Edi!" She raised the ring in raw defiance. "Blame your frizzled girlfriend when that fairy's tiny body shrivels up and—"

A wet cough tore through her words, spattering crimson across her lips. Her body convulsed as her threats died mid-sentence.

Rafe's blade pierced her spine with swift finality.

"Bitch," he spat.

Charmagne collapsed, striking the ground with a final, silent thud. Motionless. Defeated at last.

Edius knelt above her, breathless, chest heaving in stunned silence. Though fully healed, he still trembled as he steadied himself on the ground. With careful deliberation, he pried Ascian's ring from her lifeless grip, turning it over in his palm before sliding it onto his finger.

Windley rushed forward, gripping Edius's wrist. "What do you think you're doing, mate?"

Edius lifted his gaze, quiet resolve shining in his eyes. "Dropping the hexes. What else?"

"All of them?"

"All but one," he murmured.

Gwen's.

Bracing himself, Edius closed his eyes and began muttering in a low, rhythmic undertone. A dark gleam flickered along the ring, then spread like ripples across his fingers. One by one, sparks crackled and vanished—Ascian's twisted curses unraveling beneath Edius's careful hand. Forced bonds snapped in succession, each marked by a sudden flash, until only the hex binding him to Gwen remained—a faint, pulsing glow he left untouched.

Yet in dismantling those spells, he also severed a lock he never should have touched.

Across the lawn, Pip released a piercing, harrowing scream as the sky above him darkened. Something ancient had just been unleashed.

5

PIPSQUEAK

Collective cheer, captive ones, for Charm's end.
        Think me wicked if you must, but of all deaths
I've witnessed, this one brings a certain fondness.
It's all right if you feel the same.

The child Pip had used as a shield now lay still at his feet.

As the ring's hexes collapsed, a swirling funnel of darkness engulfed the Spirite youth, then tore away to reveal something else entirely—something monstrous.

Pip no longer resembled a teenager. He stood tall and broad, his once-soft hair now parted by razor-edged horns. All-black eyes gleamed, set in a face far older than the boy we knew.

"What is he?" yelled Rafe.

But the Spirites among us were just as bewildered.

"That is not a beastling!" Vita's warmth flared frantically against my chest. *"It's something older, something ancient!"*

"Something?" I cried. "What kind of something?"

"But they were destroyed when the angels fell! How did one survive?"

"Vita—tell me what he is!"

"The first of the Drakaina's children!" Vita's voice shook urgently. *"Before beastlings, a fiercer race was created—so powerful they could wipe out humes. We forbade the Drakaina from making more and sent angels to extinguish the existing ones. Your kind called them Dracons."*

"Dracons?"

Windley shot me a sharp glance. "What did you just say?"

"Dracon," I repeated breathlessly. "Vita says Pip is a—"

Windley lunged, pressing desperate kisses against my forehead, wrists, neck—fiendishly coating my skin with his scent.

"Edius, mark the magician!" he barked.

But Rafe and Edius merely exchanged tense glances, then turned toward Pip, sword and fists at the ready.

"Windley, what are you—?"

"Dracons," he muttered quickly against my skin. "Our lore says they nearly wiped out humans long ago. They're insatiable predators. I'm trying to make you less appealing."

Any other time, I'd have gladly welcomed it, but the air around us had darkened swiftly.

The creature Pip had become exuded an aura so thick it suffocated the forest—heavy and stale, laced with death—while dark clouds pressed downward from the sky as if even the heavens recoiled.

"I remember now," Pip said calmly, tone unwavering and chillingly self-assured—nothing like his earlier timidity. "All these years, I thought you two were my big brothers. But really, I'm yours, aren't I? All of yours—even that fool who dared make me call him 'master.'"

His voice—once a hesitant trill—now dripped icy confidence, keen as his chiseled features.

Never had I seen him so focused, his bearing so commanding.

He extended a hand toward Edius. "Thank you, Edi, for releasing me. I'll take my ring back now."

"*Your* ring?" Windley's eyes narrowed.

"Before it was stolen by that cur, Ascian."

Edius clutched the ring protectively. "Yeeeah, that's not happening, Pip. Besides the obvious—that you're a complete psycho—Gwen's still attached. Nobody's touching this ring until I see her."

Pip's mouth curved slightly. "Because you know she'll fall dead the moment her hex drops. There can't be much life left in her, Edi. You don't want to see her—not like that. Give it to me."

"You don't know that!" Edius growled.

"Perhaps not. But I'm not leaving without it." Pip's soulless gaze shifted toward me. "And I'll take the girl, too."

Windley shoved me firmly behind him. "Like hell you'll take her!"

Pip's smile deepened. "Cute. My little brothers, acting as though they have a choice." He stretched lazily, rolling his shoulders as if shedding invisible restraints. "After spending a century in that diminished form, I'm not open to negotiation. I'll take the ring, and the girl, and gain leverage over those meddlesome goddesses."

"Leverage for what?" Rafe demanded, glancing anxiously at the sky, where Soleil's comforting glow had vanished, giving way to moonless night.

Pip shrugged casually. "To free our mothers."

"You mean the Drakaina?" Windley stiffened. "Why would you want them freed?"

"So you can return to your true natures," Pip said, like it should be obvious. "Gods, you were all so much more entertaining before our mothers were imprisoned. Brutal. Merciless. Cunning."

The Drakaina. Ancient serpent beings, among the first to rise from the void, who warred with the goddesses before being cast out beyond realms of life and death.

Horrid things. The reason beasts desire to devour one another.

Long ago, before we evolved beyond base instincts, humans were our prey...

Windley's brow knitted fiercely. "You want them freed...so we become feral?"

Pip smirked. "Among other things. The world's gone soft, and I'm tired of being the lone Dracon. Let our mothers breed again—fill the realms with new spawn and rekindle that old hunger in you and the rest of your shackled kin." His eyes thinned to slits. "Humans as mates? Protectors? Friends? That was never our mothers' design."

His Dracon gaze speared into mine, and I plunged helplessly into its abyss.

"Queen lion—come."

My body betrayed me at once, feet gliding toward him as though seized by a riptide.

"No, love!" Windley's arms cinched around my waist. Rafe seized one shoulder, Edius the other—

—But Pip's spell moved through me like a command. I stamped hard, the ground bucking beneath us and flinging my companions aside. Their shouts echoed as I lurched forward.

Windley scrambled upright, only for a flick of my wrist to raise a wall of thorny hedge between us.

"Your Majesty!" Rafe burst through the foliage—roots instantly coiled up, snagging his ankle and yanking him down.

Windley clawed at the thorns. "Pip! How could you do this?" he cried, raw and desperate. "We were brothers. I've been trying to reach you all this time!"

Pip barely spared him a glance. "Keep your sentimentality, Windalloy. The brother you knew is gone. I have his memories —none of his fondness. Still, you may yet earn a sliver of favor..."

His arms opened in triumph, and—helpless—I drifted straight into them.

"If you surrender the ring and stop meddling with the girl," he finished, voice velvet-soft.

Heat spilled from his touch, like sinking into hot springs after winter chill.

"Excellent. Easy enough, yes?" he murmured, savoring the win. "Now—let's sample the prize."

His breath skimmed my jaw, nose grazing sensitive skin as he drew my scent in deep.

"Mmm." Lips parted, brushing the hollow beneath my ear. "A blend of worlds—goddess, fallen goddess, human. Resisting the urge to devour you will be...difficult."

His tongue traced slowly along my throat; shivers rippled under my skin.

"But what a satisfying first meal you'll make."

His mouth sealed hungrily against my neck—

—Until a low, territorial growl ripped the moment apart.

Windley.

Pip ignored him.

"You want to come with me, don't you, queen lion?"

I had no choice. I yielded—like a fly drowning in honeyed poison.

"Let's make it real," Pip breathed, voice silken. "Seal it with a kiss."

His lips hovered a breath from mine. I was trapped inside

myself, a silent witness while muscle and instinct betrayed me. His breath brushed my mouth—ruin wrapped in sweetness— and then I devoured him.

The kiss obliterated thought.

His presence hit ten times harder than any Spirite's. Freedom—forbidden and intoxicating—lingered on his tongue, and his iron arms welded me to his chest.

If Spirites were fashioned to tempt humans, Dracons were forged to destroy them.

I would have shattered gladly to keep tasting him.

He crushed me closer, unyielding, before breaking the seal. I was left panting, ravenous for more.

Pip licked the memory from his lips, decadent. "Oh, I think we're going to have fun together, queen lion."

I felt dizzy, lost in a tide of instinct and submission.

Windley, Edius, and Rafe shouted, their voices distant, muffled beneath layers of Pip's influence.

Pip's gaze flicked toward them, amusement glinting in those abyss-dark eyes. Tilting his face to the sky, he murmured, "I'll be back soon for my ring."

And then—

I braced for him to launch skyward, dragging me with him.

"MERRIN!"

Vita's shout speared the fog around my mind—plaited with a second, darker timbre. One goddess Pip could muzzle; a duet he could not. Light and shadow fused, shearing through his command and snapping the trance.

In the next heartbeat the horizon split—golden fire in the east, argent frost in the west. Day and midnight collided, and four divine voices thundered where even one had been silenced moments before.

Four goddesses—each driven by her own design, yet united in recognizing the gravity of this ancient threat.

"Soleil!" Rafe gasped. "And...Luna?"

Sun and moon ripped Pip's conjured darkness apart in a burst of blinding brilliance. The goddesses ringed their quarry, power flooding the breach like a tidal wave.

I hovered at the eye of the storm—a living conduit between eclipse and dawn—swallowed by warring light and devouring shadow.

"NO!" Pip recoiled as their twin powers struck, dropping me like hot iron, clutching his hand as if scorched. "You shouldn't be capable of that while bound!" he snarled, horns casting jagged shadows in splintered light.

"Focus, little royal," Vita urged. *"His eyes can't ensnare you while my sisters share the sky—but one brush of his skin still can. Keep your distance, draw the Destroyer, and never speak her name."*

I pulled the goddess-mantle tight, compressing it to a single black star that burned in my palm.

Pip circled, predator-still, waiting for the smallest slip. Overhead, sun-fire grappled with moon-frost.

Crack.

Thunder like shattering glass split the sky.

An ice spear plummeted and punched straight through Rafe's chest.

My breath vanished; the star winked out, the mantle sputtered. In that gasping beat Pip lunged, iron fingers clamping my elbow.

"Behave, queen lion," he crooned, "or the next one finds your heart."

Hatchets screamed toward us. Pip yanked me in front of him—a living shield—and the goddess-roar collapsed, caged by his touch.

Ice shards clattered to the earth and, when the mist cleared, Rafe still stood—unharmed. One eye blazed molten gold, the other glimmered moon-silver. Power thrummed through him, his blade now blazing with twinned fire and frost.

"Dual-wielding now, chap?" Windley called, almost gleeful. "Has the moon forgiven you, then? Pretty sure she doesn't know you shared her sister's bed."

And when Rafe moved, he blurred—faster than thought— lunging straight for the Dracon.

Pip swore and flung me aside to dodge the oncoming eclipse-blade.

The instant his hand left mine, the goddess-cloak surged back, catching my fall in a whirl of light and shadow. The trance shattered; I gulped air, lungs trembling. Windley whooped somewhere behind me, but every sense tunneled onto the Dracon.

"If he snares your gaze again, I'll seal your sight myself," Vita warned.

I gritted my teeth, summoned Exitium's darkness without hesitation, and hurled it at Pip. He vaulted skyward, wings of deepest shadow snapping wide.

Windley's hatchet followed.

Rafe's flaming blade followed.

But only my shadow connected.

Pip roared furiously, clutching at his calf as darkness devoured his flesh.

Cursing bitterly, he shot a final glare our way—then vanished into the sky.

The heavens bled back to blue; sun and moon drifted to their rightful thrones.

Yet something had shifted irrevocably.

Far off, the forest birds remained silent—as if the world itself were holding its breath to see what a reborn Dracon might do next.

There was much to say, but one thing came first.

"Edi! How's your chest?"

Edius had ripped sections from his shirt to form a makeshift bandage. "Should hurt like hell," he said wryly, "but I feel strangely okay, highness."

"He will not perish from this," Vita assured. *"Charmagne's life fills him now, sustaining him beyond mere healing."*

Charm's death felt sweeter knowing she'd given life back to Edius.

Edius rubbed his chest, a grin like a crescent blade overtaking his face. "Does that smile mean you forgive me for bedding a cheap imitation of you?"

"Edius!" I snapped.

True, nearly losing him had dulled the sting—but I wasn't ready to let it go just yet.

"Too soon, mate." Windley cuffed the back of Edius's head.

Meanwhile, Rafe stepped forward, carefully scooping up the child Pip had abandoned. Released from the oppressive aura that had pinned her down, she began to stir.

Rafe drew her close, murmuring in a low, protective tone, "You're safe."

And the voice that so often dripped with boredom carried no trace of it now.

He was a fortress, one hand sketching slow circles across the girl's back, shielding her from the grim scene nearby.

"I have sisters," he added softly—the first sliver of his past he'd ever offered.

"There's another child inside," I reminded him, recalling the faint heartbeat. "Can you retrieve them, Ed?"

Edius nodded and slipped into the cabin, returning

moments later with another girl—round-cheeked and too small to speak.

"Oh, poor darling." I took the child from Edius, bouncing her gently on my hip. "Those must be their parents."

"No," Edius said, nodding toward the bodies. "They don't smell related. Neither do the children, for that matter."

I stiffened slightly. "You can...smell whether people are related?"

"If the relation is close enough," Edius confirmed.

I glanced at Windley, but he was preoccupied with the older child.

Whether intentionally or not, I couldn't tell.

Because if Spirites could smell blood relation...

My fingers brushed over the necklaces dangling at my chest.

"S-so these people had two children unrelated to them?" I asked.

"Yeah," Edius replied, voice sober. "And there's no child's belongings inside, from what I could tell."

I passed the tubby little one back to Edius and crouched down before the older girl, carefully brushing tangled strands of hair from her storm-gray eyes.

"Hello there. My name's Merrin. Can you tell me yours?"

Dirty-cheeked and cautious, the girl curled tighter into Rafe.

Softening my voice further, I tried to coax her trust. "It's all right, little one. You're safe now. I'm a queen, and these—" I gestured at the others, "—are my royal guards."

Her eyes drifted toward my hairline, clearly expecting a crown.

"Ah, of course—" I rummaged in my pack until I found the ivy crown Albie had thoughtfully packed weeks earlier, delicately placing it atop my head.

"See?"

She shifted in Rafe's grip, curiosity sparking.

"Would you like to wear it?"

Eyes wide as saucers, she nodded eagerly.

Smiling, I set the crown upon her small head.

"Well, look at that! It appears we have another queen among us."

Windley bowed extravagantly, playing along. "Tell me, little highness, is this your home?"

She shook her head slowly.

"No? Do you know those adults who were here?"

She shook her head again.

"They were strangers?"

A small nod.

Oh, dear.

"Were they...kind strangers?" I pressed.

Instead of answering, she buried her face deeper into Rafe's chest. He responded immediately, holding her more securely, mildness in every careful movement.

I took Windley's sleeve, guiding him a step away. "What's happening here?"

He hesitated, exchanging a knowing glance with Edius, who awkwardly held the younger child, stiff and cautious, as if afraid she might shatter in his grip.

Windley exhaled reluctantly. "Charm probably chose this place deliberately."

I folded my arms tightly. "You think these people were the ones who...bought her?"

"No," Windley said, shaking his head. "I've heard plenty about that place, and this isn't it. These people seem more like peddlers—these children were either stolen or sold."

A painful lump formed in my throat. "How awful." My heart cinched tight, urging me to keep the children, carry them home to the Crag, fill their lives with sweets, warmth, and glittering comforts.

Windley knew exactly what I was thinking.

"You saw Pip, Merr. We can't have littles around. We passed a road to a city yesterday—there should be some of the Crater's guards there. Send a decree ordering the children to be delivered safely to Queen Sneha's castle. She'll ensure they're cared for; I hear she's a good queen."

It was a practical plan.

But still...

"We don't have time to bring them ourselves," I said quietly.

"No," Windley agreed. "And you and I should avoid cities. Ed, too. But especially us—Pip will return, and it's better if no one else gets caught in the crossfire. Dracons were known for their cruelty."

Something raw tinged his voice—hidden, but unmistakable.

He was mourning.

Because this Pip meant his friend was gone.

Forever.

He was carrying grief.

Just as I was carrying grief.

"Rafe and Ed will bring the children to the city," I decided. "You and I will stay. I still have to rejoin the Nemophile's Crown, and you..."

"Yeah." Windley's voice lowered. "There's something we need to discuss. Alone."

That sounded ominous.

I quickly relayed our plan to the others before approaching the girl in Rafe's arms once more. "We'll get you something warm to eat, then my guards will escort you to safety. How does that sound?"

I didn't blame her cautious stare.

"Don't worry," I assured her gently. "They're trained specifically to care for queens. And you, my little highness, can borrow my crown for now. Alright?"

That did the trick. Her little shoulders relaxed slightly.

"Rafe, your gallop is steadiest—we'll swaddle the younger one to you. Edius, would you mind holding the older girl?"

But the older child eyed Edius—intense, brooding Edius—and instead pointed straight at Windley.

"Oooh, yes," I gave a sunlit laugh. "He *is* quite handsome, isn't he?"

Windley's grin turned wickedly bright. "Ha! You see that?" He scooped the girl from Rafe's arms with practiced ease, giving her a playful whirl before gathering her close. "Come here, little sovereign. You know, I've got a special weakness for queens, but I have to stay here and watch *this* one." He angled his head toward me, lowering his voice in a conspiratorial aside. "She gets into terrible mischief if I'm not careful."

Adorable. Unbearably adorable. Seeing Windley cradle a child with such natural grace tugged fiercely at instincts I wasn't yet ready to acknowledge.

But ours was a love that could never produce such miracles.

Windley continued, playfully coy, "Ed might seem intimidating, but he's truly a softy underneath. He's even got a secret. Ed, show her."

Edius shot me a wary, uncertain look before letting out a begrudging sigh and—

"E-Edius!"

He smiled.

Not his usual smirk or a half-hearted grin—but a genuine, radiant smile. It softened every angular line of his rugged features, revealing a glimpse of the warm-hearted person he might have become, had life dealt him a kinder hand.

A sudden compulsion to run to him surged through me.

The girl felt it too, practically leaping from Windley's arms into Edius's embrace.

And just like that, everything was decided.

I quickly conjured golems to dispose of the bodies. We fed and cleaned the girls, wrapped the younger one securely against Rafe's chest, while the older child clung tightly—utterly enchanted—to Edius's neck. I handed Rafe a sealed scroll bearing my decree, and then Windley and I watched them ride off, leaving behind that cursed cabin and the hidden graves of two villainous humans and one malicious Spirite.

So much had happened.

So much was yet unsaid.

But the moment the last of the stags' hoofbeats vanished into the woods, Windley fell to his knees, head bowed, voice breaking in a wrenching confession—

"I can't do this anymore."

6

THE TALK

I knelt beside him and ran a careful hand along his sleeve, searching his face for the storm I knew was there.

"Windley? Is it Pip? I know it must feel as though he's—"

"Stop, Merrin."

The words came out ice-flat, detached.

I touched his arm again. "Windley, you're hurting—you never reached him, you lost your brother—"

He whipped toward me, eyes blazing. "This isn't about me. It's about you—about that maddeningly forgiving heart of yours!"

The accusation cracked like a slap.

"What?"

"You. And your total disregard for your own needs!"

"I beg your pardon?"

Grief hadn't taken him at all; *rage* had.

"Goddess damn it, Merrin! This is all my fault! Pip turning into that thing. The reason we had to end Charm. The reason you even know who Ascian is or what the Drakaina are! I'm the one who dragged this nightmare into your life—and still, you don't hold a shred of resentment against me!"

His breath hitched tightly, edged with pain.

"You just nearly drained the life from someone—you, who despises killing; you, who longs to fill the world with justice and mercy. You were nearly captured by an ancient monster, and yet you're still bleeding empathy—for those children, for Ed, for Rafe! Hell, even for Pip!"

He shook his head, incredulous. "Your dearest knight was stabbed less than a week ago, yet do you allow yourself even the slightest grudge against the one who wounded him? No! Yes, it wasn't Ed's fault—but any normal person would need those feelings to cope, to process, to heal. Yet you refuse to let them in."

His words sliced into me.

"I know you cried on Ed's shoulder—but that was for his sake, not yours. You should be cursing the heavens, raging at goddesses, hating the beastlings who dragged you into this—but you don't." His fists clenched in the grass, voice lowering. "It's always for someone else, Majesty. Always."

He exhaled harshly, like a long, grueling battle had finally ended. Then, quieter—

"I love that about you." He lifted his gaze, voice cracking. "But it's killing me."

I couldn't breathe.

"Am I hurting over Pip? Of course I am. But my pain is nothing compared to what you're facing with the loss of Sir Albie. Yet you won't even let yourself feel angry! Or irrational. Or whatever it takes to actually begin healing!"

His voice frayed, raw and pleading.

"You're wounded, Merrin. You're damn good at hiding it,

but I know you better than anyone—I've watched you for years. You're not okay. And I need you to admit it. Because you're the most precious thing in this forsaken world to me. You deserve to be acknowledged, to be heard, to be comforted. You deserve the entire damned world." He gripped my shoulders with aching care. "So enough about me. Let yourself break."

I stared at him, open-mouthed, as his words settled deep in my bones.

And he was right.

I'd been open and honest with him—but never fully.

I had kept so much inside. For his sake. For the sake of others.

My fear over returning home.

My uncertainty about my place in the world.

My hatred of hiding Windley away like some shameful secret.

My grief that he and I would never produce an heir.

My resentment toward Vita, my reluctance to accept the Crown of the Wood.

My guilt for dragging Albie into a fight that was never his.

My doubt about Albie's true relationship with my mother, the possibility that he and I were bound closer than I'd ever known.

And my grief.

My overwhelming, consuming grief, dictating every choice since stealing away my knight's final breath.

"Merrin. My lion. My queen." Windley's hands framed my face, warm as sunrise. "I know you've been protecting me by hiding your feelings. You cry so easily for others—but never for yourself. You are fierce and brave and compassionate, but there's no rule forbidding you to be selfish, to break, to feel everything. Let it out. Kick something, break something, scream until your lungs ache, cry until there's nothing left. Whatever you need—please, unburden yourself."

I couldn't speak.

I couldn't move.

And if I blinked, I'd shatter completely.

I only clung tighter, drawn into those deceptively placid eyes—darkened now, deliberately veiled so their power wouldn't breach me. Even muted, they were hypnotic; I couldn't look away.

"It's only us." He pressed his forehead to mine. "There's no image to uphold. You don't have to be a heroine here. If it means freeing you, I'd gladly share your pain."

Things always felt insurmountable, didn't they?

When hidden in the shadows.

Only when dragged into the light did we see the obstacles clearly—the paths waiting to be walked.

I gripped Windley's shoulders and let the tears fall.

The sun sank lower, bathing the lawn in twilight—

Side by side, we breathed.

Side by side, we grieved.

Until no more tears remained.

A hush settled over the clearing—as if the world had wept with us.

Beyond the cabin, sentinel pines scissored the violet sky. A lone owl loosed a tentative hoot, the note rippling across the hush like a pebble on still water. In that subdued quiet, the ache in my ribs eased, and the eve received us exactly as we were—two hearts laid bare beneath its lingering afterglow.

My head rested in Windley's lap, his fingers lazily combing through silky coils of my hair.

"Feel better?" he asked, voice a tender murmur.

"I do."

Though much had spilled from my heart while I'd wept, I wasn't yet sure how to navigate it all. The issues before us were a vast lake we needed to cross.

Windley dipped the first toe.

"You know, lion queen, it would be my greatest honor to create a child with you—but goddess, can you imagine what a terror it would be?" He tapped his chin thoughtfully. "Though I wager the little beastling would be quite the looker..."

I grinned up at him, though the topic was still too tender for words.

His voice dimmed to a whisper. "You will have children, Merrin. Even if not by me, you'll have them with anyone you choose."

A breath snagged in my throat. "And what if I don't wish to lie with another?"

He shrugged, easy as ever. "Then we'll adopt. Or rather, you will adopt. It wouldn't be unlike you. Everyone in your court knows how quickly your heart goes soft for abandoned youth." His voice dipped lower, warm against my temple. "And perhaps in the shadows, I could be—a—well, I suppose 'Pop' wouldn't work. How about their warden of mischief?"

A warden of mischief.

Not what I truly wanted.

Yet what I desired most could only come at great cost.

"My people expect an heir of royal blood," I confessed.

Windley exhaled—pensive, yet curiously untroubled. "There are other royals, Merr, and a thousand ways to trick appearances. If it came to it, I'd charm every maid and chamberlain in the castle into swearing you're with child." A playful pulse of color chased itself through his hair as he offered a forlorn smile. "An heir is the one thing I cannot give you. Everything else under the sun? I'll make it yours."

That was enough.

At least for now.

He ran fingers through my hair again, contemplative. "Now, about this Crown of the Wood business—there's no avoiding that one. Vita did what she did for your sake, for the world's sake. If you can forgive Ed, surely you can forgive her. Besides, the sooner you merge the Crown, the sooner you can be rid of all this."

"I know," I murmured. "I already decided to do it—I just wanted to complain about it first."

Windley cracked a grin. "Shall I stop trying to solve your problems, then, and simply absorb them?"

"No, no, continue. You're pretty when you're musing."

"Then I must always be musing."

Humble, to the core.

His smirk faded into quiet seriousness. "Now, I'll say something that may sting. Ready?"

I nodded, tracing the intricate lines of his face, bracing for whatever truth he'd share next.

"Sir Albie likely would have fallen protecting you one way or another—perhaps jumping in front of a runaway caravan or shielding you from a falling branch. But the fact that you literally used the last of his life to survive..." Windley exhaled slowly. "For him, Merrin, there was no higher honor."

The world fell silent.

For as long as needed.

"I know," I whispered. "And it would have been senseless for both of us to die. But having his blood on my hands..."

"It's not on your hands," Windley corrected, firm yet comforting. "It's on Ed's."

That hit like a punch to the ribs.

"You've already forgiven him," Windley continued evenly. "Why should forgiving yourself be any different?"

I hadn't thought about it like that.

"Who knew you were so wise?"

His smirk returned, warmer this time. "Well, *I* did, for one."

We exchanged flirtatious glances, his lingering longer than mine.

And since we'd already touched upon Albie... I clutched the two coral pendants against my chest. Was I brave enough?

Windley pressed a finger lightly to my lips, knowing me as well as ever. "Before you ask—are you certain you truly want to know?"

I hesitated.

His palm rested against my cheek, as if shielding me from whatever pain waited behind the question.

"He loved you, and you him. All your memories together..." His thumb swept affectionately over my cheekbone. "What happens if you learn he was your father? And what if you discover he wasn't? You would love him no more or less," Windley assured quietly. "Your memories would hold the same meaning."

I swallowed thickly. "You already know, don't you?"

Windley gave a single, simple nod. But his expression revealed nothing. "Think on it, and let me know."

I want you, and I would give up everything to have you, so... think about that and let me know...

Albie's memory was perhaps too fresh a wound to prod further. I'd think, and then I'd let him know.

But there remained another topic—

The deepest one.

The most forbidden one.

I was questioning my role as queen. *Dreading* the idea of tucking Windley away like a shameful secret.

And he wasn't mentioning it—because he knew how easily swayed I would be.

He loved me too deeply to ever ask me to run away with him.

"What?" He tilted his head. "You look like you want to say something."

"Since we left the Crag, you've opened up to me completely, Windley. I've seen a new side of you—one I never would have guessed, for all your teasing. You're a thoughtful partner. How do you know how to treat me so well?"

His mouth twitched, pleased by the compliment.

"It comes naturally, queenie. I spent years imagining how I'd treat you if you were mine—played it endlessly in my head." His eyes shimmered with emotion reserved solely for me. "Besides, when someone cares as purely and fiercely as you do, it's easy to return the favor."

I felt closer to him than ever before. I skimmed my fingers along his jaw, thumb grazing his cheek—and he pressed a kiss to its tip.

"What color's my hair, queenie?"

"Yellow."

He closed his eyes, exhaling through his nose, shifting it slowly into scarlet.

Like the wood.

Windley rubbed his cheek into my palm.

"W-Windley! You have stubble! I've never seen you with stubble!"

He chuckled, lazily nudging into my touch. "Mmm. Spirite survival tactic. Have to adapt to all preferences. We've been courting weeks now—must keep things spicy."

I squinted skeptically. "You can just...grow facial hair at will?"

He smirked wickedly. "Not just facial hair."

"Windley."

"Whatever it takes to woo our prey." His teeth teasingly grazed my thumb.

I rolled my eyes but let him play, though the word prey lingered in my mind.

For a moment, only fond silence hummed between us.

Then, hesitant—

"Windley, is Pip... Are Dracons truly as bad as they sound?"

He let out a low breath, warmth skimming my skin. "Worse, probably. Bad enough for the moon to hand Rafe her power again. The angels wiped them out, didn't they? No idea how he slipped through. But you saw—Spirites make formidable foes." His smirk eased. "Or rather, you and Rafe do."

My thumb lingered at the corner of his mouth. "You handled those hatchets like they were a part of you," I murmured.

Windley's smile curved—half pride, half tease. "Careful, lion queen. Praise like that is how you *start* trouble."

I ignored the invitation and pressed on, needing to be sure his own storm had settled.

"How are you—truly? About Pip?"

His fingers stilled; he let out a slow breath and tilted his gaze to the sky.

"Honestly? It's a relief."

"What do you mean?"

His mouth twisted faintly. "I felt guilty. Thought leaving him behind created the monster he became—all those people at Abardo, guests at the castle, Sir Albie..." His voice trailed briefly, then steadied. "But seeing what he truly is—that wasn't my doing. He was never just some defenseless kid. Knowing that...absolves a lot of my guilt."

"But you cared for him once, didn't you?"

His jaw ticked. "Sure. But the more I see what he's capable of—the Cove, what he put you through—the more I realize the Pip I knew is already gone." Sadness flickered briefly behind his eyes before he quickly hid it. "I mean it, Merr. I'm getting by."

Evening settled crisp and cool, the sky streaked in molten oranges that bled into bruised violet.

For a heartbeat I only watched him—the shy dimple that tried to hide whenever he fought a smile, the steady lift of his chest, the pulse ticking in his throat almost in time with mine—until the hush between us felt alive and waiting.

"Merr," he breathed, a question without words.

I answered with a kiss—soft at first, then searching.

He tasted of dusk and freedom; when our lips parted he lingered, close enough for me to feel each exhale against my mouth.

Around us—

Tall grass bowed, a green hush of privacy.

Beneath us—

Spring-soft moss rose to cushion every shift.

His hand tucked a curl from my brow; my nod sent a quiet thrill through him. He moved slowly—unfastening a clasp, smoothing fabric from my shoulder, letting the night air kiss new skin, always pausing for the smallest sign of hesitation. There was none.

Thought unraveled; instinct took the reins.

Skin on skin.

Shared breath growing warmer, quicker.

He eased me back against the moss, guiding rather than

leading, every touch an invitation rather than a claim—teaching my body how to want without fear.

Yet a warning pricked:

He's working hard to tame himself for you...

"I don't want to tame you," I whispered, voice snagging as a distant ocean rose inside me—afraid I might turn his restraint into a cage.

"Tame?" he echoed, breath rough.

"Is it true you wish to lie with other people?"

He stilled instantly.

"Absolutely not," he said—almost offended. "I have *you*. Why would I want anyone else?"

I shifted to straddle him, and the tide inside me surged anew.

"I just...needed to be sure," I confessed, pulse unsteady. "If you won't claim ownership of me, I won't lock you in a cage."

He held my gaze for a long, electric heartbeat—then his hands tightened at my hips, eyes flaring brilliant emerald.

"Merrin," he growled, voice rasping with heat, "I have never felt more *free* than when I'm with you."

I felt the same—and told him so.

His hands moved with an artist's patience—tracing, coaxing, drawing helpless sounds from deep inside me—never once crossing the fine line between mastery and care. When pleasure threatened to outpace me, he slowed, murmuring praise into my hair; when curiosity nudged courage, he answered it with gentle surety. Each time he breathed my name, half-worship and half-promise, the wide, wild world shrank to the safe harbor of his arms. By the time we were tangled and breathless, the urgency felt both brand-new and long overdue.

One deft motion rolled me beneath him again, his soldier's body solid, commanding. His lips brushed mine, a spark poised to blaze.

"Want to see a trick only Spirites can manage?" he whispered, breath smoldering across my lips, our foreheads almost touching.

His gaze pinned me from inches away, dark and decadent, lips curling in a wicked tilt.

I wanted to nod—

But the ocean inside me roiled dangerously close.

Waves rose—crested—

Then simply hung there, relentlessly suspended at their peak.

Windley watched over me, drinking in every gasp, every desperate cry, every helpless shiver as sensations danced unbearably at the edge.

I uttered countless embarrassing things—curses, his name, animalistic sounds—

All while trembling from pleasure too intense to contain.

And then—

"Alright," he whispered huskily, after long, exquisite minutes. "Too long? Too short? You can critique my timing later."

Then—with one decisive, bone-deep thrust—he shattered the restraint he'd woven, and this time I wasn't the only one who cried out.

We collapsed together, sweat mingling, hair damp, our limbs interlaced in the pillowy moss.

I was too breathless to speak.

When I finally could—

"H-heavens..." I rasped. "Only Spirites can do that?"

Windley answered with a slow, smug nod, satisfaction humming beneath his skin.

I lay back, bold and bare beneath the endless sky, hair wild in the breeze, chest still trembling for breath. A grin tugged at my lips.

"No wonder half the Cove queued up to bed Edius."

Windley's hand closed in my hair—possessive, just shy of pain—as he tipped my head, baring my throat.

"Don't say his name while looking like this."

Deliberately, he dragged his tongue from shoulder to ear, predator-sharp teeth grazing the curve of my lobe, breath scorching against my skin.

"Wait until you see what else I can do, lion queen."

"Goddess help me."

7

MENDING THE CROWN

"Mmmm." Windley held me from behind, cross-legged in the spongy moss, as we watched dusk bleed gently into night. He kissed my shoulder, nuzzling into my neck. "If I could freeze time, I think this moment would be my pick. Don't you agree?"

"Yes. Although, there was that other moment just a short while ago...but if you want me in working condition, this one might be better."

He squeezed me playfully between his knees. "Liked that moment, did you?"

Very, very much.

We watched the day's final colors fade until night sounds began whispering around us, wrapping the woods in a cool hush filled with unseen life.

"Windley?"

"Yes, love?"

"My heart still aches terribly for Albie, and I'm anxious about Pip, but despite it all...I'm happy." I turned to him, my palms cradling his face, tracing the strong line of his jaw.

"Me too, queenie. More than I ever imagined."

"Merrin?"

A voice like wind over wheat, a hush that seemed to fill everywhere at once. Vita.

"I do not wish to interrupt your moment, for your warmth is tangible, but it is precisely because of your warmth that I must. Your heart is perfectly prepared to mend the Crown of the Wood."

I sighed, tapping my ear dutifully. "Goddess stuff."

Windley's fingertips skimmed my shoulder as if disrupting the still surface of a pond. "Mm. Harder and harder to let you go, queenie..."

The chill left in his wake told me the feeling was mutual.

He withdrew, heading toward the cabin to search for supplies, leaving me beneath the slowly darkening sky, where the earliest stars had begun to wink awake. It was autumn, northern autumn. Perhaps tonight we'd be treated to auroras of gold and scarlet.

"Are you ready, little royal?" Vita coaxed with quiet tenderness.

"Not quite yet. There's something I need to say first."

I had practiced this, yet in practice, the words had always faltered.

"You need not say it aloud, Merrin. I already know."

"I need to say it," I insisted, determined. "For myself. To prove I can."

"Very well, Merrin. Proceed."

Gathering courage, I breathed deeply. "What happened with Albie—the way you forced my hand...it was awful. It wasn't my choice, and I don't know if I'll ever truly reconcile with having stolen his final moments."

Vita remained quiet, patient, letting me continue.

"But that's my heart speaking. Logically, I know why you

did it. I know it was senseless for both of us to die." Another steadying breath filled my lungs. "I wanted you to know that I forgive you—but not completely. I don't think I can ever forgive you fully. I need to hold on to a sliver of anger—just enough to keep me standing."

"Humes are complex beings," Vita answered, voice like a hush between heartbeats. *"Your feelings are natural. I willingly carry the weight of your anger."*

"Thank you for keeping me alive, Vita."

"It was necessary for the good of all," she responded. *"And... I did not wish to see you perish."*

Warmth flooded through me, pressing away any lingering bitterness toward the goddess and her actions—all but a small, cold abscess I would keep guarded in my heart. A pocket of anger and regret, proof that I was imperfect. That we all were.

"Okay," I said finally. "Now I'm ready. Tell me how to restore the Crown of the Nemophilist."

Vita wasted no time.

"Hold my light in one hand and the destroyer's shadow in the other. Ground the soles of your feet in the pulse of the earth. Lift your gaze to the heavens. Listen to the whisper of the forest, heed the will of the sea. Picture clearly the broken halves of the Crown and imagine how you might mend them."

I followed Vita's instructions, picturing one half of the Crown held in shadow-dark fingers, the other nestled in an emerald glow.

Suddenly, I was no longer in that pine-filled clearing; instead, I stood in a shimmering space scented like springtime.

My soul.

Relief washed over me to see it unchanged by Exitium's presence, that no violent hunger writhed within.

Each hand gripped a half-crown—one a glittering lattice of crystal, the other a mirror-dark shard of jet. When I tried to join them, they slammed apart again, repelling me like twin north-poles of a magnet.

From deep within my soul, Exitium's laughter hissed in mockery.

But Vita's voice rang louder, steady and unwavering.

"Bend them to your will, Merrin. Feel it—in marrow and muscle. Desire it fully, and it shall be."

With every ounce of determination, as I had when first expelling Exitium, I commanded the pieces to reunite, pushing against their resistance, wishing it more than anything. Not from altruism, but from a purely selfish desire to complete this task and move forward.

Yet it worked all the same.

The destroyer's hissing laugh became a scream of frustration as the resistance gave way.

"Yes, Merrin!" Vita encouraged triumphantly.

The halves collided, erupting in brilliant, blinding light, overwhelming my senses. When it faded, the Crown was no longer in my hands.

It rested heavy and whole atop my head.

In my veins bloomed new, radiant power—like golden sunlight breaking through endless winter. Strength, arcane and ancient, wound sinuously through my core.

"Now, Merrin, you are the true bearer of the Crown. Now, we may banish the destroyer to the end of days."

The end of days.

An intangible concept, as intangible as the Crown itself had seemed moments ago. I ran fingertips along its jeweled edges.

"It's a literal crown. I always thought it was a metaphor."

Vita tinkled a laugh, as though humoring me. *"Not one existing in your physical world, but yes, an actual crown, hence its name."*

"Why was it created at all? And who created it?"

"*I did,*" Vita answered simply. "*It was a way to bind the destroyer's will to that of a mortal.*"

The truth felt strangely obvious now, though I'd never considered its origins deeply before.

"*It surprises you? Then allow me to tell you how it began,*" Vita offered. "*Before the first pages of time were written, there was only void. We were many, a host, countless beings existing as one.*"

Nameless goddesses, drifting in the heavens like embers—Windley had once spoken of them.

"*Within the host, I envisioned a world yet to exist and breathed life into it. But creation must always have an end; with my breath came another force, a counterbalance—the destroyer. She was not yet fallen, only necessary. Creation and destruction, inseparable. Yet as I built, she grew restless. Destruction came too soon, ruin scattered in the void. Time and again, I created life, only to have it prematurely undone, for creation cannot exist without destruction.*"

"How did anything ever survive?" I asked, intrigued.

"*Time,*" said Vita gently. "*Time as you know it was created to separate us. I would remain at the beginning, and she would wait at the end. For eons, we balanced each other from afar, watching life bloom.*"

"And then?"

"*The mothers of beastlings turned against us.*"

"The Drakaina?" My pulse quickened. "They existed already?"

"*Those you call Drakaina existed before the turning of the first page,*" Vita explained. "*From within the void arose a lineage distinct from our own. Though they aided in the forming of life, their vision did not match ours. They sought to mold creation in their image, turning beast against beast, forging creatures that* upset the balance we had carefully sown. War erupted, and the stirrings of destruction drew the destroyer from her resting place."

Vita's voice lowered, heavy with memory. "She fed off the bloodlust rippling through creation and grew stronger, refusing to return to the end of days even after the war had been won. But as she grew, so did I, until I forged a vessel strong enough to contain her—the Crown of the Wood, for in the wood, my breath thrives strongest. But binding the destroyer also bound myself."

"So you created a way for that vessel to attach to a mortal, so they could carry her there for you?"

"Not just any mortal," Vita corrected softly. "Only those I had cradled in my hand longest, those whose blood carried divine energy, for I knew their will would protect all of creation. You, little royal, possess such a will. That is why you must be the one to deliver the destroyer to the end of days."

And that was when I realized I had unwittingly agreed to a task far heavier than I'd intended.

Vita continued solemnly. "At the farthest edge of your world, there is a cave from which crawled the first spark of life. It exists outside your mortal realm, beyond living and dead—a passage leading to the end of days, where the Drakaina remain in banishment."

"Wait—" My pulse quickened. "The Drakaina are at the end of days?"

"It was the only suitable place to exile them."

No wonder Exitium didn't want to go back there, if half of what I'd heard about them was true.

"And just where exactly is the farthest edge of the world? Can it be marked on a map?"

"For you, it lies in the direction known as south."

"South? But Vita, we've just come from the south! I don't

even know how far the south extends! And now Pip's after us—"

"*The Dracon poses a significant threat,*" Vita conceded yet didn't sound worried, "*but not for much longer. To cast the destroyer into the end of days is also to put an end to the Drakaina and their offspring.*"

Realization struck me, sharp as a blade.

"By offspring...you mean only the Dracons, right?"

Vita did not answer.

"Vita?" Panic rose, tightening around my heart.

"*Destruction belongs at the end of days,*" she said quietly. "*The Drakaina exist there in exile. To end the Drakaina would erase their breath from the world. And when the Drakaina fall, so too will their offspring—Dracon and beastling alike.*"

Next time, I'd demand every detail before setting out on an epic quest.

"What?!" My heart slammed painfully against my ribs. "But—but you adopted the Spirites—the beastlings—when you banished the Drakaina! They're your children now! How can you ask me to be the vessel for destroying an entire species? You know the depth of my love for Windley, the warmth I have for Edius!"

"*That is the duty of she who bears the Crown of the Wood,*" Vita said evenly. "*Will you accept it?*"

Absolutely not.

The line between good and evil was far too thin.

"Destroyer!" I called inwardly, my desperation boiling over. "Can you hear me? I refuse to utter your name, but I wish to speak with you!"

"*Merrin! Do not call for her!*" Vita flared urgently. "*She will bring you nothing but ruin!*"

"What choice do I have, Vita?" I shouted, furious. "I would

never willingly destroy an entire race of people—I will not condemn Windley to death! What is wrong with you?"

Another presence slithered into my awareness, silky and venomous. *"Hello, Merrin,"* Exitium purred. *"Are you ready to awaken to your true nature once again?"*

"No!" I snapped. "I won't be your conduit for destruction— but neither will I be Vita's vessel to erase an entire species. Is there another option?"

"I do not wish to be banished from this world either," Exitium hissed. *"The end of days is but a distant dream. Split the Crown, cast me out, and I shall leave you be."*

"To find another host you can use to end the world?"

Exitium offered no reply.

I growled in frustration. "No! My only choices can't possibly be 'destroy the world' or 'destroy the Spirites.' I refuse both outcomes! Logic dictates that in a universe of infinite possibilities, there is always another path. Choosing the lesser of two evils is never fitting for those who forge their own destiny!"

"Yes," Vita murmured approvingly. *"Now you are thinking like a creator. Two choices have been offered. If you desire a third, you must create it yourself. You know, I found it quite humorous your soul chose a beastling for its counterpart. Perhaps it was always meant to be. I shall watch in silence, little royal. Luck be yours."*

With a playful giggle, Vita's presence slipped away, leaving me back in the woods beneath a tapestry of starlight.

An irritated Windley jumped from the porch steps, hurrying toward me.

"Took your sweet time, didn't you?" His voice was tight, but the arms he wrapped around me were tighter—"Oh, well, wait. Your skin feels...delightful, Merr. Can't describe it exactly, but it's like seeing light at the end of a long, lonely tunnel. What happened? Did you repair the Nemophile's Crown?"

I recounted everything to him, leaving nothing unsaid.

"Wait—Lady Life wants you to—oh my goddess! It's because she saw what I did to you, isn't it? I defiled the Nemophilist! And I defiled her thoroughly, I—"

"No." I placed my palms against his chest, quelling him. "I think this is more of a test. Almost like Vita expects me to defy her, to forge a different path." I swallowed hard, conviction building. "I still trust Vita. She must have our best interests at heart. This feels like a roundabout way to push me toward where I truly need to go—but I have no idea how to begin."

One thing was certain: I wouldn't unleash Exitium onto the world.

But neither would I carry the Crown to some ancient cave to erase the Drakaina, Dracons, and Spirites from existence.

And, deep down, I sensed Vita didn't want that either.

"Er, Windley?"

He was rubbing his cheek against my forearm as if trying to erase a smudge.

"Shit—sorry, Merr, it's just—you feel really, really good. Your spirit feels juiced up or something."

He shook his head slightly, eyes dazed, though his fingertips lingered, tracing lightly up my arm.

"I have to say, I'm relieved it was your head that Crown landed on. Plenty of royals would gladly wipe us beastlings out without a second thought. Even tamed, we could be threats. Look at Ascian. Look at Charm. Most would eagerly end a threat like us."

I held his gaze. "I've known evil humans and good humans, cruel Spirites and kind ones, vicious animals and gentle creatures. Goodness isn't determined by species."

I turned my eyes upward, tracing the glittering constellations scattered across velvet darkness.

"I will find another way."

Above us, Luna—once again round and full—began her slow, silver dance across the sky. Her moonlight spilled richly, bathing the landscape in liquid silver, casting jagged silhouettes of trees and mountains into dreamy relief.

As the autumn auroras began their delicate, twisting ballet overhead, the answer lay just before me, beautiful and intangible.

Yet I couldn't grasp it, not yet.

Beside me, Windley rested an elbow on my shoulder with loose-limbed ease, releasing a slow, steady breath.

"If anyone can rewrite destiny, it's you, lion queen."

8

PERPETUAL DAWN

By the time Rafe and Edius returned, I had little in the way of a plan. And while Windley and Rafe looked to me for direction, Edius already had plans of his own.

"I'm leaving tonight."

It wasn't a suggestion—it was final.

"What do you mean you're leaving?" I demanded.

"I wanted your help to get the ring from Charm." He nodded toward the back of the cabin, where the corpse of a golden-haired cupcake lay at rest. "Mission accomplished. So now..." His ancient eyes grazed the southern skies.

Gwen.

"Ah—" Windley narrowed his gaze at the ring on Ed's finger. "Yeah, that's not gonna work, mate."

"What?"

"Sorry, it's not that I don't trust you, but I'm not keen on letting that ring go on living. Especially not if Pip's after it. We've got to destroy it, and it just so happens we have a destroyer in our midst. Queenie's shadow power ought to take care of that, I'd imagine."

Edius guarded the master ring, hand tightening protectively. "She can't. Not until..."

Yes. Based on what he'd told Pip, he didn't want to lift the hex until he could see Gwen himself. Because he feared her fate might mirror those hexed souls in Abardo. If there was no life left to sustain a hexed person when their curse fell...

"Then we'll accompany you, Edi. To Gwen's." I straightened. "And once you're ready, I'll destroy the ring so it never again falls into evil's hands."

"Better we stick together in case Pip comes for it anyway," Windley added.

"*When* he comes for it," I corrected.

When he did, the Crown would ensure he didn't survive.

For Beau's cavalry.

For the hexed town of Abardo.

For Albie.

For every wound he had inflicted.

For every hope he had twisted into fear.

For every dream he had smothered—we would see him undone.

I turned to the only other non-Spirite among us. "Rafe? I know you didn't sign up for another long journey—"

"Until you return home, Your Majesty."

Edius's gaze flicked between the three of us. "Wait, really?"

The surprise on his face was endearing enough for me to reach toward his shoulder. "I told you, Edius. You aren't in this alone."

But my hand never reached its mark.

"Don't!" Windley cried, grabbing my wrist before contact. Sheepishly, he added, "Eh-heh. Ever since the queen mended the Crown, she feels extra good to touch. Might wanna avoid doing so, Ed, lest we feed that lust triangle of ours."

Indeed, with his hand still curled around my wrist,

Windley didn't seem capable of helping himself. He drew me closer, his grip shifting to my collarbone, pressing me firmly against him. His nose brushed my neck—his favorite spot.

Rafe didn't bother hiding his disgust. "Tch. Just what we need."

From nearby, Edius folded his arms with a dry chuckle, observing us with amusement. "Guess that means no more sneaking into my blanket for cuddles, highness."

"We've already addressed that!" I snapped, swallowing the embarrassment as heat rose to my face. Pulling away from Windley's grasp—and pointedly ignoring his satisfied grin—I faced Edius fully. "Ed, where is Gwen?"

Edius cleared his throat roughly, his humor fading to something more serious. "That's...hard to explain. But I think you might be able to get us there faster than I could alone. We'll need a wide, open area, though."

Intriguing.

"Wide and open? Like the land south of here, between the queendoms and the Emerald Wood?"

"Should do."

Rafe appeared no more in the know than I, Windley was too preoccupied sniffing me to offer any insight, and Edius was already mounting his stag, eager to depart.

From there, we traveled several hours south before making camp, watching the skies vigilantly for signs of Pip through the pine-laden trees. With the power of flight, it would be simple for him to track us. It was only a matter of time before he decided to.

But I felt no fear.

For the first time, the Nemophile's Crown was mended and atop my head. And though Vita and Exitium had fallen quiet, I could feel insurmountable power at my fingertips.

When Pip returned, I would be ready.

...Assuming it was us he pursued.

"Oh my goddess! Why didn't I think of that before?!" I blurted.

Windley, who'd been particularly grabby since dismounting our stags, had captured one of my hands and was absently rubbing my knuckles.

"You mean, what's to stop Pip from heading back north and devouring Queen Sestilia, Beau, and anyone else he crosses paths with?" he asked, far too casually for my comfort.

"Yes! How could I not have considered—"

"Because you're harboring an immense load of responsibility and grief, and you're using nine-tenths of your mind's power trying to puzzle out a third option to the quandary Lady Life presented you."

True, perhaps, but that didn't solve the issue of a destroyer of humanity running loose—one who could easily leverage our northern allies against us.

Windley saw the worry brewing.

"Chap's taken care of it."

"Rafe has? How?"

"Well, firstly, when he was in that town with Ed, he sent out directives warning the surrounding queendoms, including Queen Beau. But that's of little use if we're dealing with a Dracon. More importantly, he's asked his mistress to help."

"Mistress? Soleil?"

"Mm. The sun's invested in protecting the queen and that divine babe she's carrying. You saw how she and Luna jumped in to shove Pip's influence away before, yeah? They'll do so again—Luna guarding Rafe's clan, and Soleil protecting her unborn heir. It'll be perpetually dawn in the queenlands until Pip is disposed of, which should prevent him from using whatever spell he cast on you."

That effortless beguiling.

"And the lands south of royal domain?"

"Will have you and those two goddesses in your head to guard them."

Two goddesses who'd grown eerily silent now that the Crown was whole.

I hummed in understanding, narrowing my eyes playfully. "And just what is it you're doing with my hand?"

"Ech!" Windley dropped it as if burned—unwise, considering he'd been rubbing it against his neck. "Apologies, lion queen. You're especially irresistible now. Best that no other Spirites lay hands on you." His jaw tensed until the muscles visibly stood out.

Curious. "What does it feel like?" I asked.

He exhaled sharply, clearly debating whether to answer. "It's like pressing into a sore muscle with just the right amount of pressure, or that moment just before..." He trailed off, biting down on his lip with a forced laugh.

To be looked at that way was not a bad thing.

"You can touch me all you'd like—" I leaned in, lips nearly grazing his ear. "Later."

"Fffuckkk."

With the smile of a temptress, I left Windley behind to check on the others.

"Ed, come here a moment?"

His tent-making skills had improved drastically since we'd left Flora's cottage all those days ago. It was with the correct side of the canvas in hand that he teased, "Do you really think now's the right time for a cuddle?"

"Edius!"

He grinned like a scamp.

A good sign. Hopefully, it meant I'd get a good answer to the question I was about to ask. Drawing him away from the others, I led him into a sparse stretch of woodland.

"I heard about the plan from Windley," I began. "It sounds like the north will be protected by celestial goddesses, but not the south. And I wanted to make sure...I was worried that..."

"Spit it out, highness."

I swallowed. "Pip—does he know where Gwen is?"

Edius's face betrayed nothing, his crafty stare unreadable. "No one knows where Gwen is except me and a few trusted others. Had to stow her away after..."

That perpetual dawn was settling in for a long stay, amber light reflecting in his dark eyes, turning them nearly the color of Rafe's.

"Will you tell me about her?" I asked, choosing my words with deliberate restraint. "And about..." I let my gaze drift to the ear tips hidden beneath his hair. "Will you tell me?"

He released a sigh heavy enough to crack mountains, staring off into some distant memory before returning to me. "You've got that golden glow right now, highness. Like the light can't help but find you. It's pretty."

I was not pretty—I was dirty and worn, frayed from the day's events.

I let his words sit briefly before kindly shifting the topic.

"I want to know about her," I said quietly. "This woman who made you give up your freedom and your values to follow an evil messiah. The one who softens your eyes at the mere mention of her name. She must be very special indeed, and I'd like to know."

Gwen.

Once we found her, perhaps the lust triangle would diminish. Perhaps I could build a relationship with him akin to the one I shared with Rafe—one where I didn't feel the urge to crawl into his bed at night or notice the sculpt of his shoulders and the shape of his jaw.

He exhaled through his nose, arms folding as he leaned back against the stiff bark of an evergreen.

"Yeah, I'll tell you about her—figured I would, someday." He drummed a finger on his bicep, gaze sliding off to nowhere. He let out a thin breath through closed lips.

And then he told me.

Finally, he told me.

"Gwen and I were dumped in the same piss-poor orphanage before Ascian picked me up. I was the lone Spirite, she was the lone Seelie—so yeah, I kept an eye on her. We both knew what it's like when people stare because you're 'different.'

"Kids with her sort of power usually get whisked away fast, but Gwen can't walk—born that way. There's nothing to 'fix'; it isn't a sickness. It's just who she is. Guess that's why nobody claimed her. Hell of a joke, right? A kid who can patch up half the world but can't swap out the one thing in herself that doesn't even need changing. ...Listen to me ramble.

"In the beginning I figured Ascian was rough, sure, but not a monster. Same lie the rest of us swallowed. If we're decent liars, he was a gods-damned poet. He dangled one thing none of us had ever tasted—a home.

"Look, my parents were Spirites, yeah, but they weren't exactly model citizens. Got themselves caged before I was old enough to learn their names. After that, every orphanage wrote me off—said the blood must be 'faulty.' That's what originally led me to do this—" He swept his hair aside, revealing one of his clipped ears. "Thought if I didn't look the part, maybe some-one'd take a chance."

"Oh, Edi!"

He put up a hand. "Told you—that wound's ancient histo-ry." A beat. "Gwen hated it, though. Said carving yourself up so somebody'll keep you is backwards." His thumb grazed the blunted point, then slipped into a fist as if to shove the memory away.

"Anyway." He exhaled through his nose. "So there I am, hungry for a roof and someone who wants me, and Ascian purrs, *You belong with me.* Felt like getting picked first after a lifetime of last. The nuns all but packed my bag for me, so I walked out—and, yeah, I left Gwen behind."

Regret flared in his eyes, raw as an open nerve. "Idiocy number two? I bragged to Ascian that I knew a Seelie. Thought he'd be impressed, maybe proud. Had no clue what kind of hell he'd make of it." He ground his teeth. "Been trying to undo that one stupid sentence ever since."

A Seelie. Gwen was a Seelie—one of those with light in their veins, able to heal ailments both magical and mundane. The very Seelie Ascian had used as his personal gauze for years. The one he'd drained to heal Charm on the beach. The one Pip had used to heal me in the spider's lair.

"Ed..." I reached for him but stopped short. "You know it isn't your fault, right?"

He didn't answer, but his expression hardened.

"I mean it. Children are taught to trust their elders. To be offered a home after never having one... You're a good person, Edius. Windley is too. You both fell victim to the words of a man who coerced you into unspeakable acts. But you aren't a villain, and you're no longer a victim. You're a survivor, as Windley is a survivor. And you've done so much to repay the debt you feel you owe."

"A romantic idea, highness."

"It's one I believe."

He kept his eyes on the dying light. "Soon as Ascian got wind of her, he breezed in, slapped that damn hex on, then tossed her aside like trash. When I hit seventeen I stole her back—forged the papers, signed the ledger, the whole bit—and hid her in a place only a couple of kids from the home and I knew existed. Spent every coin I'd ever squirreled away making sure it stayed off the maps. Haven't dared visit since—figured he'd sniff her out the minute I showed. But we wrote, every month, like clockwork. Right up 'til..."

"Until I destroyed Ascian."

His head dipped once. "Yup."

"Wait," I said. "You adopted her?"

"Gotta be seventeen down there before you're considered an adult. Gwen was younger than me, so it worked out to get her outta there earlier than she could've on her own."

"So you're legally her...father? I imagine that must be strange."

He chuckled softly. "'Cause you're still thinking of her as my fiancée? Yeah, imagine that would be strange."

The fall of his face came quickly.

"Well, anyway, Ascian promised he'd let her go if I did what he said, but I did what he said, and he still used her power whenever he damn well pleased. Seelies aren't bottomless wells; they burn out like anyone else. Took me too long to see he'd use her up before ever letting her go. That's when I started looking for ways to steal the ring. Tried a few times. Got beat. Was biding my time when you fell into my lap. Felt like a gift wrapped up in a bow."

Edius exhaled through his nose, finally meeting my gaze—unflinching and searching. The shadows stretched behind us, the sun ahead, and guilt coiled uneasily in my stomach.

"Sorry, hon. Ever since we caught you in those woods, I always meant to use you to free her. Always figured it'd be you... Being around you...it felt inevitable. So did being in your service."

As he spoke, something shifted in his expression: a subtle dip of his brow, a catch in his throat, a hint of restless longing.

"People don't just like you—they orbit you. I once joked you collected broken boys, but the truth is broken people collect you." He released a humorless scoff. "My life's a black ocean: a handful of sparks flickering on the horizon. Gwen— she's one of them. Steady, but far. And you?" Awe tugged at the edges of his voice. "You're the gods-damned sun, hanging bright right over that water."

Oh. That was quite a thing to say. A thing for which I had no adequate response.

"Please don't compare me to the sun," I managed, my heart willing itself to slow. "As you've seen, we have history."

A fleeting smile—disarming, not threatening. "Sorry, that just slipped out. Really not trying to use my 'charm' or what-ever you'd call it as a human. It's just hard not to with you. Seeing you like this..."

A flicker of emerald flashed in his sunlit eyes.

"I don't mean to stir up that triangle. Just—thank you. Danger trails you everywhere, yet being near you feels...right. I haven't had 'right' in a very long time."

Something painfully sweet, coming from someone so... untamed. I was glad he wasn't touching me. My heart was Windley's; it always would be.

Still, I sensed it—that plum-pit ache inside him, twisting tighter as he fought it. Perhaps my fault for choosing the loveliest hour of day to dig at a tender memory.

"Ed?" My voice cracked.

"Hm?"

"A Spirite can only love once." I swallowed. "Please—don't waste it on me."

A breathy laugh escaped him, but it never reached his eyes. "Not planning on it." His throat bobbed; one hand flexed against his arm. "Just...not sure how much choice I really have."

9

UNDER THE DUSKY SKY

It was with mutual understanding that Edius and I kept our distance during that camp and the next—not that it was difficult, as our rest stops were consumed by exactly that: rest. We made decent time, riding as swiftly as our stags allowed, slowed only slightly by the fact that prancelopes were no longer an option unless Rafe wished to share one with Edius —which would surely never happen.

Our destination, by the sound of it, was that expansive stretch of outlands beyond the last queendom but before the Emerald Wood. Edius insisted we choose a place beyond outskirts towns and lonely farmsteads—somewhere seldom traveled. Apparently, there was a trick to reaching Gwen that I could help with, though Edius remained tight-lipped about it, eyes continually flicking skyward and backward, scanning for signs of Pip.

If Pip was trailing us, he was doing an exceptional job of remaining hidden. So much so that I might've worried about the northern queendoms if not for the immobile sun and moon stationed at either horizon, standing a protective vigil. The farther we traveled, the dimmer the sky became, and it occurred to me that if the royal domain was perpetually bathed in dawn, everywhere else was doomed to perpetual dusk.

It was beneath this shroud of twilight that we stopped for camp near a grove of drippy willows, anticipating open fields the following day—though the word "day" hardly mattered now that Soleil and Luna were fixed in place.

Rafe spent some time lifting his sword toward the two celestial bodies, charging it with their power before tending the vegetable garden I'd conjured for his stew-making needs.

"This would've been helpful on the way down," he remarked, fingers buried in damp soil as he unearthed a potato to accompany his collection of carrots and leeks.

Indeed. But it wasn't a power I intended to keep. I would relinquish the Crown as soon as I figured out what to do about Exitium.

Yet I'd made no progress.

I was distracted by a dozen other things: defeating Pip, reaching Gwen, destroying Ascian's ring—and managing the two predators traveling with me. One avoided me for fear of accidentally touching my flesh, while the other had already touched me and was working very, very hard to be respectful.

Not that I minded Windley's persistent hands seeking my skin.

But out of consideration for our companions, we tried our best to remain apart.

He was looking at me from across the fire with lowered brows and an adorable pout when he offered, "You touch her, chap. See if it's the same for you or just us."

Rafe looked up from his stew, wary. "What?"

"Touch the queen and see if she feels...different, will you?"

Unenthused, Rafe leaned over and poked me once in the forehead.

Both Spirites stiffened, aware of what that spot represented. But not Rafe. Rafe had no reason to hesitate. "She feels normal."

Windley let out a long-suffering sigh. "As I thought. It's just us." He propped his chin on his fist, prodding at the fire with a lazy stick. The flames responded by spitting sparks into the dimming sky.

"Your moping is annoying," said Rafe, waving away the embers. "Woman up."

"Wait, *woman* up?" questioned Edius.

"Northern expression," Windley muttered, releasing another exaggerated sigh.

"Ugh, it's not like you can't touch her," said Rafe. "Just do so without groping her."

"Exactly the problem," Windley groaned dramatically. "The two have become one and the same."

Rafe rolled his eyes. "Fine. Mope." He shoved a bowl of steaming stew into Windley's hands before handing Edius and me ours with significantly more care.

We'd moved too quickly in previous nights for Rafe to showcase his culinary prowess, but now, as Edius took his first bite of Rafe's cooking...

"You're a good cook," he admitted.

"Isn't he, though?!" Windley chimed in, entirely too proud.

Rafe eyed them both suspiciously, searching for hidden ridicule before tentatively accepting the compliment. "Thanks."

"What spice is that?" Edius poked curiously at his stew.

"Red garlic. Usually only found in the far north. The queen grew some for me," Rafe said, a subtle note of pride in his voice.

From the corner of my eye, I caught Windley chewing anxiously at his spoon. When I tried to meet his gaze, he quickly looked away. He had definitely been staring, and that poor spoon was suffering the brunt of his frustrations.

I was determined we'd find time alone tonight—and reward him for his admirable restraint.

It felt cruel to flaunt, knowing Rafe missed Beau terribly and that Edius struggled daily to keep his heart closed to me. So in secret, we would find our moment.

And then, perhaps, I could take that spoon's place.

That lucky, lucky spoon.

Windley caught me grinning and couldn't help but grin back, though he clearly had no idea why.

"Let's scout around, eh, Ed? See if we can't catch Pip skulking about?" Windley tapped his hatchets together, restless.

"Are you certain that's wise?" I asked. Of the four of us, only Rafe and I wielded power bestowed by the goddesses.

"We won't go far, queenie." He winked. "Besides, I need some time away from you to collect myself." Steam puffed through his nose like the hound he was.

"Let him go," said Rafe, sounding exhausted already. "Please."

"Don't worry, highness. I'll protect him," Edius said dryly.

"Ha!" Windley crossed his arms indignantly. "Says the one without a weapon."

"I have a weapon," Edius countered, reaching instinctively toward his belt—then freezing mid-motion.

The short blade.

The one I had gifted him.

The one he'd used to kill Albie.

The three men turned toward me, carefully gauging my reaction.

But the cork in that bottle was dangerously loose—so loose, it was best left untouched lest it unleash a devastating flood.

"Be back before dark," I called sweetly, knowing full well dark would never truly arrive.

Windley hesitated only long enough to scan me for hidden pain before flashing a reassuring grin and calling Edius along. I watched them vanish into the brush—Windley chattering away, something amusing enough to make Edius snort.

The atmosphere grew notably quieter without my unbearable soulmate around.

"Queen Merrin?"

Unlike Rafe to begin conversation.

"I'm fine, Rafe, but thank you for asking."

I wasn't fine. And I wouldn't be fine for a very long time.

Grief was a beast that settled deep beneath the skin. Even buried, it could flare at any moment.

But in some ways, I was fortunate—distracted by our quest, by blooming love, by ridiculous lust triangles, danger, and the unknown. These distractions kept the wound from reopening.

"Mmkay," said Rafe simply. A quiet presence, much like Ruckus, who grazed contentedly nearby.

Rafe was a rock—a calming, tranquil rock. Sometimes, the stoniest souls provided the most comfort.

I soaked up the stillness, searching the sky for stars—a sky barely dark enough to reveal them—and reminisced about the first time we'd traveled through these willows. Back when the world was smaller, simpler.

Back before I'd experienced so many things.

I felt aged by it all. Tired. Ready for an end, but not necessarily ready to return home.

I didn't know how everything would play out, but I had confidence that I would end Pip, destroy the ring, and find a suitable fate for Exitium.

And afterward?

Two great paths stretched before me.

I was a good queen, after all. There was something to be said for duty, legacy. I loved my people, my court, my queendom, and the good I was able to accomplish through my station.

And I loved Windley enough to know I could never tuck him away.

I mused over it—over years spent with him just out of reach, over all the ways he'd shown his love from the shadows, over the countless signs I'd ignored.

The chains around my neck clinked softly—perhaps evidence of others' sins.

Early in this thing between us, I'd come to understand love didn't abide by rules, and the longer my heart went untamed, the more unruly it grew.

There was no taming it now.

No stopping a love like this.

I loved Windley with a love that deepened daily. Because of how he treated me. Because he believed in me. Because I could simply be myself in his presence. Because he was skilled and sexy and gifted at so many things. Because he was both charming and clever, hard and soft, polished and rough. Because he could settle my heart just as effortlessly as he could send it racing.

I loved him so damn much.

And I had a decision to make.

"Rafe, can I...ask you something?"

The Spirites had been gone for a while, and Rafe was busy plucking things from the garden for later use. He looked up at me, wiping dirt from his brow. "Sure?"

"It's about Windley."

"Uh..."

"Something I'd normally ask Beau."

"Oh no."

My eyes found refuge in a stalk of carrot. "When we...met bodies for the first time—"

"Oh *no*."

I barreled onward. "He did other things to me, aside from the obvious, to make me feel...er, I-I was wondering, are there things I might do for him as well?"

Rafe delivered the flattest, most vacant stare he'd ever summoned.

"I'm sorry, Rafe! I'm inexperienced in these matters, and there's no one else to ask! I worry Edius might become...aroused if I approached him."

Rafe's expression didn't budge. "Why not just ask the man himself? He's the expert."

"B-Because I don't think he'll tell me. I don't think he'd want me to...lower myself for him. But I do...want to. With me, he used his fingers and his m—"

"STOP. Stop. I get the picture." Rafe looked as though he wished to cease existing, but my obvious desperation seemed to evoke his pity. With a sigh toward the heavens, he relented. "Whatever he did to you, do it back to him and see if he likes it. It's...pretty intuitive."

"You don't think he'll be alarmed?" I pressed.

"He will be elated."

"But—"

"*Elated*, Your Majesty."

"Oh. Thank you, Rafe."

"You can thank me by never asking anything like that again," he muttered toward the garden.

Fair.

My intention was clear: I would take Rafe's advice.

While the others slept, Windley and I would steal away to be together. I would show him my desire, and he would be elated. And then I would tell him the full extent of my love.

That night, I did show my desire.

And the recipient was, indeed, elated.

But Windley was not involved.

10
NIGHTMARES

Ever since my cuddle mishap with Edius, Windley had cycled out of guard duty to stop me from pursuing Edius's scent in my sleep—a command none of us had forgotten.

Which was why the guards were all the more confused when I suggested Windley take second shift during our stay among the willows.

"You sure, queenie?" Windley glanced cautiously toward his Spirite brother.

I nodded firmly in front of the others and leaned closer, whispering warmly into Windley's ear, "Wake me when it's your turn. You won't be disappointed."

"O-oh?" Windley's confident expression faltered, becoming boyishly adorable. "Can't decline an ask like that. You heard the lioness, mates. Ed, first shift; I've got second, yeah?"

As always, I formed a pair of vigilant golems to help keep watch before ducking into the tent after Rafe. I nestled next to Windley beneath layers of blankets, cuddling without skin contact so neither of us would be too distracted to sleep. His warmth enveloped me protectively, his scent soothing.

But the dream I fell into was anything but.

Beau and I stood hand-in-hand deep in the Scarlet Wood as inhuman echoes reverberated through the bleached bark of the trees. Crimson leaves beneath us clung wetly to Beau's gown— blood had painted the wood scarlet.

In the darkest corner of the forest, a pair of familiar, dangerous eyes gleamed. I released Beau's delicate hand and stepped forward, knowing this time exactly whose gaze awaited me. "Exitium."

Or so I thought.

"Wrong," came a voice—light, calculating—as the owner of those obsidian eyes stepped into Luna's silver glow. Dark, curling horns sprouted from spun-sugar hair. Pip's cruel, black gaze met mine, his mouth twisted smugly.

"I've found you, miss queen lion," said Pip, "found you in a place you can't hide."

"Hide?" I laughed. "I have no desire to hide. Face me! Let's end this now!"

Pip's smile stretched wider. "Even though you can't use your magic?"

"Wha—?"

He was right. I lifted my hand to conjure destruction—but nothing came.

"I'm...dreaming?" I realized.

"Yes," Pip purred. "But just because you can't use magic here doesn't mean I can't use mine. Come to me, Merrin."

Dream or not, my feet moved against my will. "Wait!"

The plush ground, the papery bark of the trees—if this was a dream, why did it all feel so painfully real?

"Because it is," hissed Exitium's voice from everywhere and nowhere. "And the only way to save yourself is to vanquish the enemies of your blood. I told you, when we smite this world, the beastlings shall be first."

"No!" I shouted. "Never!"

Yet darkness was already swirling, pulling me closer to Pip.

"Release your bloodlust, Merrin. Release it and watch them fall, starting with your favorites."

Pip extended a hand, each finger crowned by a blackstone ring. "Come and let me suck the power from you. I'll start slow, highness. I'll start real—"

"Highness?"

My eyes snapped open, heart pounding, panic cresting in my chest. I spun, desperate to run—only to find I was no longer in the tent. A weeping willow arched overhead, branches brushing the earth like trailing fingertips. The evening air caught in my lungs, and I whirled—

Right into the solid warmth of a figure behind me.

"No!" I gasped, panic spilling free. "I won't kill them!"

Strong hands caught me by the shoulders, steady and reassuring.

"Hey, hey—relax. You're safe. Just a nightmare, highness."

My legs nearly buckled with relief, and I clung to his shirt, breath still unsteady.

"E-Edi?" My voice wavered.

"Yeah." His low rumble resonated through his chest—a warm vibration against my cheek. "Tried to wake you sooner, but you were really out of it. Didn't wanna scare you."

He brushed a hand through my hair, each stroke unhurried and grounding.

"You good now?"

"Yes," I whispered, not entirely sure. I hated realizing I'd wandered here asleep, laid bare to buried fears.

He went taut beneath my fingers—the first time we'd been this close since I mended the Crown.

His fingertips drifted, feather-light, over my shoulders—soothing, almost tentative. The simple tenderness sent warmth skimming across my skin, and I leaned into it before I could think; his breath hitched in a sharp, shaky inhale.

"Gods above," he murmured, voice rough, eyes wide. "That feels...far too good."

Something raw flickered in his voice—dangerous for both of us. Slowly, I eased back, relieved when he let me go.

But then I met his gaze and froze.

His eyes.

His eyes, *his eyes.*

Something shifted behind his expression—confusion or curiosity, I couldn't quite tell. His brows knitted slightly. "What? Why're you looking at me like that?"

Words dissolved on my tongue. I couldn't answer him.

"Highness?" he asked, leaning closer—precisely what he shouldn't have done, because it brought those eyes even nearer, glittering beneath dark lashes. My heart stumbled.

My fingers lifted on their own, tracing lightly over the softness of his lips, tracing the curve of a smile he rarely revealed.

I wanted to know his mouth.

He jolted back, startled. Uncertain. Yet beneath that uncertainty lay an unmistakable hunger.

"Merrín?" His voice was lower now, almost pleading. "What...what's this about? Are you even awake?"

In answer, I cradled his face between my hands and claimed his lips.

He stiffened briefly, shocked—but quickly surrendered, one hand sliding firmly along my jaw while the other tightened around my waist, drawing me flush against the burning heat of his body.

His lips parted, breath shuddering against my skin as he broke the kiss, a faint tremor coursing through him.

"Damn it, highness," he whispered, breath jagged, mouth hovering achingly close. "I don't know what's gotten into you, but you're making me forget how to behave."

Then he captured my mouth again, deeper, with feverish desperation—like a man determined to savor something he'd long denied himself.

It wasn't the kind of kiss I'd expected from him. This was fire—slow, intoxicating, deliberate—heat that sank into my bones and promised devastation.

His whole body burned beneath my palms, muscles coiled tight as he fought for control. And when he drew me closer, the hard, undeniable ridge of him pressed against my belly, leaving no doubt about what he craved.

"You have no idea," he breathed roughly, forehead pressing to mine, "how hard it is to be near you. Every time you smile, it takes everything in me not to give in."

His lips found my neck, igniting trails of heat that drew an involuntary gasp from deep within me. My fingers traced greedily along his frame—the taut cords of his arms, the breadth of his shoulders. He felt strong, built for this moment, and every touch made me ache for more.

And beneath it all, that cocoon in his chest twisted in desperation, as though clawing for release.

A breathless sigh...

A shiver passing through us both...

The faint metallic clink of a belt buckle loosening—

Suddenly, Edius went utterly still.

Awareness flashed vividly in his eyes. "Wait. Wait, wait—WAIT."

He drew in a shaky breath, pressing a single trembling finger firmly against my lips, stopping me. "Merrín—hold on. What...what are we doing?"

A fair question, truly.

"You don't want me, highness. Your boyfriend practically offered you permission, and you turned it down. So why this? Why now?"

But I couldn't reply, because Edius had told me to *wait*—and that single, firm command held me utterly still. My lips remained pressed obediently against his fingertip, gaze locked on his, spellbound.

His body flinched, eyes flaring with sudden horror as he wrenched his hand away, cupping it hastily over his face. "Shit —I didn't even realize I was—" He staggered back, terror plain on his features. "Everything just now—that was purely carnal desire?"

Without meaning to, Edius had ensnared me completely. His stare shimmered verdant emerald, filling my mind until I could see nothing but him, think of nothing but touching him again.

He dragged his fingers roughly through his hair, shaken. "Gods, Merrín, I'm sorry. I swear I wasn't trying to ensnare you. I...I like Windley. I never wanted to betray either of you. Oh gods, we can't come back from this—"

"Edius," I managed at last, voice uneven from the aftershock of his influence, "I know you need reassurance, but right now, I have to speak to Windley. I need him to know what happened here. I know this wasn't intentional—not for either of us—but you're not my first concern. We'll deal with the rest afterward."

I dreaded it. Windley had expectations about tonight, hopes. This shattered them.

Edius caught up to me, shoulders set, halting me. "Let me do it."

"Edius—"

"None of this was your fault." He eyed the red marks on my neck, my tousled state, guilt etched into every line of his face.

I swallowed hard, noting his unbuttoned shirt and the bruises faintly forming on his skin. "Thank you for stopping before—"

"Don't thank me." His voice wavered. "I could've hurt you a lot worse."

Before I could respond, he was gone, leaving me scrambling for how to confess any of this to Windley.

Moments later, Edius returned, towing a sleepy, disheveled Windley behind him. Windley's eyes lit upon seeing me—

Until he noticed my dirt-smeared feet, my tangled hair, and finally, my swollen lips.

His head whipped toward Edius. "Why does the queen look like she was just *tussled*?"

Edius exhaled heavily through his nose. "Let's talk." He caught Windley's arm, guiding him a short distance away— Windley craning his neck toward me the entire time.

I couldn't make out Edius's exact words, but I saw Windley's fist connect squarely with Edius's jaw.

"Windley!" I sprinted after them, panic flaring. "It wasn't just him! I was sleepwalking, and we accidentally touched, and—"

Windley whirled, hair wild from half-sleep, eyes rimmed with exhaustion and something deeper. His gaze pinned me in place, one heartbeat away from unraveling us all.

"I understand why it happened!" he lashed. "Doesn't mean I can't be upset! The fucker beguiled you without your consent! And don't feed me shit about not being able to hold back! If a pubescent version of me could deny her, then you damn well should be able to, *Edius!*"

Edius didn't refute it.

Windley fumed visibly.

"Are you in love with her?"

A question that struck perhaps harder than his fist had.

Finally, Edius pushed him away. "No."

Windley's gaze drilled into him. "Are you falling in love with her?"

Edius went quiet.

Every time you smile, it takes everything in me not to give in.

"So you decided to beguile her against her will?" Windley's voice dropped dangerously low.

"That's not what—"

"And what about you, Majesty?" Windley swung toward me, voice raw. "Seems like you're more concerned about us than about yourself being violated, which is...frustrating, but expected at this point."

He was right.

I was more concerned about them.

Because I didn't feel violated.

Because...

"Ah. You liked it."

Windley voiced the secret I'd tried to bury.

A muscle jumped in his jaw. "Well, can't say I blame you there either. You're built to like it."

"Windley—"

He raised a hand. "Let me make one thing clear. I might be willing to share you with a boorish royal for optics and producing heirs, but I will *never* let your affections be stolen by another predator. Physical recreation is one thing, but this?

He's not just after your body, Merrin. He's after your heart, and his is dangerously soft for someone in his line of work."

That was why the cuddle had upset me so deeply.

That was why I'd been distraught over the nuzzle.

Small moments had huge impacts.

"My affections haven't been stolen," I said sternly. "You should know me better than to think I'd allow that."

Windley's eyes remained guarded, but warmed a touch. "I wasn't implying they were."

Edius, meanwhile, was a storm barely contained. "I'm not after her heart. I know she's yours—or rather, you're hers. Whatever's happening to me...it's not something I want." His gaze flicked briefly to mine before he stepped closer to Windley.

Windley squared his shoulders, standing his ground. "You know what would happen if it became serious," he warned quietly, holding Edius's stare. "I'd have no choice but to challenge you—and I'm exceedingly adept at dueling."

"Which is why this alliance is over," Edius finished firmly. "After we deal with Pip, I'm getting the hell out of your lives."

Windley lowered his fist, tension draining from his expression. Edius had become his first Spirite friend in ages, and over recent weeks, the three of us had bonded deeply. Shared experiences forged powerful connections.

Selfishly, I'd come to see him as a trusted guard.

Selfishly, I didn't want him to leave.

"Your growing feelings will fade once I relinquish the Crown," I offered hopefully. "You've never known me without it."

Pity tempered Windley's anger. He sighed heavily. "Dunno, queenie," he muttered. "I fought and lost that battle too—you do have a few..." He pinched his fingers together playfully, a tiny gap between them. "Other things going for you besides the Crown. But it's worth a shot."

He placed his hand on Edius's shoulder. "I know your intentions are good, Ed. Lesser men wouldn't have stopped where you did. But I've loved her for a long, long time, and it was hell to get her to see it. I need you to lock that heart of yours back up, even if it kills you."

He eyed the damage he'd inflicted. "Sorry about your face, mate."

"And I'm sorry about..." I struggled for the right words.

Windley waved it off. "It's common in the south to share lovers, especially among our kind. Not bothered by that. It's the 'being forced' part I don't like. And feelings from an unpracticed predator toward the woman I love? Could do without those."

As could I.

As could we all.

It was with mixed emotions that we resolved to move past the incident.

No one else ever had to know what had transpired.

No one else—

"Well, that was entertaining," said a voice like wind through reeds.

We three messy people spun to see a pastel-haired fiend drifting down from atop the nearest willow, shadowy wings half-extended.

Pip.

"Is that what they call drama?"

Windley stiffened.

Edius exhaled sharply.

"But don't worry, brothers," Pip murmured, eyes glittering in the dusky gloom. "Love was a gift from the goddesses. When our mothers awaken, that gift shall be returned."

II

ALL HANDS

"Though it does say quite a lot about them," Pip continued, kicking Rafe's canteen casually across the campsite. "The goddesses, I mean. They let you Spirites love so you could relate to their other creations—but only once, unlike their own children who can love again and again. Do you have any idea how much pain that's brought your kind?" He folded his arms leisurely behind his back, gaze sliding wickedly between us. "If you died tomorrow, Windalloy, your human would fall in love with Edi. And if he died, she'd fall in love with another. Such is the shallowness of her affections. You deserve better." His eyes found mine, sharp as razors. "Come to me, queen lion."

In the land of dusk, beyond Soleil and Luna's protection, my feet began to wander toward him.

"Argh—no! Snap out of it, Merr!" Windley lunged to restrain me, only to be rewarded by the nearest willow lashing violently at him. He shot a glance at the canvas wall a few paces away. "Rafe—out of the tent! Bring that flaming sword, *now!*"

"Really?" Pip tilted his head mockingly. "Dragging another liability into this?" He motioned toward me as I continued drifting obediently closer.

Edius sprang forward, but my golem intercepted, charging from the perimeter, stronger than even the strongest Spirite. Edius grappled against it, muscles straining, finding no leeway. Windley hacked at the thrashing branches, but each severed limb regrew instantly.

There was nothing they could do against my magic.

There was nothing they could do against Pip.

Lucky for them, I wasn't truly spelled.

The moment Rafe burst from the tent was the moment Pip laid hands on me—and exactly the moment I unleashed the shadows I'd silently conjured.

Chains of destruction whipped around the Dracon, binding his arms to his sides.

Windley, still tangled in branches, let out a triumphant cheer.

I freed him and commanded my golem to retreat from Edius as Rafe rushed to my side, disheveled but gripping a sword encased in frost and tipped in flame.

"What?!" Pip hissed, struggling fiercely. "You should be helpless—the sun and moon aren't here to aid you!"

True enough, but the Nemophile's Crown was restored. A glove of emerald creation climbed my skin, mingling with destruction swirling eagerly in my palms. Pip was bound before me.

The Dracon was captured.

I was going to kill him.

"Restrain her," Pip spat viciously at the only other human present. "And if you can't restrain her, kill her."

"Don't look at him, Rafe!" I shouted desperately.

But it was too late.

Rafe's blade swung ruthlessly toward my chest.

I stomped into the earth, hoping to topple his balance, but he stood firm, fire licking dangerously at my shirt. Windley was there in an instant; the sharp clang of metal announced at least one hatchet intercepting Rafe's blade.

"Wound my brothers, mage," Pip ordered Rafe calmly, eyes never leaving mine. "But keep them alive if possible."

Rafe moved swiftly, practiced slashes cutting air—physical blade merely the decoy to deliver devastating waves of frost and flame.

Windley knew his moves.

Edius did not.

Edius dodged the blade's edge but caught the full blast of fire in his stomach.

"Argh!" He howled, tumbling backward, desperately smothering the flames eating at his clothing. Windley tried reasoning with Rafe while dodging precise strikes, but Rafe was unresponsive.

Pip knew we wouldn't readily hurt one of our own.

"Golems! Restrain Rafe, but don't harm him!" I commanded urgently.

The clay figures charged, but Rafe's skill was unmatched. He evaded their grasps fluidly, rolling and springing again—this time toward Edius, who still fought off lingering flames.

Edius anticipated the fire, but the frost caught him unaware, slicing deep into his arm and staining his sleeve crimson. "Fucking hell!"

"Get behind me!" Windley shouted, charging forward. "I know chap's tricks!"

My focus jerked back to Pip as the shadow chains weakened. He flexed powerfully, shattering them like glass.

"No matter," I growled. "I'll do it again—"

But Pip's hand snatched my wrist.

And I dropped to my knees.

Crown or not, his touch was consuming.

"Oh, I see that still works," he murmured, hauling me upright by my throat. "Oh?" His tone melted, reverent—then his breath caught, eyes widening with realization. "O-oh. You feel rapturous."

His fingers tightened possessively around my wrist, as if testing the fit of shackles. "I'd hate to end you here, should my brothers misbehave. These wrists were made to be bound."

He lifted my arm slowly to his lips, brushing them tenderly over my pulse before placing his teeth lightly against my skin.

"*Unhand* her."

Windley's voice was a pure, deadly snarl. He'd abandoned his battle, leaving Edius to manage alone as he raced toward us, hatchets raised.

"Not another step, Windalloy!" Pip's fingers pressed tighter against my throat, just enough to make me choke.

"Merrin!" Windley skidded to a halt, teeth bared, glare darker than midnight. "I swear to goddess, Pip, I'll carve off those hands if you don't release her."

Meanwhile, Edius desperately dodged Rafe's enchanted blade, my golems sluggishly trailing, helplessly outmatched by Rafe's speed and precision.

"Damn it, Pip!" Edius snarled as frost skimmed his thigh, ice crackling dangerously over fabric and flesh.

"Stop, mage," Pip called mildly, as if bored. "Leave Edi alone. Turn the blade on yourself."

"NO!" My scream ripped through the clearing as Rafe's body obeyed, the sword's blazing tip angling ominously toward his own throat.

"Edius, get away from him!" I shouted frantically, thrashing against Pip's hold, but my limbs betrayed me, melting willingly beneath the devastating softness of his touch. If a Spirite's contact could cause a swoon, a Dracon's threatened to obliterate entirely.

Pip barely acknowledged my struggles, voice steady. "Give me the ring, Edi. Now—or I'll have him finish the job."

Edius hesitated, gaze darting between Rafe's blade and my weakening form, before choosing his own path—defying us both, lunging at the enthralled magician.

"End yourself, mage," Pip commanded Rafe coldly.

But Edius reached Rafe just in time, tackling him fiercely to the ground, wrestling desperately as the enchanted sword flew from Rafe's grasp, scorching the grass as it landed out of reach.

Still not enough.

"Shit—he's holding his breath!" Edius cursed, realizing the beguiled sorcerer fought internally to obey Pip's command.

"Let him go, Pip!" I writhed against Pip's deceptively lean body, but my traitorous limbs craved the feeling, lulled dangerously by the Dracon's overpowering touch. Every nerve, every instinct betrayed me, urging me deeper into his embrace.

Pip smirked, eyes alight with twisted amusement. "Wow, Edi. You must not care about her after all, if you're unwilling to trade the ring for her safety."

"Oh, shut the fuck up, you little psycho," Edius barked. "Of course I care about her. But if there's one thing I've learned about the queen, it's that she can take care of herself!"

True.

But sometimes, even magical queens could use a little help.

My mind struggled valiantly against Pip's influence, but my body—my human body—was steadily weakening beneath his touch.

And while Pip was distracted toying with Rafe and Edius, he hadn't noticed Windley.

Windley, whose eyes had never left mine.

Windley, silently urging me, without words, to look at him.

Windley, who didn't even need glowing eyes to ensnare me completely.

Pip's touch was all-consuming—

But the moment Windley's gaze flashed vibrant green, Pip's spell shattered.

I drew in a ragged breath, and darkness erupted from every pore of my body, engulfing the entire grove.

A frantic cry split the night, followed by the hiss of searing flesh; when the shadows thinned, Pip was gone.

Rafe hunched nearby, gulping air. Windley slid an arm beneath mine just as my knees buckled, propping me upright.

"Where did he go?" I breathed, clinging to him while the last shreds of darkness drifted skyward.

"Flew off, I'd wager. He'll be back—nothing else to entertain him, and he wants that ring even more than he wants you." He drew a slow, steadying breath, then pressed a kiss to my forehead—dirt, sweat, and all. "Nice work, queenie."

"Likewise." I squeezed his arm. "You...saved me, Wind."

"And why," he teased, "do you sound so surprised?"

I rested my cheek against his chest. "Because I've never read a story where the incubus gets to be the hero."

He huffed, mock-affronted, and brushed a kiss across my forehead. "Hero? Hardly. I'm the scoundrel you house-broke. Flash that smile at any halfway-decent rogue and he'll be polishing a shield by dawn."

I tipped my gaze up. "Cute—but no. I've seen how the others look at me, and I've seen how you look at me, and the two are not the same."

Windley stilled. Something hungry lit his eyes. He slid his fingers into my hair, giving just enough of a tug to make the world narrow to that single point of contact—sharp, commanding, exquisite.

"Say it again," he breathed, voice ground down to gravel and heat.

A shiver rippled through me. "They aren't the same."

His answering rumble was half-purr, half-warning. He pressed a lingering, claiming kiss to the crown of my head. "Good girl."

Silence stretched while his grip eased—but his thumb traced my pulse, possessive.

I bit my lip. "About that kiss, Wind... I know it doesn't bother you much, but it matters to me. I never would have done it if I hadn't been compelled."

He let out a rueful huff. "I know, lion queen—I have never once doubted your loyalty. But instinct can be treacherous, and I should have shielded you from it. I understand you don't need guarding, and I've no right to claim you, yet...there's a balance I have to master. For all your ferocity, there's a softness in you too easily missed."

His palm settled over my heart. "You love so freely."

I closed my eyes, groping for the right words. "Maybe I've simply been fortunate—maybe fate stitched me to seek the good in everyone. But, as you said, loving isn't difficult when you already feel loved. And yes...I care about Edius; you know exactly why. Yet, Wind—if I could behold only one face again, share every secret with one soul, fall asleep beside a single heartbeat for the rest of my days—it would always be yours."

Tension eased from his shoulders; he pressed his forehead to mine. "That's all I needed to hear."

He tried to hide how hard his heart was racing, but I felt every thrum. A breathless laugh escaped him.

"You know," he murmured, throat bobbing, "I was a respectable guard before all this."

"Respectable?" I cocked a brow. "In what sense of the word?"

"Respectable-*adjacent*," he conceded, grin sharpening. "Point is, you could snap a collar on me and march me through the barracks—let every soldier see I'm claimed—and I wouldn't care an inch, so long as they knew whose man I am. That's what you do to me, queenie. The price feels laughable next to the reward."

Now my own heartbeat was the one to hide.

He had a gift for closing the space before I noticed—one palm settling at my waist, his mouth hovering indecently close. His thumbs skimmed the livid marks Pip had left on my throat and wrists, cataloguing every bruise as though it were sacred.

"I'll kill him," he murmured, tilting my chin upward. "For *this*."

The dark promise sent a thrill racing down my spine.

"If you don't, I will."

A twig snapped to our right; footsteps crunched once through the leaves—

And Edius's dry baritone sliced through the heat between us.

"Alright, highness. Break-time's over."

Windley eased back—reluctance written in every line of him—yet he kept our fingers laced when we turned to his Spirite brother.

Edius's gaze flicked from the heat still staining my throat to Windley's possessive grip. "We found a spot west of here last night. If we start carving the labyrinth now, Pip won't have time to regroup."

"...Labyrinth?" I echoed, pulse still racing.

Yes. *Labyrinth.*

12

THE LABYRINTH

Edius's devotion to Gwen was clear from the lengths he'd gone to keep her safely hidden. I wasn't sure why his heart hadn't been fully claimed by her yet, but all the time, sacrifice, and scars...they spoke of something deep and pure. Perhaps those feelings would become the blade to sever the thread that bound us improperly. Maybe, once he saw her again, his heart would finally beat as it was meant to. Maybe...

"She's where?" I asked as we stood at the edge of a sprawling, unobstructed field where not even rabbits roamed.

"The lighted realm," Ed replied gruffly.

"Wait, that place actually exists?" Windley raised an eyebrow, dusk tinting his hair blue.

"Yup. A little pocket of pure light surrounding this world. You can only enter if you're Seelie, or if you're invited by a Seelie."

"Or if you use a labyrinth?" I clarified.

"Kinda. The labyrinth's just how you reach the door," Ed explained. "So, we need you to grow us a large one, make sure it's suitably challenging, and—think you can sprout a door in the middle?"

I'd never grown a non-organic object before. "I'll certainly try. And when we reach the door, we just...knock?"

"Yup." Ed shrugged as if this were perfectly ordinary. "Gwen'll open if she hears my voice. As long as..."

As long as the hex hadn't yet drained her life.

"A labyrinth?" Rafe muttered quietly, eyes pinned to the expanse of bronze grass and wilderness beyond.

"Something the matter, chap?" Windley cocked his head.

Rafe didn't answer.

"And if we fail this labyrinth challenge?" I asked, shifting my focus back to Ed.

"Then we starve, I guess." Windley tugged me to his hip, flashing a confident grin. "But don't worry, love. I won't let Edmond devour you."

"Tch. If anyone's going to devour her... Besides, she can conjure food and uncover water, right?" said Edius.

"And forge a path out," Rafe quietly noted.

"Ah! Good point, *Rafael*," Windley sang. "Then why do you look so..."

Anxious?

Come to think of it, Rafe wore an expression I'd rarely seen on him.

"I've...never seen a labyrinth," he finally admitted, gaze averted. "Besides printings."

"Ahhh. So that's your version of *excitement*?" Windley elbowed me playfully. "Queenie, have you ever seen chap excited before?" Then, under his breath, he whispered, "All the wonders we've witnessed these past weeks, yet it's a maze of plants that finally does him in?"

"As opposed to you, who gets excited whenever the queen so much as sneezes," Rafe countered dryly.

Windley shrugged casually. "I enjoy watching her lose control."

A casual comment on Windley's part, but...

I fought to ignore Edius's sudden, uncomfortable stare at my neck. Windley caught it too and subtly shifted to stand between us, pretending it was part of his continued teasing of Rafe.

He was protecting me without smothering me, and my heart swelled at the thought.

My knave.

My devil.

I stepped forward, slipping off my shoes and digging my toes into the dry autumn grass. I closed my eyes, feeling Vita's breath flowing beneath the ground, pulsing through roots hidden in the soil. With the restored Nemophile's Crown atop my head, I willed them to weave upward, forming a sprawling maze filled with twists, turns, and endless corridors.

Hands rising slowly, I pulled hedges and plants through the earth, disrupting the ground far ahead with a beautiful labyrinth of greenery. Sweat beaded along my brow and trickled down my neck from the sheer effort.

When I finally opened my eyes, the field before us was transformed into an intricate warren of lush, dense hedges stretching endlessly onward.

"W-whoa," breathed Windley.

"Yeah," Ed said, clearing his throat. "That should definitely do it."

Rafe simply stared, silent and transfixed.

"Edius, you said it must be challenging, right?" I dusted my hands together. "I suppose that means no cheating once inside. What if we get an aerial look beforehand, though?"

"I'd say that'd be fair," Ed agreed. "The labyrinth I've used before is down in a valley. Hard to avoid glimpsing the layout beforehand."

Exactly what I'd hoped for. "Then tuck down," I instructed the three men.

"What—?" Edius started, only to trail off when the ground shifted beneath us. A plateau of earth gently rose, lifting us high enough to peer over the entire labyrinth.

I'd done this mostly for Rafe's sake and was richly rewarded by another rare expression—pure wonder spread openly across his features.

My smile quickly faded into mild astonishment. The maze was...immense.

"Definitely challenging," Windley murmured appreciatively, scanning the endless green paths winding into obscurity.

"Yeah, might've gone a little overboard, highness," Ed added.

"Shall I scale it back?"

"No," Rafe said firmly, turning his back to us. "We'll be fine."

Windley threw an arm around Rafe's neck, grinning. "What chap really means is that he's thrilled about the challenge."

Rafe shrugged him off with an irritated grunt, and I carefully lowered us back to solid ground. We bid our stags a temporary goodbye, entering the labyrinth shortly after.

But we didn't make it far before delay struck.

"Er, highness?" Only a few steps inside, Ed had stopped, eyeing the walls curiously.

"Oh!" He was staring at the tiny flowers dotting the hedges. "I thought we could mark where we'd been like this." I brushed a hand along the nearest wall, and yellow petals burst forth. "Still challenging enough, isn't it?"

Edius plucked one, eyes widening in surprise. "They...smell

like you." Instantly, embarrassment flooded his face, and he shook his head, looking away. "Yeah. Still challenging."

Rafe, at the front, looked impatiently over his shoulder. "Coming?"

Windley took my elbow, leaning in conspiratorially. "Chap's an explorer," he whispered—though it was really an excuse to keep Edius at a distance.

Behind us, Edius quietly studied the delicate flower dwarfed by his palm. I knew he wasn't in love with me, yet...

That look held longing at the very least, bordering dangerously on something deeper. My chest ached to know I'd put it there, despite my careful intentions.

Danger trails you everywhere, yet being near you feels... right.

There had to be another way. There was always another way.

Another way to banish Exitium. Another way to remain friends with Edius. Perhaps Gwen could provide answers to the questions haunting us.

"He's right, you know," Windley said in a hushed tone, breaking my reverie. "The whole maze smells like you. This might be...difficult for Ed. Any chance you can fix it?"

I shook my head in a small, uncertain motion. "I didn't intend it, and I'm not sure how I'd even undo it."

Windley released a resigned breath. "He'll manage. Just... stick close to me, alright?"

"I feel terrible," I whimpered.

"I know. Just remember you've done nothing wrong. It isn't your responsibility to keep us from our natures. That's on us." Windley's fingers curled around my arm in a tempered clasp, grip as taut as the cut of his jaw, before he forced himself to let go. "Still not used to how bloody good you feel now. Fighting the urge to whisk you into the brush and...delight you."

Well, that sounded lovely.

"That grin of yours isn't helping, queenie. Go on up with Rafe. I'll keep Ed company." He gave me a playful nudge from behind.

I hurried ahead, joining Rafe just as he paused at our first fork in the path. "Hope you don't mind if I walk with you a bit, Rafe. We had an incident earlier while you slept, and it's best I keep my distance from Edi for now."

"Of course, Your Majesty." He glanced briefly back at the two predators, deep in quiet conversation.

"Take the left path!" Windley called cheerfully, catching Rafe's glance.

Rafe blatantly ignored him, turning right instead.

"Ha!" Windley crowed triumphantly. "Exactly the way I wanted you to go!"

Rafe's shoulders stiffened. "Ugh. That guy. I still don't understand it, Your Majesty."

"He can be charming, you know," I teased gently. "And sweet. And supportive. And...kind of irresistible."

Rafe flicked a fleeting, skeptical glance my way but didn't argue.

We reached another fork.

"Take the right!" Windley called again.

This time, Rafe obediently turned right.

"Oh-ho, worked again!" Windley sang out gleefully. "You thought I meant left, didn't you? But I really wanted right this time!"

I was growing increasingly convinced Windley couldn't care less about which paths we took, so long as he could needle Rafe. Judging by the tension in Rafe's jaw, he was realizing it, too.

"We could leave him behind," Rafe deadpanned.

"Only him?" I asked wryly.

"The other one's quiet. He can stay."

I smiled as Rafe navigated the next junction. With my flower-marked hedges, neither Spirite would lose track of us.

"I bet you're eager to get home," I said softly, glancing sideways at him. "You should know how much it means that you came along this far. And for dealing Charmagne's final blow."

"I wasn't much help against the last one, though," he muttered.

"Pip's different," I agreed. "But we'll finish him when we see him again—I'm certain. And then we'll finally return to Beau."

The flowers surrounding us bloomed brightly at the thought.

Rafe eyed them curiously. "May I ask you something, Your Majesty?"

"You can always ask me anything, Rafe. I feel I owe you that much, especially after—"

Elated, Your Majesty.

He gave a tight nod, expression flat in uncomfortable remembrance.

"S-sorry," I stammered, heat rising in my cheeks. "Please, go ahead."

"Are you going to run away with him?"

"W-what?" I sputtered. "With Windley? Why would you think that?!"

My reaction—too swift, too flustered—told him everything he needed to know.

Rafe studied me quietly, then looked away down the long, green corridor. "It would be a shame if you did, Queen Merrin. Your people like you, and..." He paused, more reflective than usual. "You've done a lot of good in just the few years since I arrived. The Crag would mourn you leaving. The Clearing, too." He hesitated, frowning slightly. "Take it or leave it."

"Oh, Rafe!" I hugged myself, knowing how deeply uncomfortable he'd be if I embraced him instead. "That was incredibly kind of you. Especially after all I've put you through—"

"Don't sell yourself short, Your Majesty," he cut in graciously. "You've always treated me well. I wouldn't be here if I didn't want to be."

A wholesome moment—perhaps the purest we'd ever shared.

"I don't intend to leave," I confessed, my voice as soft as dusk settling over the maze. "The choice is difficult. I know I'm a good ruler, and I owe it to my mother—and to A—"

The name faltered on my tongue, the wound still too raw. "To everyone, really, to fulfill my birthright. But..."

Windley's laugh drifted up behind us, perfectly timed. "But I love him, and I want the world to know it."

Silence stretched comfortably between us.

I forced a laugh. "I don't know why I'm explaining myself, Rafe. You and Beau are in the same situation, after all."

"No." He shook his head slowly. "He's harder to hide. And you and Beau—you're very different people."

Both statements were painfully true.

Rafe studied me longer than usual. I pretended not to notice until finally he spoke again. "Do you like being a queen?"

"I do."

"Keep that in mind, Your Majesty."

I would, though it wouldn't make the decision any easier.

But, in a world as vast as ours, surely there was always another way...*right?*

13

GODDESS BLESS RAFE

"Hm." Windley was musing. "Hmmm."

"Just come out and say it already!" lashed Rafe.

We were tucked into a small alcove of the labyrinth, resting amid flowered shrubs that shielded us from wind and chill.

"I'm just surprised Pip hasn't descended on us yet," Windley admitted, scanning the gloaming sky with an apple in hand. "Seems strange. I'd have thought..."

"Yeah," Edius agreed warily. "Me too."

"Of course, he could be gathering backup," Windley added.

"Backup?" I asked.

"Finding a settlement, entrancing humans to use as hostages or ammunition." Before my expression could sour completely, he amended, "Not that I think he will. It would slow him down significantly."

True enough.

"Could be recovering," Edius suggested. "Your smoke

power hurt him last time. We didn't see the aftermath. He could be wounded."

We could hope.

I glanced upward, the sky thick and stagnant. "Do you really think Ruck will be okay out there on his own?"

"Yes," Windley said flatly. "That naughty, naughty stag will be just fine. Ed and I ordered them to stay close to the labyrinth's entrance. They'll be waiting when we exit. And if, for some reason, we don't exit, our beguiling will wear off eventually."

"Not that your stag was easy to reason with," muttered Edius.

"Yeah, but it's a coward and should stay close to the others," said Windley.

"A coward!" I scolded. "I'll have you know Ruck is a pure-bred stag of the finest royal lineage."

Windley flashed an overly charmed smile. "That just proves lineage means shit." He offered his fruit toward me. "Bite of my apple, lion queen?"

"For the last time, I do not desire your core!"

His fingers hooked beneath my chin, tilting my face. "You sure? It tastes like me now."

I let my gaze drop to his mouth. "I prefer the source, not the sample. Pity—I'm already full."

Hunger flashed in his eyes; he swallowed it, then gave my chin a playful jiggle. "Tragic."

"How are you holding up, Edi?" I pivoted, voice low and soothing. "Does it bring peace knowing Gwen is nearby? Or anxiety?"

"Little bit of both," he said, eyeing the ring that had steadily siphoned her life. "Little bit of..."

His trailing words were enough to wrench me. "We're all in

this together, Edi," I reminded him. "We'll do everything we can once we reach her. We can talk through your worries if it helps."

Rafe and Windley nodded their agreement.

Meanwhile—

"Fuck." Edius gripped his chest, which had just pounded once acutely toward me.

"E-Ed?" My empathy must have shown, because he quickly turned away while his heart beat again—twice more.

"Don't. I know it's your nature, but I can't take you looking at me like that, Merrín. It's too soft, okay? Gives me the instinct to comfort you."

And comfort from Edius had never turned out well for any of us.

"Very well." I hugged my knees, aching at having no comfort to offer.

Rafe misread my posture as cold and summoned a compact flame from his sword. "Here, Your Majesty."

Windley squeezed my palm, then moved to Edius's side, drawing him away with distracting banter. Two hearts beat there—one strong; the other faint, weakening by the moment.

"I just thought of something, Merr," Windley called over once Edius's heart had closed completely. "Your flower trail makes it easy for Pip to track us, but you'll sense his heart, right? No chance of an ambush?"

"Actually, no," I admitted. "When Pip transformed into his Dracon form, I could no longer sense his heart. It's as if he lacks the breath of life now."

Windley swore. "I guess that makes sense. The goddesses modified us after adoption, but they never touched the Dracons."

"How'd he survive all this time?" Edius questioned. "The

angels wiped them out, and he survived? Thousands of years alone?"

Windley shrugged. "Ask angel boy."

Rafe looked exasperated. "Why do you keep calling me that?"

"That angelic face, of course."

Rafe stared at me pleadingly, and I dipped my head in a quiet nod.

"Vita said magicians descend from angels, allowing pacts with Luna and Soleil—the astral goddesses. Royals were the first humans, stained with divine energy by Vita herself, allowing us to host Vita and...the destroyer." I avoided saying Exitium's name aloud.

"So Soleil and Luna are different from Vita and the destroyer?" asked Rafe.

"They're all celestial beings, same as the Drakaina, but Luna and Soleil are astral. They were never meant to enter the physical plane, only observe. Vita and the destroyer belong here —Vita to create life, the destroyer to end it. The destroyer became fallen by repeatedly forcing destruction too soon, restarting the cycle prematurely."

That endless cycle had forced me to create Flora.

"That's everything I gathered from Vita. She's been quiet since I restored the Crown. They both have."

Because this was a problem I needed to solve alone.

"What will you do about it?" Windley asked, almost under his breath.

"I won't drag the destroyer to the edge of the world to wipe out all the Drakaina—and the Spirites by extension—if that's what you're asking. Ethics aside, I won't sacrifice you or Edi. I refuse to save one race by destroying another."

A silver drizzle kissed Rafe's flame with a soft hiss.

"Rain?" Rafe opened his palm.

"Seems so," said Windley, hopping up. "Hard to see it coming."

"There's not enough room for the tent," Ed noted.

"We don't need one." Kneeling, I pressed my fingers into the lush clover, channeling Vita's breath. "Stand back."

Rafe jumped away as the earth trembled, giving birth to a squat tree whose wide, fan-like leaves shielded us from the downpour.

Windley studied it curiously. "What kind of tree is this?"

"It's an...umbrella tree."

"She made it up?" said Windley.

"She made it up," said Edius.

They weren't wrong, but it served its purpose.

"I'll fill canteens," Rafe volunteered, holding out a hand.

"And I'll wash," I announced. Rain was falling in sheets, soaking the labyrinth. I raised the alcove floor slightly to prevent flooding.

Edius tended to the fire—a skill learned from Windley in the Emerald Wood.

"Ed?" I asked sensibly. "Mind closing your eyes a moment?"

I intended to strip to my undergarments, modest enough but best left beyond his view. He took in my figure quickly from head to toe before shielding his face. "C-course."

Windley hurriedly stepped between us. His voice dropped low, hopeful. "Is this a solitary, reflective wash or an I'd-like-help-reaching-my-back wash?"

"I can reach my back just fine," I bantered, watching brief disappointment cross his features. "But I'm not opposed to company—if that company is you."

I handed him my outer layers, and he folded them neatly before beginning to undo his own ties with the smirkiest of smirks. My folded clothes landed with a faint thud. Behind us,

Edius's chest pulsed once in quiet response. Guilt blinked through me at the sound.

Windley noticed immediately. "Jealous, Ed? Don't worry—you can have your turn with me next," he offered generously.

"Ha. Ha," Edi deadpanned.

Windley shrugged nonchalantly. "I can reach my own back, but there are plenty of other bits I can't."

"Tch." Edius tried to sound grouchy, but a reluctant chuckle escaped anyway, shaking his head as Windley shot me a triumphant wink.

A good friend.

A bastard and a scamp, but a good friend.

I loved him fiercely.

My affection radiated so openly he scratched his neck awkwardly. "Eh...heh."

That awkward, repressed laugh of his was enticing on its own. Unable to resist any longer, I grabbed his hand, tugging him swiftly into the downpour, past disapproving Rafe and around a tall wall of hedge. Windley didn't waste a single moment grabbing my waist, pulling me flush against him, mouth finding mine, possessive, claiming.

Rain slicked our bodies quickly, drenching Windley down to his knickers and soaking my thin shirt and shorts until they clung revealingly to my skin. His eyes devoured me openly, hungrily, hands gliding with deliberate hunger over my recently mended chest.

"You feel damn good, lion queen. Almost too good." He released a frustrated growl. "It'll be nice when you're back to normal. It was already torture to restrain myself before, but at least I could take my time. Now..."

He ground his teeth, cupping my breast in a tender squeeze, then pressed his mouth fervently to my neck, sucking hard enough to leave me breathless.

I shivered at his intensity. Edius had been right—if anyone were to devour me...

My palms pressed lightly against his chest, halting him. Windley pulled back immediately, eyes cautious, worried he'd gone too far. "Too much? Sorry. I'm trying not to be an animal."

"No, it's not that." Warmth flooded my cheeks. "It's just... there's something I'd like to do for you." My pulse quickened, nerves and excitement mingling. "*To* you?"

His eyebrow lifted, intrigued. "Go on."

A fresh wave of heat warmed my face as I placed a slow, careful kiss to his cheek, his collarbone, down to his chest, sinking to my knees beneath the chill of falling rain.

Windley tensed sharply, breath hitching. "Q-queenie? What are you—h-hooh—okay."

I was taking Rafe's advice.

And it was the first time I had ever knelt before another mortal.

"Ah—" His voice cracked softly in disbelief. "F—" He sounded entirely undone, his voice barely recognizable. "*Fuuuck.*"

I took my time, savoring each tremor, every shuddering breath. Rain cooled my flushed skin while heat rippled through him; his fingers tightened in my hair—guiding, never demanding. His gasps climbed, rough and desperate, until a guttural groan tore free. His body jerked, one hand darting for a hastily snatched handkerchief as he convulsed, spilling hard into its folds.

When it was through, he rewarded my efforts tenfold, claiming my mouth with grateful hunger, pulling me tightly against him, his breath fusing hotly with mine.

Several minutes passed as we stood there, lightly panting, bodies warm beneath the cool, steady rain. Windley brushed the wet hair from my face, his thumb tracing along my jaw. He marked my forehead tenderly before tipping my chin upward, his gaze blazing with warmth and adoration.

"I hope you know," he murmured huskily, "you've just ruined me for anyone else."

"Good," I whispered, smiling breathlessly against his lips.

Rain continued to pour, cloaking our stolen intimacy beneath its rhythmic hush, keeping the world at bay just a little longer.

Eventually, thoroughly chilled and drenched, I summoned a bed of leafy moss beneath broad leaves to shield us from the steady drizzle. We settled together into its lush embrace, limbs tangled comfortably, listening to droplets pattering around us.

"Well, that was...unexpected," Windley murmured, gently stroking my hair. His voice turned teasingly curious. "Where exactly did you learn to—"

"Rafe."

He blinked, staring blankly at me for several moments. "Come again? It sounded like you just said the world's greatest cockblock taught you how to give a—"

"N-not exactly." Heat rushed to my cheeks. "He just offered a small piece of advice, from which I...figured it out myself."

Windley dropped his head back against the moss, incredulous and deeply satisfied. "Goddess bless Rafe."

I laughed at the sheer contentment that spread across his face.

"You're quite the little vixen, Merr. Never did I imagine—" He paused, reconsidering. "No, that's not true. I imagined it all the time. All. The. Time. It would scare you to know the things I've thought about you."

"I did have a naughty dream about you once," I admitted shyly.

That immediately captured his attention. He leaned closer, eyes gleaming mischievously.

"Once?"

"More than once."

His mouth quirked in wicked amusement. "How naughty?"

"Mild, I'm sure, compared to the 'things you've thought' about me."

He gave a low chuckle. "We'll chalk that up to your lack of experience, with the promise that your future dreams will be far, far naughtier." He placed a gentle kiss on the tip of my nose, then gazed at me quietly, twirling a damp curl of my hair between his fingers. His expression warmed in a way he rarely allowed. "I love you, my queen. More than I know how to say."

He didn't need to say it. The cage that was his bones could scarcely contain the thunder of it.

"I never thought I'd be lucky enough to have you," he went on, voice no louder than a thought. "Even in my fantasies, I knew I'd have to share you, but..." The words faded; his gaze slipped aside.

I framed his face with both hands. "Say it."

"It's selfish and complicated," he murmured.

"I don't care."

He rested his forehead against mine, breath trembling. "I don't want to share you—not with a royal, not with some future paramour, not with anyone you might marry. I thought I could bear it, but moments like this make me doubt my own strength." His throat bobbed. "Sharing lovers is normal in the south, and I've never met a queen without...side hobbies. My mind knows that, yet here I am—jealous of a political marriage that doesn't even exist, one I've braced for since the day we met."

The vulnerability in his eyes—something he'd show no one else—sent a sweet, bruising pang through my chest.

"I don't deserve you, Merrin. I have no right to claim you. But after seeing the way Ed looks at you...I can't help myself. I want you. Only you. Always."

He drew a slow breath that lifted his shoulders. "Which is selfish, knowing I can't give you children—knowing the kind of heart you have."

Silence settled between us as memories stirred.

I'd been young—barely fourteen—when Beau invited me to the Clearing to meet her newest guard. My first thought upon seeing him had been that he was cute; my second, that his scarlet-colored hair was striking; my third, amusement, as he botched a trick with his hatchets, embedding one into a castle turret. Even then, he'd simply thrown up his hands, flashing a charming grin and announcing, "Ta-daaa!"

We'd only just met, yet it had felt as though the three of us —Windley, Beau, and me—had always been friends. Falling for him had seemed the most natural thing in the world, as if our souls were simply meant for each other, as if our meeting was woven into fate itself.

My fingertips traced the scars along his back, voice quiet and sure. "It has always only been you, Wind. It will always only be you."

He kissed me deeply, desperately, and when he finally pulled back—

"Marry me, Merrin." His voice was suddenly earnest, soft, filled with raw sincerity. "It doesn't have to be official or known to anyone else, but marry me? I...don't have a ring or anything, but I will."

At that moment, clarity settled graciously into my heart— the answer to something that had troubled me deeply. Yet, I held it close a little longer, savoring the tender look in his eyes.

"Ask me again when this is over," I whispered, brushing another silken kiss across his mouth.

He smiled against my lips, accepting this promise.

He held me close as we lay beneath the whispering canopy of leaves, listening to the rain until it finally ceased to fall.

14

IS IT WORTH IT?

"Your hair's really long."

That was Edius.

"It lengthens when it's wet," I said.

"Didn't notice before." Because he had been looking at me much more intensely in recent days. He exhaled his reluctance over what he was about to say next. "It...looks nice."

Meanwhile—

"Chaaaap. Chap? Chap!"

"What do you want, you pest?" lashed Rafe.

"Just checking in on my favorite magician. Need any help roasting that corn, mate?"

Rafe narrowed his eyes at Windley's sudden devotion—his dazzling grin, his abrupt eagerness to assist. Then, with a slow, dawning horror, his attention flicked to me—which I hastily averted—before burying his face in his hands.

"Oh my goddess. You told him."

"Told him what?" asked Edius.

I clapped loudly. "Let's all name a fruit we'd like for dessert! I'll go first! Cherries!" I stomped my feet, and a tree erupted from the ground, its branches heavy with ripe, glistening red fruit.

"Raaafe." Windley slung an arm around the sorcerer's shoulders, giving him a hearty shake. "How about you, chap? How do you like your dessert?"

"Next time, I'm staying home," Rafe grumbled. Then, turning to me, he added darkly, "Never again, Your Majesty. Never again."

But in friendships destined to last as long as ours, never again was an impossible promise. I would accept many more morsels of Rafe's advice through the years—though perhaps none quite so scandalous.

It was best that Edius remained blissfully unaware of the joke. Quickly, I grew him the southern fruit known as pineapple.

"Did I get it right?" I asked, shaking out my damp hair, which had begun curling at the ends.

"You've...never seen a pineapple before, have you?"

"So I did not get it right," I concluded.

"Eh, close enough." He stabbed at the prickly thing with his knife, giving me an amused look. "Though it tastes more like an orange." Catching my crestfallen expression, he raised a reassuring hand and grinned. "It's fine, you little mirefox. I like oranges."

I enjoyed Edius.

I did not enjoy how long our gazes lingered after he said it. It was difficult not to get lost in eyes like those—impossible not to smile back at a mouth like that.

Windley gave my shoulder a reassuring squeeze. "Oi, Ed. Care for a walk, mate?"

He was a good friend.

A good partner.

A good person.

Sometimes the sweetest gifts came wrapped in the most unexpected packages.

Dinner, dessert, and rest accomplished, we ventured deeper into the labyrinth.

At the front like a steadfast captain, Rafe attempted to discern some logic to the maze's layout. "Your Majesty, when you built this, did you have more of a contemporary design, classical design, or perhaps a meander design in mind? I recognize it isn't circular or seeded, but those styles can still serve as a foundation—"

"To be honest, Rafe, it feels as though you've just spoken an entirely different language. I had no design in mind; I merely envisioned a labyrinth from a storybook I adored as a child."

Rafe rubbed thoughtfully at his chin. "That would explain the inconsistency."

"I always knew you were a nerd, but chap, you are such a NERD." Windley gave Rafe a roughhousing pat on the back, clearly delighted by this newly discovered side of our stoic guard. Rafe had always preferred solitude in the courtyard, quietly absorbed in his books. We'd understood he enjoyed peace and contemplation, but never realized how deeply he adored puzzles.

To unfold the layers of someone was a beautiful thing.

"This way," Rafe announced confidently, pointing ahead with an explorer's determination. "I'm sure of it."

Edius passed me a subtle smirk. It felt entirely natural to return it—and equally painful to realize I had.

These close quarters of the labyrinth proved perhaps the most challenging stretch of our journey. Each brush of our arms, each stolen glance, each shared word was an ongoing battle against a pull driven by magic, instinct, and the unseen lure of something tantalizing.

How could a heart remain steadfastly committed to one yet

find itself so helplessly enticed by another? Even the best among us could be tempted. The world was not built of constants. And hearts? Devious, plotting things.

I was lucky to have found someone who understood that.

"Hey, Merr?" Windley had tilted his head skyward again, neck long and temptingly exposed.

A true lion would have bitten it.

Instead, I feigned interest in the skies alongside him. "Hmm, I think we're too far south to see it."

He turned his gaze to me, intrigued. "See what?"

"Oh, I assumed you were searching for every color on the skyline," I said lightly. "Considering how low the moon and sun have dipped."

The others had moved ahead—an unconscious effort on all our parts—and now Windley's glittering look was solely for me. "Listen here, Your Majesty, everyone knows that obsession is yours and yours alone." He tapped his chin thoughtfully. "Though, admittedly, I have found myself paying extra attention to sunsets ever since you first mentioned it to me..."

"And when exactly was this first mention? Surely, I've hardly spoken of it."

"You mean you don't vividly remember every single interaction we've ever had?" He feigned exaggerated hurt.

"I actively try to block out the more insufferable ones."

"You wound me, lion queen." His demeanor was carefree, effortlessly charming. "I suppose that gives me the advantage, then. Wiping your memory clean leaves ample room for absorption. My first, second, and third impressions of you? Crisp." He tapped his ever-changing hair. "But this particular one? Especially good."

And that was that. No elaboration. No smug retort. Just silence.

Because he wanted me to beg him for it.

But I was every bit as stubborn as he was.

We walked quietly side by side for several long, increasingly agonizing minutes until he—the absolute ass—started whistling.

"Argh! Fine. Tell your story, Windley."

"What story?"

I whipped around to face him. "I swear to goddess—either tell it, or I'm leaving to analyze this maze with Rafe."

He smirked, lacing his fingers casually behind his neck. "Well, if you insist. You, my darling, were visiting the Clearing —for something terribly boring and official—while Queen Beau was off being an oracle, doing oracle-y things. You know, the usual."

I narrowed my eyes playfully. "Is that all you think we do?"

"Well, aside from saving worlds and scandalizing the royal bloodline?"

That earned him a swift swat.

"Shh. No more interruptions," he said, winking at me. "I was stationed in the throne room with a few other guards when you burst in, hair looking as if it had just endured a war. You practically yanked my arm from its socket, dragging me away from the others—just to show me the sunset through those enormous windows at the back. I remember because it was the first time you ever took my hand. Evidently, you'd escaped some meeting or another specifically to see it from that view, and—you chose me as your victim, knowing full well I'd be the one blamed when you were inevitably caught."

I stared at him before releasing a laugh loud enough to make Rafe and Edius glance curiously back at us. "You really think that's why I showed it to you?"

He shrugged, nonchalant. "Why else?"

Somewhere deep in my chest, a chord was delicately plucked.

"Windley...of course I remember that. How could I not? You were still quite new to the queendoms then, and I knew you hailed from somewhere far away, though you were reluctant to share exactly where. I took your hand and showed you the hidden colors of that sunset because I wanted you to feel at home."

He gave me a curious look. "...Why would a sunset make me feel at home?"

"Because it contained every color."

One brow arched slowly upward.

"Much like your hair," I finished, the words barely grazing the air.

Adoration overtook him. "Oh, you sweet, unworldly, sweet thing."

"I was young!" I protested, cheeks burning.

"Those dots were far too distant for me to connect, lion queen, but—" He clutched at his heart dramatically. "You liked me and wanted me to feel at home. That's adorable."

"Patronization does not suit you," I said dryly.

In an instant, his gaze darkened, dangerously rakish. "Everything suits me."

It was annoyingly true.

"Psh." I waved away his confidence. "If not the sunset, then what were you searching the sky for? You were about to ask me something before this tangent."

The teasing charm fell swiftly from his face. "Afraid I wasn't thinking of anything nearly so pleasant, queenie." And there was only one topic that could shadow his expression so completely—

"Pip?" I guessed gently.

He surrendered a grim nod.

"What about him?"

"You said you can't feel Vita's breath inside him now, right?

But you could feel it before—back when he still looked like a Spirite?"

"Right," I confirmed slowly.

Windley turned suddenly. "Oi, Ed! Mind coming back here a sec?"

Ed pivoted immediately to join us. Rafe, deeply absorbed in his maze-solving, made no such adjustment. Quickly, I closed the flowers around us, which were surely emitting my telltale scent.

"Relax," said Edius, amused by my frantic gardening. "I'm not that fragile. I can handle some fuckin' flowers." He rolled out his neck and cracked his shoulders. "Getting real cooped up in here, though. And Rafe knows a ridiculous amount about mazes. More than is strictly normal."

"I quite like it," I said. "It's rare to see him this excited. Is there something you get like that over, Edius?"

Edius shrugged casually. "Sex, probably." Before I could formulate a proper response, he turned swiftly to Windley. "Why'd you call me over?"

"I'm trying to understand something," said Windley thoughtfully. "Pip changed forms when you dropped the hexes in Ascian's ring, so it's safe to assume he was being held in Spirite form by some sort of hex. But what kind? And could we possibly use that to our advantage?"

"Well, when I dropped 'em, there was one bigger and darker than the rest. Guess that was whatever Ascian used to keep Pip that way. Could've been a suppression curse. But Ascian never shared that one with me."

"Nor me," said Windley, rubbing his chin in contemplation. "And if it was a hex, I'm surprised it held someone like Pip for so long."

"I believe I saw Pip begin to transform once," I interjected softly, then corrected—"Twice."

They both turned sharply to face me. News to them.

"At the manor," I continued, more cautiously now. "When I was locked in the room with him, he was searching within me for...the destroyer, and I saw him begin to shift. And again before healing me in Sestilia's chambers."

Windley's eyes narrowed in thought. "He was using your goddess juice to free himself?"

"Though it didn't seem he knew what he was doing at the time," I clarified quickly.

"Interesting," murmured Windley. "I mean, we've always known he was different. A normal Spirite wouldn't have been able to hex a wraith the way he did with that spider creature. And he was always strangely attuned to hearts and physicality —far more than any of us. Not to mention powerful enough to hex entire towns alone..."

Among us, one had fallen quiet.

"Edius?" I tapped lightly at his shoulder with my canteen. "Are you all right?"

Edius grabbed a handful of the closed blossoms around us, tension rippling across his shoulders, his throat visibly tight. "I'm the one who locked you in that room with him. I took someone like you and trapped you with someone like him. What the fuck was I thinking?"

Windley exchanged a worried glance with me. "H-hey, you've more than made up for that, mate."

Yet the cloud hovering over Edius refused to lift.

Of the many tangled threads that composed Edius's being, guilt was woven deepest—guilt over Gwen, guilt over Albie, guilt for kidnapping me, guilt for kissing me. Guilt for a hundred sins carried over from a life no longer truly his.

But I clung stubbornly to the belief that people could change. There was no rule that forbade a person from claiming a second chance.

"If you think I would not have done precisely what you did if Windley had been the one trapped within a hex, then you're sorely mistaken," I said firmly. "Judgment is hardly impenetrable. And love?" My voice fell to a gentler register. "To me, it seems the sharpest arrow of all."

I had meant to comfort him. Truly, I had.

But my words struck deep, causing Edius's heart to thud once heavily. He curled forward, gripping his chest.

"Come on, Ed." Windley gave him a knowing tap on the back. "Let's take that walk, yeah? Clear our heads a bit?"

As the two of them disappeared around the corner, I caught the beginnings of a conversation not meant for my ears.

"I swear to gods, Windley, I'm not after her. It's like I have no control over—"

"I know, mate. I've been there."

"Does it always feel this shitty?"

"That's only at first...and then off and on," said Windley quietly.

"And that's worth it?" asked Ed.

"My answer to that question would only make your situation worse."

15

INTO THE LIGHT

When the Spirites returned, high spirits returned with them. Edius was composed, his heart small, cold, and carefully closed. And there it stayed—long enough for me to feel comfortable sharing a quiet conversation with him again or offering him my canteen. Whatever he and Windley had discussed, it seemed to have silenced the murmurs stirring in his chest.

We carried on through endless dusk, setting camp, getting lost, turning this way and that. Not once did we catch a glimpse of Pip. The longer his absence stretched, the more sharply we anticipated his sudden return, yet those faded wings stubbornly refused to grace us again.

Through all this, Windley and Edius made frequent time to slip away, Windley quietly helping Ed navigate the shifting terrain of his troubled heart. I was glad for it; Ed always returned with his chest clasped tighter, his mood lifted noticeably brighter.

But then there was one time, near the end, when I caught the pair discussing...something else.

"It isn't the ending any of us would pick," Windley was murmuring, voice pitched so low the words almost dissolved in the labyrinth leaves. "But if that's where the path bends—and she says yes—I've no right to block it. I trust her compass."

A pause; Edius's reply was too soft to catch.

Windley let out a slow breath. "No one else can unpick that knot, Ed—and the magician isn't exactly an answer we can woo."

Knot? And I was practically the only "she" they both knew.

When Windley saw me nearing, he masked his quiet discussion with an obnoxious burst of enthusiasm that startled a hidden bird from the leafy wall. "Ed wants you to grow him a beanstalk, Merr!" he called out loudly, waving dramatically. "One that goes right up to the sky! I tried to tell him it won't support his weight, but he insists."

From the coded glance he sent my way afterward, he knew I was onto his cover-up. But I trusted him enough to know it was with good reason, so I played along, growing Edius a beanstalk of only moderately acceptable proportions.

Days deeper into the labyrinth, we finally reached the inner sanctum—a spiraling path growing narrower and narrower until the verdant hedges brushed insistently against our clothing and Edius had to angle his broad shoulders sideways to avoid getting snagged.

"Figure you didn't have me in mind when you grew this part, highness," he muttered archly.

I was fairly sure I must have. With a wave of my hand, I bent the hedges away from him, coaxing them into blossoming with bright pink flowers as he passed.

"Cute," he drawled.

And the ground too. The ground burst cheerfully into bloom in the exact shape of his footprints.

"Oh, for fuck's sake."

"He's practically a wood nymph," I cupped a whisper in Windley's direction, loud enough for Edius to hear.

"Oh-ho, careful now—that's my line, highness."

With the sly mouth of a born schemer, Windley leaned over and murmured something mischievous in my ear. I nodded eagerly, and moments later, my peculiar version of pineapple plants sprouted vigorously behind Edius with every step he took.

"I can't believe you're responsible for thousands of lives," Ed deadpanned, earning an enthusiastic cackle from Windley.

Then suddenly, ahead—

"It's here!"

Possibly the liveliest phrase ever uttered by Rafe.

The rest of us had been lagging behind, teasing, laughing, and feeling rather pent-up from too long spent in close quarters —but upon reaching the end of the spiral, all humor swiftly drained from us.

Because we knew precisely what awaited us beyond the door at the labyrinth's heart.

The door wasn't truly a door at all. It was hewn into ancient tree-stump—cracked, withered, and worn as though it had died decades ago, despite having sprung into being only days before. Its bark was weather-scarred, the top gnawed by wind and sun. Even the knob was only an illusion: a shallow relief chiseled into the wood, nothing more.

Edius entered the small clearing at the labyrinth's center, placed his palm against the wood, and lowered his head solemnly. Any lingering mirth in the air faded instantly.

Gwen.

We were nearly to her.

"Edi—"

Windley carefully intercepted my hand as I reached out to comfort Edius, pressing a kiss to my knuckles before replacing my touch with his own upon Edius's shoulder. "You all right, mate?"

"This'll work." Edius patted the weathered bark but didn't turn to face us. "Gimme a moment."

Windley's subtle nod told Rafe and me to occupy ourselves elsewhere, and he leaned in closer to Edius, voice dropping low to offer consolation I could not.

"Aw, Ed, that's..." I heard Windley murmur. "But you won't know until you see her, right?"

Edius's reply was indistinguishable.

"I know you mentioned that before, but let's not jump to conclusions, mate. Especially now that you've got..."

It wasn't meant for me to hear, and it was unbecoming to listen further.

"D-did you have fun, Rafe?" I asked, motioning vaguely to the labyrinth.

He arched a skeptical brow. "Did *you* have fun, Your Majesty?"

The flush rising rapidly in my cheeks made him roll his eyes.

"There's a branch in your hair," he muttered dryly, flicking his wrist in vague annoyance.

"Shh, I was seeing how long it would take her to notice," Windley cut in smoothly. With Edius composed once more, he had sauntered over to join us.

I plucked the branch—still flush with leaves—and swatted him before stepping up to join Edius at the door. His jaw was taut, his stare unwavering. Whatever Windley had said to him, it had left him...tight.

"What now?" I prodded with care.

"I have to knock," said Ed.

Yet he hesitated, afraid there might be no answer.

I fought every urge to embrace him. "Take all the time you need, Edi... Would it help if I grew you another beanstalk?" A weak attempt at lightening the mood.

He shifted his gaze to me, managing a bittersweet smile. "That might help." Then he turned back to the door, muttering quietly, "Gods damn, I'm a coward."

"Everything you've done to reach her proves otherwise," I answered quietly.

With a steadying breath, he tentatively knocked against the aged wood.

"Gwen, dove, it's me."

Silence from within.

"G..." His deep voice fractured painfully. "Gwen? Wake up. It's Edi. Came for you, at las—"

He got no further. Upon speaking his name, a sharp click echoed from inside the tree, followed by the carved outline suddenly blazing with a murky blue glow.

"That's promising, yeah?" Windley observed.

Edius was too shaken to answer. His eyes downcast, he pressed his fingers to the carved knob and pushed inward. The door silently separated from the bark, revealing an opening filled with languidly swirling, luminous blue mist.

"Is this what they call a portal?" I whispered.

"Think so." Windley's voice was nearer than I'd anticipated.

Ed's face revealed nothing as he gazed into the unknown. "Brought some friends with me, Gwenny. And, uh, I look different now. Just to warn you." He locked his sphinx-like eyes briefly with mine before nodding stiffly to the others and stepping through.

I moved to follow, but Rafe caught my shoulder, hand

resting pointedly on his sword—as if to say just in case—before trailing Edius through, leaving me alone with Windley.

"A moment, Merr?" Windley's hand settled on my back, the pressure barely there through my shirt.

The air between us grew thick with unspoken tension.

"Going to explain now? About that beanstalk nonsense?" I teased, narrowing my eyes. "I thought your kind was supposed to excel at deception."

He swallowed, a hint of strain tightening his features. "I have difficulty lying to you. That was the best I could manage."

Stalling, clearly.

"I assume it relates to whatever you were whispering to Edius by the door?" I asked.

He neither confirmed nor denied. "Look, what I said before, darling—about not wanting to share you—that still holds. But...there may be situations..." His voice wavered. "I understand why you might want to allow it. Why you'd both want to...under certain circumstances."

A riddle.

"I haven't the faintest idea what you're talking about."

Windley released a quiet breath, gaze drifting toward the swirling blue glow. "Just...be ready to bend the rules if you have to. And if it comes to that, you'll have my blessing."

I frowned at him, puzzled, but before I could question further, his arms closed tightly around me—as if anchoring himself—before we stepped into the light.

The other side was nothing like I'd anticipated.

"The forest fortress?" I gasped.

Edius glanced slightly over his shoulder. "Is that what you see?"

Yes. The portal had spit us into the entryway of the treetop refuge I had visited my entire life.

"But how are we here? There's my riding cloak hanging up, and that's Windley's chair." I gestured toward the corner.

"Wait, my chair?" Windley echoed, brows rising.

"Well, it is your favorite, isn't it?"

His smile curled at the edges—the kind that began at the mouth and ended in his eyes.

Ed watched our exchange curiously. "Is that what you see, too?"

"What do you mean, see?" Windley asked.

Edius turned toward Rafe. "What about you? You see something different, don't you?"

Rafe hesitated, cheeks darkening. "I'd rather not say."

Windley and I exchanged intrigued glances before he threw a hand dramatically onto his hip. "Wait a second, Ed. Are you saying we're all seeing different places right now?"

Edius nodded. "The light realm isn't tangible, but your eyes need something to perceive, so your mind fills in the gaps with whatever place it cherishes most." He paused, his voice lowering slightly. "Apparently, that place can change."

Windley's devilish eyes narrowed in on their prey. "Out with it, chap. What do you see?"

Rafe stiffened instantly. "Shut up."

"Oh my goddess—it's Queen Beau's bedchamber, isn't it?" Windley feigned horror. But I barely paid attention, because—

I saw it.

Edius's heart had begun to shift.

My voice softened, edging carefully around the moment. "What do you see, Edi?"

He wouldn't meet my eyes. "That's...not something you wanna know, highness."

Oh.

"W-where's Gwen?" I asked instead.

Edius nodded down the hallway lined with antique frames, chosen by long-dead royalty. "This way."

"How do you know?"

Ed tapped his nose knowingly.

Ah.

He pinched at thin air, lifting it as though parting a flap only he could see, then sidestepped an unseen obstacle and walked straight through the center of a table—solid as ever when my palm brushed it.

Existence within the lighted realm was undeniably strange.

Behind us, Rafe and Windley continued their bickering.

"Ooh, no—you know what I bet it is?" Windley's smirk widened. "The *labyrinth*."

Rafe sighed long and thin, utterly exhausted. "Why would it be the labyrinth?"

"I don't know, chap—you're the one who was all hot and bothered by it."

"Leave me alone." Rafe shoved past, sidestepping something invisible to the rest of us.

Meanwhile, Windley's fingertips brushed fondly over a painting of a thunderstorm on the wall, a small smile playing on his lips.

"I'm glad we see the same place," I murmured. "Glad you cherish our times here as much as I do."

"Oh, sure—I've always loved coming here because it means getting to see—" He lifted his brows. "Chap."

"Chap. Mmhmm." I tugged playfully at his sleeve, pulling him along behind the others—until he abruptly sidestepped something as well.

I froze.

"Wait." I pivoted back. "What was that?"

"Hm?" Windley glanced at the empty floor behind him.

"You don't see it?" His expression fell slightly. "You don't... nothing, Merr. Just leave it."

"No, no. What is it?"

I thought back to our last visit to the fortress. Before Beau's confession. Before Rafe showed me how to charge his sword. Before...

I knew exactly what Windley had just stepped around.

Something my mind had spared me from seeing.

Realization struck like a blow. I doubled over, gripping myself tightly. "His armor," I managed through a rush of sudden grief. "That's where Albie left his..."

Pain twisted inside me, scorching and fierce. It never truly went away. It dulled, yes. Slept even. But it lingered, always waiting.

"Shh." Windley's lips grazed the crown of my hair as he cradled my head. "I'm sorry, Merr. It's okay."

The fortress smelled of my knight. When I looked around the familiar entryway, he was everywhere. Sitting in chairs. Leaning against walls. Polishing his sword. Puffing thoughtfully on his pipe.

I could hear the gritty comfort of his voice, feel the scratch of his mustache against my forehead.

I understood then:

Albie was the ghost destined always to haunt this place.

"You deserve to grieve, my queen," Windley murmured, tone low and steady. "But now's not the time. Not when..." He tipped his head toward the hall where Ed and Rafe had disappeared.

He was right. Ascian's final victim still awaited rescue.

"Here." With a touch no heavier than a drifting petal, Windley tapped my temple. "Let me blur the edges for now, yes? You'll have all the time you need later. I'll ensure it's so."

One small nod, and the sweet haze of beguilement slipped through me, tempering the ache.

"Think of another place," he murmured, voice threading like gossamer between us. "You have many favorites."

At once, the world around us dissolved.

The air thickened with salt, sky rumbling overhead beneath storm-laden clouds, coastal waves crashing against the cliffs of the Crag.

"There." Windley released me and drew a long, grounding breath. "Feels good out here, doesn't it?"

I studied him carefully. "It...changed for you as well?" I asked. "How is that possible?"

"My favorite place isn't a place, Merr."

It was at my side.

And he said it with a sincerity I'd seldom heard from him.

Warmth welled in my chest—perhaps a touch intoxicating —before I followed him down the shoreline, trailing after Edius and Rafe's footprints. The sand eagerly formed ours alongside theirs, sucking greedily at our boots.

But this place wasn't safe either.

I remembered running this beach as a child, wild in the wind, a certain dutiful knight—mustache more gray than white —calling after me to slow down.

I remembered tea picnics. Etiquette lessons. Poetry readings.

Poetry.

A thought struck. The pages Albie favored most—scribbled over, worn edges, bound lovingly in leather that smelled distinctly of...lilies.

Windley noticed my hesitation. "You all right, love?"

I shook off the residual daze. "Yes. My head's a bit foggy thanks to you, but I was just thinking..." My fingers grazed lightly over the pendants at my chest. "Those poems Albie read me growing up—I think my mother may have written them. When we return home, I plan to search his chambers."

Windley's expression shifted, something unfamiliar darkening his features. His gaze wandered to the horizon, stormy waves churning beneath skies the exact shade of his eyes.

His silence held layers.

When we return home.

Cupping his cheek, I murmured with a velvet tease in my voice, "It's a shame seeing a look like that on a face like yours."

He stiffened. "That's exactly something I'd say, queenie."

"You're rubbing off on me. Mother Poppy will be horrified." I motioned toward the sand ahead. "Let's go."

But instead, he caught my wrist, slowly guiding my hand down the curve of his jaw until my palm rested warmly against the base of his throat. He shivered, exhaling unevenly, absorbing the magic of the restored Crown through my touch against his skin.

I felt the goosebumps rising. Felt how he almost couldn't bring himself to let me go.

"Sorry." His voice was rough as he released me, fingertips dragging reluctantly away. "I'll behave."

"What happened?" I whispered. "You've been managing so well."

"Ha! Is that what it looks like?" He rubbed roughly at the back of his neck, focus darting anywhere but at me. "I told you —men are generally weaker than we let on. Walk a few paces ahead of me, would you? It's been building." Under his breath, he muttered bitterly, "I'll be glad when we're rid of that goddess-damned Crown."

Ahead, Edius ducked beneath nothing, sidestepping ghosts only he could see. Rafe's head tilted oddly, as though something beyond our reality tugged at his attention.

And then, abruptly, Edius broke into a jog.

Then a run.

Then a desperate sprint.

We followed—because we saw it too.

A glow. The glow surrounding a body.

Later, we would each recount seeing her somewhere else entirely: Rafe recalled a velvet couch in a throne room that wasn't mine. Edius admitted he'd found her curled inside a lantern-lit travel tent, blankets bunched exactly as they'd been the morning we woke tangled together. Windley and I remembered her on the sand of a well-trodden beach.

But in that moment, the one vision we all shared was her.

Gwen.

Her face was framed by fabric drawn snug around her hair, eyes shifting from blue to lavender with each tilt of light. Her warm umber skin carried quiet, rich undertones. A murmuring aura of pulsing blue wrapped her—Seelie magic alive in her veins—and at the center of her forehead a small incandescent jewel shimmered.

Yet the moment my eyes fell upon her, I suddenly understood—

Why Edius had never fallen in love with her.

16

GWEN

"She—She's a child!" I gasped.

And she was—no older than eight, fragile, delicate.

Edius wasn't fit to explain as he frantically dropped beside her, scooping her limp body into his arms and giving her a desperate shake. "Gwen? Gwen!"

"Oh, shit," Windley swore quietly. "Is she—"

"Ed...di?" The smallest of voices, wispy and cracked, shattered our worst fears. Her tiny arms curled weakly around Edius's neck. "You came back," she whispered. "I knew you would. You always keep your promises."

Edius buried his face against her shoulder, his broad back trembling visibly. "H-heya, Gwenny. Sorry it's been so long."

A wave of relief should have followed. After all the dread, after Ascian's torment, after the uncertainty of her fate—the hex hadn't taken Gwen's last breath.

But when Ed finally turned toward us, his eyes dark and stormy, I nearly buckled beneath the force of the realization.

His heart was thrumming—not in desire or longing, but in a rhythm I recognized all too clearly.

The way Albie's had for me.

Oh, Ed.

My chest ached with the weight of it.

"When you said you adopted her..." I pushed out the words, my voice shaking. "I assumed it was just a loophole, but you—you're really more like a father to her?"

"Seelies don't grow like humans," Edius said, his voice scraped raw by grief. "In twenty years she's aged maybe two. I wasn't really a father—more a brother who kept growing while she didn't." He swallowed hard. "Every word of my story was true."

"Edi?" Gwen's voice cracked, little more than a breath. "I'm tired all the time."

Edius stiffened. "Yeah, hon?" Anguish flashed across his face. "That's the hex. The man I bargained with died and, at the end, he drained you hard. Then the curse landed in even crueler hands, and—" His voice broke. "I'm so sorry, Gwenny. I never meant to let it get this bad."

She curled closer against him. "It's okay," she whispered. "I didn't feel anything. I've just been sleeping." Her fingers brushed the tiny, dim jewel set in her forehead. "See? No matter how hard I try, I can't make it brighter."

Edius's jaw clenched. "We'll get your light back, dove. I swear it."

Windley and Rafe stood still, their expressions unreadable, though comprehension glimmered briefly in Windley's eyes. His slight nod confirmed some suspicion.

And in that moment, I understood completely.

Edius hadn't been hiding this. The signs had always been there—I just hadn't wanted to see them, blinded by my own wishful thinking, hoping for a savior to keep his heart from rooting in the wrong place.

"Gwen, think you could fix this?" Edius gestured around

himself vaguely. "Not sure why this is the place I'm seeing, but it's...less than ideal."

He was referring to the vision he was witnessing inside the realm of light.

Feet dangling, Gwen nodded gently and pressed a small finger to the jewel at her forehead. Instantly, the surrounding beach rippled like heat waves. Sand and foam dissolved, replaced by a small chamber whose walls shimmered with the same iridescent blue as her eyes.

The ground was lush with plush poufs and draped silks, and at the center stood a small fountain that flowed with thick, opal-bright light.

Edius carefully placed her onto the cushions. "These are my friends, Gwen. They helped me get ahold of the ring. Can you see 'em okay?"

The girl's gaze drifted, unfocused. "No," she whispered. "But I can feel them."

She...couldn't see us?

Pulse quickening, I stepped forward. "Hello, Gwen. My name is Merrin. I've been hoping so long to meet you. You must be especially dear to Edius for all he's done to find you."

But she gave no response.

Edius ghosted his fingertips across her elbow. "Can you hear a lady's voice, Gwen?"

"No," she admitted weakly. "It's too distant. What is she, Edi? She's not human."

My throat constricted.

"That's...complicated," Edius murmured, glancing briefly at me before returning his attention to her. "She is human. Just...super-charged at the moment. Nothing to fear. She's the one who's going to help us."

I stiffened instantly.

I was?

Edius's expression turned grave.

Windley saw it too. He hesitated, stepping forward to press two fingers to Gwen's forehead.

The moment stretched painfully.

And then—

Windley pulled back, face ashen. "Yeah...not much there, is there?" He exhaled harshly. "So this is that worst-case scenario you mentioned?"

Edius gave a single, barely perceptible nod.

Then, in one smooth motion, he slipped something into Windley's open palm. A worn, dark-metal band glinted dully in the half-light. Ascian's ring? My stomach twisted at the sight.

Windley's grip tightened around the band. "Shit. Ed..." He trailed off, staring at the cursed ring as if answers might be hidden there. "And the kid?"

"She can bend the light here, so you won't have to carry her until you're out in the mortal world," Edius explained, voice eerily steady. "We had a rolling chair back home. Make sure she gets one—"

Windley's brows knitted. "Ed, are you sure about this?"

Edius met his eyes, unyielding. "Do you know another way?"

Windley inhaled a loud breath. "Not one I can live with."

"Yeah. That's what I thought."

My fists clenched.

Edius turned slowly toward me. "A word, highness?"

Heat rushed up my neck. "Only if you tell me exactly what's happening. What are you and Windley plotting? What are you asking me to do?"

But Edius merely walked past me toward the far edge of the chamber.

"Windley?" My voice sharpened with demand.

Windley hesitated—then raised his hands apologetically. "I

know you're going to be pissed at me, Merr. But I understand where he's coming from. I told him I'd only help him if you were okay with it. Both decisions are yours, really."

I stiffened. "What decisions?"

Edius halted at the distant wall, his voice low. "Come with me, highness."

I turned to Windley, searching his face urgently.

Regret shadowed his expression. "Go with him," he nudged in a whisper, unable to meet my wolf-like stare.

Rafe exhaled irritably. "I knew it. Bad move, Windley."

"Oh, fuck off, chap," Windley snapped back. "It's not that simple. You don't know what it's like carrying that sort of blood on your hands." A faint waver in his voice. "Only we know that truth—how no amount of scrubbing ever washes it away."

Rafe's jaw flexed.

Windley drew a breath. "Go with him, Merrin."

I paused, caught between anger and dread, unsettled by their cryptic exchange.

Then I followed.

At first, it felt ordinary, our footsteps echoing in velvet pulses, the air cool and luminous, brushing my skin like a whisper. But gradually the world dimmed, becoming translucent and dream-like, as though reality had been stretched thin. The others faded silently into nothing, leaving only vague impressions of where they'd stood, blurred shadows that dissolved when I tried to focus. I never saw them leave. Instead, the corridor lengthened in secret, walls shifting like liquid glass, drawing us onward with an unseen tug, until we stood isolated in an endless, shifting expanse of argent light.

Edius slowed, pressing a palm to the shimmering wall. Light rippled around his fingers like water. "Trippy, isn't it?"

I tuned him out. "Tell me what's happening, Edius."

His lips curved. "Going to command me, highness?"

My jaw locked. "Fine. I command you—tell me what's going on."

His grin twitched wider, yet his humor was bitter. "Surprised you didn't pull that earlier."

"I don't appreciate games," I snapped. "Why is your mood so grim? What are you and Windley plotting? And why can't Gwen see us?"

Finally, Edius met my eyes fully. "Because, highness," he said mournfully, "we're not really here."

I stilled. "What?"

He raked a hand through his hair. "Only those with light in their veins can truly exist here. Gwen can't see you because you're still back in the labyrinth."

My blood chilled instantly. "Our bodies are just lying there?!"

Edius released a wry chuckle. "No. We're at the doorway, so to speak. The mortal world can't touch you, but you're not truly in the light realm either. Ever feel something in the dark you can't see? Right now, for Gwen, you're exactly that."

I shivered. "What about you?"

"I have traces of light in my veins. Gwen lent me some once, so I could stand here without fading." He tapped the spot just above his heart, tugging the fabric a finger-width away. "I can show you—"

"No!" I threw up both hands before he bared so much as a button, nerves sparking. "You found her, you can break the hex —so what's this really about?"

His voice dropped, heavy as an anvil. "I want to finish what we started." Eyes ancient and intent, he leaned in until his breath grazed my lips. "If I asked for one last kiss—without the beguiling—would that be all right?"

My pulse leapt.

He was serious.

"Edius, I can't. It isn't productive—or safe."

"What if it couldn't touch your boyfriend?" The words came out like a dare, rough around the edges. "Then could you?" His gaze dipped to my mouth. "We're only echoes here," he added, phantom heat stirring my skin. "It wouldn't even be real."

"It still counts."

A thin, stubborn thread of fondness tugged.

In the next heartbeat, he angled in and pressed a quick, sand-papery kiss to my cheek—brief, unpolished, gone before I could flinch.

I jerked back, heart hammering. "Edius, what is this? What are you doing?"

He caught my wrist. "I'm about to ask something you'll want to refuse, but I need you to agree. It's life-or-death, Merrín, and I know exactly what I'm asking."

My throat tightened. "What?"

"Before you surrender that Crown of yours...I need you to give my life to Gwen."

Air punched from my chest. I stepped backward until the shifting wall steadied me. "Are you mad? Absolutely not! She's weak, yes, but she can still recover."

"I wish that were true." His voice held no anger, only grief. "If I take her out of here like this, she'll fade. Charm timed it perfectly—left just enough spark for me to see Gwen once more before it gutters out." He swallowed hard. "She's been sleeping to save what's left. Woke up the moment we arrived, but the instant I touched her I felt it—her spirit's a trickle, not a river. Next time she drifts off, I'd stake my life she won't wake up."

I jerked my head hard. "Then we lend her energy. She doesn't need a sacrifice. Just enough to—"

"That won't work," he cut in.

"Yes, it will!" I fired back. "I wasn't the one who ended

Charm—Rafe dealt the final blow. We didn't trade her full life to replenish yours then. Same with when Pip healed me! Why should this be different?"

Edius's mouth tipped in a weary half-smile. "Always chasing a fix. That's why they made you queen, huh?"

"For the last time, I was *born* into it."

He pressed on, calm but unrelenting. "What you and I had —those were wounds of the body. Fatal but physical. We just needed a surge—call it a few heartbeats' worth of somebody else's charge. Gwen's running on less than one percent. You'd have to pour in everything you've got, and she'd start dwindling again the instant you stopped. Ascian drained her spirit a sliver at a time every time he healed. Borrowed time won't patch that. She needs a full replacement."

I trembled, voice thinning to a whisper. "Did you know— on the way here—did you know this might happen?"

"Not for certain. But once I wore the ring, I felt how faint she was. I knew I might need you." His tone sank. "And I knew you'd only come if I kept the ring, so..."

My stomach knotted hard. "You set me up? And Windley *knew?*"

His jaw tightened. "Last-ditch plan. Windley didn't figure it out till later—save the fury for me." He softened, almost pleading. "Merrín, I know how awful this is. But you're the only one who can save her now."

"So I'm cornered." My pulse thundered. "If I don't give her your life, she dies. You kept quiet because—"

"Because I knew you'd never have come."

Something in me snapped.

For the first time, I didn't hold back. I struck him—hard.

Edius barely flinched, crimson blooming on his cheek. When his eyes lifted again, there was no anger—only grief.

"How could you, Edius?!" My voice splintered. "After what I—what I had to do to Albie—you—"

"I know," he whispered, rubbing the sting slowly. "I'm a bastard. I always hurt what matters most." His gaze dimmed further. "When I said I was leaving after this, I never guessed how far."

He hooked a scarred finger under one of my curls, let it spring free. His gaze was raw, voice scraped thin.

"Can I kiss you, highness?"

The word hung there, tight as wire.

"I know you're still juiced," he went on, visibly wrestling himself down. "I'll keep my hands where they belong—swear it."

I drew a shaky breath. "Why?"

His fist settled over his chest, as if bracing the riot beneath. "Because I've never loved anyone. I'd like to feel it—just once. And the only person it could ever be is you."

Pain cinched tight in my ribs.

"I tried to fight it—you can see how well that went." He dragged in a ragged breath. "Yeah, it's selfish. Unfair. But before I go, I want to feel it—and I'm close."

"You're not going anywhere," I snapped. "Not like this."

His gaze searched mine. "If one kiss would send me off happy—would you?"

"No. I mean—" The words snagged. "In that awful scenario, yes, but you're not *dying*, Edius—"

He heard only permission.

His mouth found mine—warm, fiercely restrained—then it was gone before the kiss could deepen. A battle-scarred hand cupped my neck, tender yet already pulling back.

It felt heartbreakingly familiar. Cherishing. Remembering.

He brushed my chin with his thumb. "Hard to stop, highness. In the old days, I wouldn't have."

I pushed his hand away, breath shaking. "Edius—saving Gwen is one thing, but I can't—"

"Then come with me," he rasped. "If there's any spark at all, drop him. I'll keep you safe—love you how you deserve. One chance, Merrín. Let me steal you away."

Love.

It was love in his stare, love in his hands enclosing mine, love in his heart pounding defiantly against fate.

Oh, Edi. You absolute fool.

"No." My whisper was broken. "I would never."

His lips quirked—not surprised, not bitter—expectant and understanding. "I know," he murmured. "Wouldn't have let you say yes. But for myself, I needed to hear it." His grip loosened. "Easier knowing I'm leaving nothing behind."

I knew exactly what he meant. I hated that I did.

"And thanks," he murmured, pressing a hand over his chest as if feeling the wreckage beneath. "It feels..."

Warm? Freeing? Like home?

"Awful," he finished quietly. "Feels fuckin' awful."

Yet, somehow, he smiled. He rubbed absently at his erratic heartbeat, as though attempting to soothe it into submission. And I officially became the worst well-intentioned person in all the realms.

"Alright." He turned slowly. "We need to do this soon."

But I hadn't agreed yet. If he thought I'd accept this quietly, he was a bigger fool than I realized.

Rafe and Windley, attuned to unspoken truths, already knew what was unfolding.

Windley—torn between fury at Edius, shame toward me, and sorrow for his friend's impossible choice—watched helplessly.

But none of us—the restless, reckless, broken ones—would let a child die.

"I'll give her a year, Edi," I said tightly. "Enough time to find another way."

Edius shook his head slowly. "My Queen, that won't work. It'd take ten of my years to give her one. Just take 'em all. Let me repent—for Gwen, for Albie, for everything."

I looked to Gwen, bathed in weak, flickering light. "So your whole life is five or six years for her?"

He opened his hands, surrendering himself entirely. "It's all I got."

No. There had to be another way.

There always was.

But we wouldn't be able to solve it yet.

Just then, Ascian's ring—perched snugly on Windley's finger—began to smoke.

17

THE VILE ONE

It was with an open heart that Edius rushed forward, gathering the sleepy, fragile Gwen into his arms just as darkness began seeping into the light-washed chamber.

"What the hell?" Windley yelped, jerking his hand back as the ring began to smoke. "What'd I do? Is it reacting to something?"

Rafe, ever the pragmatist, didn't waste time theorizing. He shoved me behind him, sword drawn.

"Will that even work?" I asked hurriedly. "If we aren't really here, can we fight off a threat?"

"We aren't really here?" Rafe echoed.

Gwen stirred weakly in Edius's arms, fingers curling feebly into his tunic. "Edi...what is that?" Her voice was fragile as paper. "It's something bad. Something that shouldn't be here!"

Edius tightened his grip protectively. "Just hold on to me, Gwenny."

But his heart—his newly awakened heart—was thundering straight toward me.

Still cradling Gwen, he joined Rafe, forming a wall

between the threat and us. Windley, pale-faced, ripped the ring from his finger and tossed it to the ground.

The wrong choice.

The instant the cursed ring struck the floor, darkness surged violently around it, writhing into a humanoid silhouette before solidifying to snatch the fallen object.

With a shattering burst, shadows exploded outward, revealing the one person none of us wanted to see.

Pastel hair. Hollow, gleaming eyes.

Pip!

"Well, that was easy," he crooned, casually sliding Ascian's ring back onto his finger.

At least three of us cursed at once.

"What the hell, Pip?! You were inside that thing?" Windley shouted in disbelief.

"Of course I was," Pip replied, amused, as if the answer were obvious. "It's a refuge, crafted from the bones of our mothers. Now, give me the queen. And I'll take the Seelie, too."

Windley bared his teeth. "So that's how you survived extinction when the angels came? Hid inside jewelry while the rest of your kind were slaughtered? Pathetic."

Pip shot him a bored look. "Watch yourself, Windalloy. Naturally, I crafted rings for my brothers, too—but they declined and were destroyed. All I asked in return was that they share their power with me. Our mothers meant for me to rule. Shame they lacked faith in my abilities."

My breath caught. Pip was the last of his kind. The last Dracon.

He'd survived through cowardice.

"Yet your ring was stronger than theirs," I accused, stepping around Edius and Rafe to face him head-on. "You forced them to feed you magic in exchange for protection. That's not leadership.

True rulers give to their people—they don't take. You're responsible for the suffering those rings caused Windley, Edius, Charmagne. You'll never be forgiven, Pip. And you won't exist in a world that no longer wants you." My spirit pulsed with shadow, wrapped in creation's shimmering glow. "Today, Pip, I end you."

Every fiber of me meant it.

Pip merely grinned. "No," he whispered, vanishing in a blur.

Suddenly his hand was at my throat.

"I will end *you*, miss queen lion," he countered, fingers tightening cruelly. "And because my brothers repeatedly failed me, I'll do it in ways that stain their memory and haunt them in the dark."

Windley was there instantly, hatchet slicing toward Pip's arm, but Pip was faster. With a flick of invisible wings, he hurled Windley aside as if weightless.

I didn't hesitate. I pushed—a surge of will—and all the shadows I'd gathered slammed into Pip like a storm.

The impact rocked the chamber.

He released me.

But unlike last time, Pip didn't fall.

He laughed.

"Excellent." He flexed his fingers, admiring the ring. "My shield is restored." Satisfaction curled his lips. "And you've left me a gift inside."

A strangled cry escaped Gwen's throat as Pip clenched his fist.

"Stop!" Edius roared, anguish visceral in his voice, gripping Gwen as if sheer desperation could shield her. "Leave her alone! She's suffered enough!"

Pip's expression darkened. "Then help me, Edi. I'll let you keep your little Seelie—if you help tame the lion."

The thunderous pound of Edius's heart was answer enough. His gaze seared into mine, and he shook his head once.

"Go to hell, Pip."

"I've already been," Pip replied, wings fluttering faintly. "I was there when it first took shape."

Windley hauled himself upright, swiping blood from his mouth, hatchets glinting.

"Really? You think steel will succeed where a goddess failed?" Pip sneered.

He had a point; we were cornered again—

Or so it seemed, until the raw urgency in Edius's voice reached me, cajoling the tiny girl in his arms.

"Give us an edge, Gwenny. That's all we need. Just a little advantage. I know you can do it." He pressed a brotherly kiss to the crown of her head, voice breaking. "Then I'll return everything you've lost. We'll be together forever."

A dazzling flash burst into existence, momentarily blinding us. Then the world lurched. The area shimmered and vanished, replaced by an endless sky. Below us stretched a yawning gulf of pure, boundless light. We stood precariously atop a single narrow column of stone. Opposite us rose another pillar—and on it, Pip, now strangely distant.

Gwen had literally twisted the space around us.

Pip's lips curled in mocking amusement. "Cute trick," he drawled, stepping off the edge. His invisible wings flickered into view to support him—only for his ankle to yank back midair, snared by a star-lit chain anchoring him to his pillar.

He snarled, brandishing the ring. "Fine. If she won't cooperate, I'll drain the Seelie first."

"Do that," Edius warned, his voice like ice, "and none of us leave this place. Including you."

Pip hesitated, and Windley seized the moment. "What's

your plan after you consume the two humans?" he taunted sharply. "Leave yourself all alone here? You'll starve."

For a heartbeat, doubt flickered in Pip's hollow eyes.

Then his gaze locked on Rafe.

"Mage," he commanded, raw power thrumming in his tone, "kill Windalloy."

Rafe's breath caught, pupils dilating unnaturally.

"NO!" I shouted, stomping my foot in desperation. My magic—vines, branches—anything—remained silent. We weren't in the mortal realm; I couldn't grow anything here.

Pip's grin widened.

With a roar, Rafe swung a flaming sword, forcing Windley to scramble. "Ah, shit!" Windley cursed, narrowly avoiding another fiery slash.

Pip's laughter rattled through the air like a blade dragged across stone.

Edius ground his teeth, the tips of those feline canines catching the light. "Highness," he said tensely, "watch Gwen. I'll help your boyfriend deal with Rafe until we come up with a plan."

He eased Gwen's weakening form into my arms, then sprinted forward, fists raised.

I held her close, smoothing the damp wisps that had slipped free of her wrap. "Gwen? Can you hear me?" My voice was thistledown-soft as I rocked her frail body. "I'm Merrin. A friend of Edi's."

Her iridescent eyes fluttered open, exhaustion clouded yet brightened by recognition. "Merrín?" she breathed.

She shared Edius's faint accent, though hers was softer, sweeter—enough to make my heart swell despite the chaos all around us.

"Yes," I murmured, straightening the edge of her head-scarf

with gentle fingers. "I know you're tired and your magic's nearly gone, but do you have strength left for one last favor?"

She blinked up at me, brow knitting. "What is this light?" Her small fingers flexed weakly, as though trying to clutch the lambent halo surrounding us. "It feels warm."

"I've wrapped you in Vita's breath," I told her. The tranquil green aura enveloped her, restoring vitality to her drained spirit. "It's the light of a goddess. Stay within it, Gwen. Don't let yourself sink into darkness. Can you do that?"

She let out a near-silent breath, pressing closer. "It feels heavenly."

"It's safe," I promised. "And as long as you remain inside it, nothing harmful can reach you." I paused, choosing my words with care. "But there's someone here—someone dangerous. You sensed him earlier, didn't you?"

Gwen offered the barest nod against my chest.

"He wants to hurt us all," I explained in a hushed tone. "But I believe there's a way to stop him—something that can only be done here, where reality bends to our will. I need your help to make it happen. And if it's too much, we won't proceed. Will you promise to be honest with me?"

Her fingers squeezed mine with frail determination. "I always tell the truth."

A good girl. A brilliant soul.

"I know you do," I said, stroking slow circles between her shoulder blades.

Then, carefully, I told her my plan.

Her eyes widened softly, wonder sparkling in their depths. "Really? I've never met one!"

"Neither have I," I admitted, my mouth quirking wryly. "He's under a spell right now, but I think the instant you do this...it'll break."

She paused, then gave a single, measured nod.

"Do you have enough strength?"

"Yes," she replied, though her voice wavered.

I searched her expression. "Are you certain, Gwen? It would destroy Edi to lose you. It would hurt all of us."

Her lashes fluttered. "I'm sure," she whispered. "It'll take me right to the edge, but I'll stay in your light."

My chest tightened at the trust she placed in me—a stranger. "I'll remain with you the whole time," I promised.

"You're kind." A small smile curved her lips. A heartbeat passed. "Are you Edi's wyrdbound one?"

If guilt could kill, I would have perished right then.

"No, Gwen," I whispered, swallowing the ache in my throat, tightening my hold around her delicate frame. "I belong to another. But Edi is very special to me. I do love him...in my own way. And I promise I'll make sure he's never alone. He's a dear, dear friend."

Gwen's eyes brightened faintly—a flicker of hope amid her weariness. "A friend," she exhaled, relieved. "Edi has another friend. I knew he would. I'm so glad."

A bittersweet ache squeezed my heart. She had worried about him, wanted more for him.

It was a precious, fragile moment—one I loathed to end. But the clash of weapons grew louder, sharper. Windley's breath came ragged now, his evasions desperate, Rafe's sword blazing with fire—

Time was slipping away.

"We'll talk more after this is done, alright?" I promised gently.

She nodded, eyes trusting, hopeful.

"Are you ready, Gwen?"

A deep, careful inhale. Another nod.

With trembling fingers, she touched the glowing jewel at the center of her forehead—

And the world exploded.

Rafe's chest burst with blinding light.

18

ANGEL BOY

In the ancient wars, the Dracons had been wiped out by the angels. And now, in a cruel twist of fate, it was Rafe's angelic blood that had allowed him to pact with Soleil and Luna—the very celestial beings who had orchestrated that extinction.

In this world, where light could be bent and reshaped, I didn't dare let Gwen do anything directly to Pip. If he sensed her interference, his retaliation would be swift and merciless. Instead, I placed my faith in the one who had never asked for any of this. The one stolen from his homeland, where only a handful still knew the old ways of enchanting metal. The one who'd served dutifully despite the weight in his heart, and who'd reluctantly joined our journey—yet remained steadfast at our side.

As Gwen tapped the gemstone at her brow, bending the world around us, she reached into Rafe's blood—to the angelic remnants lying dormant within—and awakened them.

His transformation was instant. Where his skin had been ochre-brown, it now shimmered like burnished gold. Where his eyes had been the color of amber glass, they blazed with celestial fire. And behind him, stretching gloriously from his shoulders, were wings—not faint figments like Pip's—but shining outlines of pure, golden light.

He was breathtaking. Ethereal. Magnificent.

This was how it must have been during the first war. When angels descended from the heavens to erase the Dracons from existence. Rafe had never wished to become a weapon. Yet, in this moment, he was one. A force sent to finish what the angels had begun.

My breath caught, awed by his divine form—

Until—

"Your Majesty? What the hell did you do to me?!"

Still Rafe. Always Rafe.

"Sorry, Rafe!" I shouted over the chaos. "It's temporary. You'll revert once we leave this realm."

"Oh my GODDESS!" His voice had never held such animation. "You turned me into an angel?!"

Windley, ever the opportunist, tapped his chin and gave an approving nod. "Looking fine, chap. Imagine the positions you can attain in flight! Queen Beau is certain to be—"

"Oh, shut up." Rafe flicked his wrist, sending opposing streams of frost and flame hurtling toward Windley, who swiftly blocked them with his hatchet.

"Huh," Rafe murmured, thoughtfully inspecting his glowing palm.

"Enough!" Edius barked. "Fly over there and stop Pip before he figures out how to use that ring—"

His voice abruptly faltered.

Because Gwen's head had fallen limp in my lap.

I pressed my fingers to her pulse, my entire being wrapped protectively around her, enveloped in Vita's luminous glow. "Come on, Gwen," I whispered, giving her cheek a coaxing pat.

"You knew your limits. You said you'd be all right. You wouldn't lie to your new friend, would you?"

Edius reached out, frantic.

"No!" I said quickly. "Keep her here, in my light. She promised to stay with it. Her heart's still beating—I can feel the breath of life inside her."

Edius's hands shook as he gripped my shoulders. "Do it now, highness. Transfer my life into her now!"

Windley skidded to our side, breathless. "You okay, darling?"

"I'm fine, but Gwen doesn't have long."

"Then do it, Merrín!" Edius's grip tightened painfully. "I'm begging you—give her my life!"

"Edius." I cupped his cheek, forcing calm into my voice. "No."

His face shattered. "Gwen's life is worth more than mine. You know that, highness. And I know you. I know you won't let her die here." His voice cracked. "Windley? Little help?"

Windley's jaw flexed, and his answer was steady. "Sorry, mate. I support her choice. Like I told you—I'll never make her do something she doesn't wish to." His gaze swept tenderly over Gwen's frail body. "Never again."

"You misunderstand," I clarified gently. "I can't do it now. There's nothing to stop Pip from draining her again. We need the ring back first."

All life returned to Edius's eyes. "R-really? You'll do it?"

I nodded.

Blinding gratitude flooded his face as he leapt to his feet and raced toward Rafe, shouting commands.

Windley's hands settled on my shoulders, steadying me— he read me better than anyone.

"You're not going to do it," he murmured knowingly.

I met his gaze. "No."

His sigh was weary, but unsurprised. "I knew it."

"I won't kill Edius," I said. "I'll give Gwen five years of his life—and five of mine."

Windley's breath sharpened.

"That buys us time," I continued firmly. "A year to find another solution. I won't relinquish the Crown until I know she's safe."

Windley's gaze hardened. "No, Merr. Take mine instead. I have plenty to atone for."

My heart warmed, bittersweet. "You deserve every moment of your life, Windley. You've fought for it. You've earned it. I've lived a charmed existence—I can spare five years."

His frown tightened. "Then what about Pip? Couldn't we take his life instead?"

I wavered. "He's empty, Windley—there's no true life-spark left to claim."

"But what if the goddesses adopted him, the way Vita adopted us?" Windley pressed. "Give him a spark first—then you could claim it without cost, couldn't you?"

The thought struck like lightning. My eyes flew wide.

Windley's brow furrowed. "What is it?"

"Windley," I breathed, "that's ingenious."

He let out a short huff, trying not to smile. "Careful, Merr. You almost sound surprised."

I gripped his hand. "Go—tell Edius the plan. And tell Rafe not to kill Pip."

Windley paused, studying my face.

"What is it?" I asked, my voice low.

His gaze shifted, thoughtful. "It's rather ruthless, for you."

"I know," I replied steadily. "At the start of this journey, I never would've considered it. But my patience has run dry. Pip is beyond redemption, and this is the right decision—even if it stains my soul."

Windley studied me quietly for a long moment before his expression eased into pride. "I'm proud of you, queenie."

I clutched his hand a bit too firmly. "And I'm grateful for you, my knight."

His lips curved into a roguish grin. "Not sure I'll ever get used to hearing that one. Like calling me 'Daddy.'"

"Hmm. So 'Daddy' is better?"

His whole face scrunched. "No, goddess no."

"Go, Daddy."

"EW, DON'T."

Despite everything, I grinned. And as Windley sprinted off, I shut my eyes and reached into a place I hadn't dared visit in a long time.

"Vita? Can you hear me?"

Silence.

Yet, I felt her.

I focused deeply, calling into the quiet place I knew she lingered.

"I wish to ask for something." My voice was level, but my pulse raced frantically. "I know you already know what it is, but please consider what I've discussed with Windley. If Pip truly is the last of his kind, then his adoption will be short-lived —for I intend to use him to save this child. But I cannot do that without your breath. As it stands, there's nothing in him to take."

Still, silence.

"I understand there are things you cannot do in your current form. If you could bestow life freely, you would have done so in Sestilia's chambers instead of leaving me to other devices. I understand balance—that even gods have rules they must follow. But all I ask is that Pip be tied to the same flow of life as the rest of creation. If you do this for me, Vita, I promise I will find a way to exile the destroyer from this world. A way that is decent and right. Please—help me save this child without sacrificing another good soul."

Nothing.

No warmth. No distant whisper to tell me she'd heard.

But then—

A cry.

From across the void, where Rafe battled Pip, a sound pierced the chaos.

And then I felt it.

A dull, new beat—neither human nor Spirite. Something harder than a plum's pit, smaller than a cherry's.

My breath caught.

"It worked!" I gasped, barely restraining the urge to jump. "Windley! I feel it—it worked!"

"Oi, chap!" Windley shouted, waving wildly. "Take him alive!"

Rafe turned sharply, his glowing wings flexing as he hesitated—just long enough for Pip to seize the advantage. A spear of darkness launched from his palm, forcing Rafe to dodge at the last second, his face twisting with fury.

Shimmering like molten gold, Rafe snarled—an expression no celestial being had likely ever worn—as he plunged toward Pip, sword raised overhead, ready to strike a final blow.

But Pip was a survivor.

From liquid shadow, he conjured an obsidian blade, meeting Rafe's attack midair. Their weapons collided with a deafening clang, scattering sparks across the endless void.

"Shit," Windley muttered.

Rafe cursed louder than I'd ever heard, pressing Pip's sword back with brute force. Flames blazed in his eyes before shifting to ice, his blade forging opposing elements as he bore down.

Pip twisted, retreating just enough to unleash another wave of sludge, the dark substance streaking toward Rafe's chest—

But this time, Rafe was ready.

With a fierce roar, he flexed his arms, sending a golden pulse through his body. The darkness hissed and dissolved on contact.

"Atta boy!" Windley cheered.

Edius, tense at the platform's edge, shifted anxiously and glanced between the battle and Gwen's weakened form in my lap. He feared what Pip might do if he sensed defeat closing in —or if he won.

We balanced on the razor's edge. Timing had to be perfect.

And though angels once wiped out Dracons, the two battling before us appeared evenly matched. They clashed for what felt like an eternity—fire against ice, black against gold, blade against blade, wing against wing.

Until it happened.

One of them fell.

As the fight raged, I had quietly woven something of my own—shadows no longer capable of harming Pip directly, but strong enough to distract.

I sent them streaming across the void, waiting at the pillar's edge where gold clashed against darkness, where Pip taunted and Rafe found his wings—

Patiently waiting.

A mass of shadow crouched like a lion hidden in the grass, poised on the abyss's brink.

The instant Rafe lunged, I released it.

Pure black erupted, smothering Pip's vision like smoke from a neglected oven.

Pip reeled, clawing frantically at his eyes—

And for the first time since the fight began, he was slow.

And in that moment, Rafe struck true—

"Keep him alive, chap!"

—with an icy blast to the chest.

Pip's body locked. He crashed heavily to the ground, hands frozen over his heart.

Rafe hovered triumphantly above him, wings blazing gold.

But Pip had always been most dangerous when cornered.

Even with his life force threatened, Pip reached for one final weapon.

A sinister grin cut across his lips.

And behind me—

Gwen gave a soft sigh.

Her heartbeat—

Began to fade.

19

THE GREATEST GIFT

"No, Gwen! Stay with me!"

I had no choice—I began feeding her pieces of my life.

"Bring him over here, chap!" Windley shouted frantically as I monitored Gwen's heartbeat, slipping her minutes, hours, whenever her pulse faltered.

Edius was at my side in an instant, anguish tightening his jaw as he seized my arms. "Take from *me*, highness!"

"No!" I thundered. "I will never again steal life from someone I care for! Last time, with Albie, I was forced! I won't do it willingly!"

"You're being stubborn!" Edius roared. "You and Gwen are worth more than—"

"Your life matters, Edius! Stop lessening yourself! RAFE!" I called desperately. "Bring Pip to me—and hurry!"

A sharp crack split the air. The sound of chains shattering beneath brutal frost.

Rafe had obeyed.

Still cradling Gwen, I twisted to look. Across the void, Rafe held Pip's limp body, wings laboring to carry them toward us, his golden skin flaring brighter as he strained.

But then—

"Rafe!" Windley saw it first—the creeping blackness slinking up Rafe's torso. "LOOK OUT!"

Pip had unleashed the serpentine sludge, conjured from the rot of his ancestors' bones, and it crawled hungrily up Rafe's back.

With a furious flash, Rafe burned it away—but more surged to take its place. He fought harder, blazing hotter, but the darkness poured over him like tar, devouring his radiance.

Pip grinned triumphantly. He didn't care about survival—only vengeance.

"AAAAAH!"

With a harrowing cry, Rafe plummeted, his wings tangled and darkened.

We screamed in unison as he vanished into the chasm, his cry swallowed by darkness.

"NO!" Windley scrambled helplessly to the edge, frantic. "Come on, Rafe! Shake it off! COME ON!"

But Rafe was gone—lost to the dark depths.

Edius, tearing his gaze from the abyss, turned sharply back to me. Gwen's light dimmed rapidly—and I was pouring my life into her, just to keep her from fading completely.

"Enough, Merrín! This is insane!" By force, he ripped her from my grasp. "I won't let you kill yourself!"

"Stop, Edi!" I lunged for her. "She'll DIE!"

"Yeah? Then come save her!"

But as I reached to place my hands on her, he spun—so I placed my hands upon him instead.

"You're taking my life!" he shouted, anguished. "I know this is painful, and you'll hate me, but I'd rather that than let you die! Now respect my wishes!"

He shook violently, furious and desperate.

And behind me, warm arms curled tightly around my waist.

Windley.

He pressed his face into my neck. "I won't let you do this."

The weight of him anchored me.

"I was weak last time," he whispered, voice frayed with emotion. "Because it was your life at stake. But this time, I won't let you be forced into something you don't want. The Seelie's blood will stain my hands, not yours."

And goddess help me, I hated him for it.

And goddess help me, I was grateful.

For so long, my choices had been taken from me. And yet—

"I'll do it."

Edius froze. His stare pierced mine, waiting for me to retract my words.

I didn't.

"I'll use Edi to save Gwen," I repeated quietly.

Windley tightened his embrace, as if he could absorb my pain, carry it himself. "I know, my queen. It's the right choice. You've yet to make the wrong one. That's why we all follow you."

He released me.

Jaw tight, I stepped forward and pressed my palm to Edius's chest.

Beneath my hand, his heart trembled.

"I'm sorry, highness," he whispered hoarsely. "Truly. But I'm glad I met you. Glad I felt what it was like to—"

A heartbeat. A pulse.

There was always another way.

I closed my eyes.

Felt the flow of life in him, the rhythm of something pure and powerful.

And then—I pulled.

Edius gasped, his spirit rushing through my fingertips, into my chest.

And I broke it apart.

With my other hand, I touched Gwen's cheek, passing his life into hers.

A bridge. A tether.

I felt the moment Gwen's heart strengthened, felt her spirit surge.

And I stopped.

Edius sagged against me, blinking dazedly. "What are you doing?"

I framed his face between my palms, steadying him. "Your life means something, Edius. You don't have to sacrifice it for that to be true."

He stared, confused.

"You matter to me. To Windley. To Gwen." My voice bent under the weight of emotion, but my hands held firm. "The three of us will believe it until you do. I've given her a year"—I let him go—"and no more."

His throat bobbed.

I bent to the cool skin just below Gwen's wrap. "Listen carefully, dove."

I murmured the plan against her brow.

Before Pip could draw another breath from her—

The sky-pillar overhead shattered, air popping in my ears, and the silken chamber snapped back around us.

"AAAAAH!"

Rafe plummeted through the rippling ceiling, wings slick with tar, Pip locked in his arms.

"Chap!"

Windley lunged, caught Pip's elbows the instant the pair

hit the cushions, and fought to pin him while Rafe sprawled beside them, eyes wild, hoarfrost still cracking across his chest.

"NOW!"

I yanked Edius down beside me, fisting his shirt, one hand slapping onto the only patch of Pip's exposed skin while the other closed around Gwen's wrist.

Pip's lips curled, slow and knowing.

Because we were touching.

And he believed he could overtake me.

Of all the life I'd ever stolen, none felt more justified.

I did not ease it from him, as I had done with Edius.

I ripped it away.

Breath by breath, I stole the years, siphoning them from his flesh, spilling them into Gwen.

A hundred years. His face unchanged.

Two hundred. Hair began to gray.

Three hundred. Wrinkles crept across his skin.

I lost count after that.

All the while, Gwen's glow pulsed brighter.

Stronger.

Stronger.

Brilliant enough to blind.

And still, I pulled.

I pulled.

I pulled—

Until I felt it.

The moment Pip's life force ran dry.

His body stiffened. His head fell back.

Gone.

Windley had been right—it was brutal.

I'd considered stopping. Letting someone else deliver the final blow.

But what kind of queen would I be if I left such darkness to my guards?

Taking a life was evil.

But there was no clear line between good and evil. Under the right lighting, even villainous acts could become heroic.

The lighting in Gwen's chamber was bright.

I released them both—

Gwendol.

Pipsqueak.

Then I fell, my own vitality drained.

"Merr!"

Of course it was Windley. And Rafe. And Edius. But one voice cut through them all.

"Edi!"

As my vision cleared, small arms wrapped tightly around a much larger neck.

And as the room settled, something equally radiant unfolded.

A smile—hidden for too long—now spread across Edius's face.

Gwen was alive.

"Gwenny."

Edius dropped to his knees and folded her close, relief shaking through his shoulders. "It's you—right here." He rocked, brow resting against hers. "You'll be all right, dove. I swear it. I'm done letting go."

A moment of pure joy—of solace, of victory.

But I couldn't feel any of it yet.

I turned, arm outstretched. "Rafe—the ring."

Still breathing hard, Rafe approached Pip's withered form, fingers reaching for the cursed band clenched around his lifeless finger.

Before he could pass it to me, Windley stepped between us.

He pressed his palm lightly to my brow. "Maybe not today, queenie. You've already overdone it. You're running on fumes."

I exhaled, shaky but determined. "I won't sleep until it's done. That ring doesn't belong in this world. I need yours too— and Pip's, Ed's, Charm's. I'll destroy them all at once. I swear I'll rest afterward."

Windley dusted a tender kiss across my damp forehead, then turned to collect the rings.

Each was forged from arcane metal, adorned with the remnants of a mother race long gone.

He handed me Charm's. Then Pip's. Then Edius's.

I turned them in my palm.

For all their destruction, they felt oddly light.

Drawing shadows around my hand, I closed my fingers over them.

And squeezed.

They crumbled to ash, as if they'd never existed.

"Next, yours, Wind."

His jaw clenched, eyes heavy. He rolled the ring between his fingers, giving it one last spin before sliding it from his knuckle. He studied it closely.

The conduit of pain. The leash that had bound him.

"It's strange, Merr," he said, voice distant. "I...hate it."

Yet his gaze said something else.

"But in some ways, I don't." He turned it again. "It reminds me of what I've done—but also what I survived. Keeps me honest."

I covered his hand with mine. "Release it, Windley."

His breath wavered.

"You deserve everything you have now. You don't need reminders of your past. Those evils aren't yours to carry. Let it go."

A slow nod. A gathering courage.

Then he leaned in, kissed my temple, and relinquished it.

His ring was the sweetest to crush.

I opened my palm, revealing nothing but dust.

Windley released a long-held breath, laughing softly. "Goddess. For some reason, I expected fireworks."

"Does it feel good?" I asked.

He slapped his chest lightly. "Good, bad...hollow."

His thumb brushed the spot the ring had once occupied.

We would find him a new one.

I smiled. "I'm proud of you, Wind."

He scoffed. "It's just a ring, Merr."

I shook my head. "I'm proud of you for much more than removing a ring."

His breath stuttered, a hint of color rising to his cheekbones.

"Easy, queenie," he said, half-laughing as he rubbed the back of his neck. "Keep praising me like that and I'll start preening."

Oh, how I wanted to torment him further.

But there would be plenty of time later.

I inhaled deeply. "Alright, Windley. It's time."

The last ring.

"Drop Gwen's hex and hand it over."

His breathing steadied.

Slowly, he slipped the master ring onto his thumb, closed his eyes, and drew a deep breath.

Across the room came a gasp.

Gwen.

The hex was gone.

At last.

At last, Gwen was free.

Behind me, joy bloomed—Edius's relief surging as he clutched Gwen tightly, Ascian's final chains now severed.

I turned back to Windley, palm open.

"The last one."

And then, instead of placing it in my hand, he slipped it onto my finger.

A blink—a shock—a pulse in my chest—and then the world tilted.

That was the last thing I saw before my knees buckled.

20

OUR MOTHERS

The lighted realm was gone.

My breath was gone.

I stood in a place of purest black. Black enough that I couldn't see my own feet. Thick enough to choke on.

And in that space painted of nothing, I heard a cackle—cold, calloused, cruel.

It was a cackle I recognized—only cupcakes laughed like that.

"Charmagne?"

Around me, darkness slithered, whispering as it coiled against my ears.

"A hume? And a touched hume at that. How did a hume enter this placeeee?"

"Not a hume," said another voice, hissing gently, dripping with intrigue. *"A god-being! A god-being in hume form!"*

"No," a third voice corrected, shrewd and certain. *"The hume is only lent divinity; the hume isss not divine. The hume isss a weapon."*

"A weapon."

"The weapon."

And then—they scattered.

A presence, vast and unseen, shifted away into the black.

"Tch. Cowards," scoffed a voice unlike the rest.

A voice I knew.

And then—there she was.

Charmagne.

Rose-gold hair, a tailored waist, teeth meant for smiling— but used only for spite. She stood striking against the backdrop of nihility—a diamond buried in the blackest of dirt.

I nearly lost my footing in the nothing beneath me. "It is you!" I gasped. "Charmagne! You're alive?"

She tilted her head, examining me with that same old condescending smirk.

"Alive is relative, cupcake. One doesn't typically bounce back from, oh, I don't know—being *murdered*." She stopped a distance away, the pooling blackness rippling beneath her feet like an ink-stained pond. "You're looking...plump."

"Where are we?" I demanded. "Inside Ascian's ring?"

Charmagne rolled her eyes. "Inside a ring? Stupid. How could a person fit inside a ring?"

I had no patience for her games.

"Save your efforts, shrew," I charged. "I know the ring is a refuge. We saw Pip emerge from it."

Her gaze hooked into mine, curling like ivy. "Was he really *inside* it, though?" Her voice dipped intriguingly, as though musing over a puzzle I hadn't yet solved. "That ring is a bridge, and you, foolish human, have crossed into a place you shouldn't be."

A bridge.

At the farthest edge of your world, there is a cave from which crawled the first spark of life...

It exists outside your mortal realm, beyond living and dead...

A passage leading to the end of days, where the Drakaina remain in banishment...

Charmagne's smile spread wider, laced with sinister delight.

I knew it before she said it—

"The place where my mothers rest."

Tiny hairs pricked along my skin as shadows slithered at the edges of my vision—just out of reach, ancient and watching.

The Drakaina.

Celestial-born. Serpentine. Women of wings and fangs, their beauty twisted, their divinity forsaken.

And this was their place of exile—linked to our world by a cave.

By bones mined therein.

Bones polished into gemstone.

Bones Windley had just inadvertently slipped onto my finger.

This was the end of days.

Maybe it was fate.

I had never intended to follow Vita's instructions to come to this place. Yet here I stood, guided by means I hadn't known existed. It was as though the invisible Crown upon my head had forced my hand, leading me toward this inevitable conclusion.

But one question burned brighter than all others.

"What on earth are you doing here, Charm?"

"Excuse me, *Charm?*" She scoffed, tossing her hair like I'd committed an offense. "Since when are we that cozy? I'm here because I was murdered while wearing Master's ring. Our mothers pulled my soul the moment I took my last breath. I'm stuck here, thanks to you."

She paused, waiting for my reaction.

But the reaction I gave wasn't the one she'd hoped for.

"Wait! Does that mean Ascian's here too?"

Her scowl deepened, my lack of remorse clearly offending her. "Look at you, speaking of Master so casually—as if you have any right. As if you even knew him." Her lips curled in disgust. "True, Master was also wearing the ring when he was murdered. Alas—" she dragged out the word like a dagger across glass, "he pledged himself to that shadow goddess in his final moment, and the bitch swept him away before our mothers could claim his soul. Again, thanks to you."

Exitium.

He had joined the host of fallen echoes, those loyal to her cause. The very reason we'd been drawn to the Cove in the first place. The reason Albie had ever even crossed paths with Charm and Pip.

The reason Albie was dead.

And the puppeteer responsible stood before me—weapon-less, bodiless, Pip-less.

Anger, buried deep since Charm's death, now raged and thrashed like a black sea in storm.

"Did you summon me here, Charm?! I know I'm not dead, so there must be another reason I ended up in this place."

She sighed theatrically, as though I were the world's most tedious pest. "Oh, stop thinking yourself so important, cow." She placed a hand on her hip, looking supremely bored. "I had nothing to do with it. Our mothers felt a swell of power and pulled you inside."

Then, cupping her hand around her mouth, she called out mockingly to the shadows.

"Bet you didn't know you were inviting in a bo-omb!"

A bomb.

Vita's purpose for the Nemophilist—the very reason I'd been chosen—was to banish Exitium to the end of days and destroy the Drakaina in the process. And all for the small price of losing the man I loved and another I'd come to care for far more than I'd meant to.

Not to mention countless innocent others.

That was never going to happen.

And yet—I could feel it. Power bubbling beneath my skin. Power enough to destroy.

My fingers curled into fists. "Why, then, is it you came to greet me at the door? Do you intend to fight me, Charmagne?"

"Ha!" She flicked her hair haughtily. "So you can murder me again? No, cupcake. I came for another reason—to soak up your guilt."

My fists remained tight. I blinked. "What?"

"I thought you'd be suffering at least a *little*, facing someone whose life you drained. But no." She tilted her head, studying me, waiting for regret to crack across my face. "Guess you're more heartless than I thought. You seem to be doing just fine."

Because she had taken the knight dearest to me.

"You're right," I said, heat pricking across my palms. "I don't feel a shred of remorse for you—why should I? After devoting your life to tormenting me and everyone I care for, you're not worth the breath it would take to pity you."

Charm's lashes flickered slightly, as if my words had struck deeper than intended.

"Torment?" She mocked, tapping her perky lips. "Oh, sugar, I could have done so much worse."

I felt shadow spiraling around my fists.

"Why couldn't you just leave us alone?" I lashed out, smoke billowing around me. "Why do you hate Windley? Is it that you're jealous of him?"

"Hate?" She scoffed. "You want to know why I hate you? Easy. You killed my master. And Windalloy? He abandoned Master—after everything Master did for him. He shows up thinking he's some prince, when he should've been kissing the ground Master walked on! He was an ungrateful little shit then, and he's an ungrateful little shit now. Master Ascian saved us, and Windalloy hated him for it."

Charm was too broken to know the difference between abuse and love.

Suddenly, I felt something softer than anger.

Not guilt.

But something close.

The shadow uncoiled from my hands as my fists relaxed.

"Stop it!" she seethed. "Don't you DARE look at me with pity, you self-righteous whore!"

I kept my face even. "I'll admit, I do pity you, Charmagne."

Her jaw stiffened.

"I've heard your upbringing was anything but kind. I know you have every reason to despise my race. Then you ended up in Ascian's orbit. Some people never got a real chance. Even so, I've seen sparks of light in the blackest-painted souls, and I wonder—if you'd been offered an escape, would you have taken it?"

Her fingers flexed at her sides.

"Oh, shut up." Venom laced each word, but a tremor of something raw slipped through. "I don't need your pity sermons. Every choice I made came with a reason, whether or not it strokes your shiny little court-bred conscience. Keep your virtue for someone who asked for it."

She flicked her wrist and turned her back.

"I'm bored of you."

Yet she didn't leave.

I watched her, waiting.

"Charm?"

She barked, "What?"

"You and Pip cost me the life of someone I held very dear,"

I said, my voice steady but heavy. "Someone who was like my father. Yet...I know I did the same to you."

Charm's back stayed turned, her posture unreadable.

"What I did to Ascian, I did to protect myself. What I did to you and Pip, I did to protect those I love." I drew a slow breath and smoothed my palms over the fabric at my hips, forcing the tremor from my hands before I met her gaze. "I wish it hadn't needed to be this way."

She shifted by a hair—not much, just enough to show she was listening.

"Is that your lame attempt at an apology?" she scoffed.

"No. I'm not sorry I did it. I only wish circumstances had been different."

Her shoulders tightened.

"I believe people are capable of change," I pressed on, my words leveled to a calm, even hush. "It would have been nice to see that in the two of you."

At that, she finally turned, just enough for me to catch her sneer.

"You mean it would've been nice to see us conform to your version of what's right. Got it." She sighed dramatically, flicking her wrist again. "Good talk. Anyway—bye."

She started away.

"Pip's here too?"

I hadn't meant to say it aloud. But I knew. Felt it in my bones, in the way the shadows curled along the edges of my vision.

Charmagne halted. "Thanks to you," she said. "Albeit looking a little different these days. A lot more fun, if you ask me."

She angled her head, letting the grin—cold enough to freeze magma—unfurl, and her pupils caught the void's scant glow, flashing back a green-gold gleam, like a lynx's eyes flickering from the undergrowth when moonlight needles through the trees.

"Shame. Had I known sooner what he was, we'd be in a very different situation."

Cold dread gnarled at my core. I didn't want to know.

She turned again, her figure shrinking as she strode off into the endless black.

I let her go.

But at the last moment, I called out—

"Tell him for me?" I said, softer than intended. "That I wish things could have been different?"

She hesitated just a fraction.

Then, distantly—"...If I feel like it."

And with that, she was gone, swallowed by the nothingness.

I was left alone with things unseen, shifting just beyond my reach. The dark mothers. The Drakaina. They had pulled me here, and judging by their whispers, it hadn't been intentional.

Which meant they could send me back.

But first—

Maybe this was fate, though not in the way I'd originally thought.

I straightened, inhaled deeply, and spoke into the void:

"Drakaina."

My voice echoed and caught, like a fly trapped in a web.

"I am she who wears the Crown of the Wood."

A hush swept over the darkness.

"I have mastered the powers bequeathed by the goddesses, and I've been sent to unleash the goddess of destruction in this place—thus ending you and your children forevermore."

A wave of slithering erupted as unseen things scurried away.

"The hume is a weapon!"

"Destruction livesss within the hume!"

"You dare threaten usss, child of the goddessesss?" The voices twisted together like smoke. *"We will trap you here. Dessstroy usss, and you shall never return to your time!"*

I stood firm. "Then give me another way."

The darkness pulsed—alive, listening.

"If you don't wish me to unleash the goddess of destruction in this place," I pressed, "tell me another way to banish her from the mortal realm."

The hush deepened, unnatural stillness pressing against my skin. Then, one voice braver than the rest hissed:

"You mean to ssstrike a deal with usss?"

I steadied myself, forcing my resolve to hold. "Tell me another way to banish a goddess from the mortal realm, and I promise to take destruction with me when I leave this place."

The response wasn't what I'd expected.

The void erupted into jeers.

"The hume deceivesss usss!"

"The hume hasss already banished one god-being from the mortal plane!"

I...had?

"You mean the moon goddess?" Realization crashed through me like a breaking tide. "But she had an astral form. All I needed was to destroy her physical connection to the world and—"

The words stuck in my throat.

Because now I knew.

Knew what I had to do.

I didn't speak it aloud. Not yet.

"Send me back," I said. "I will leave you be."

This time, there was no argument. The shadows moved, and a black liquid rose, filling my eyes, my lungs. A thick, viscous substance drenching me in nothingness. I felt myself being pulled.

But just before I was completely overtaken—

"Charmagne." I called out to the edge of time.

I couldn't see her, but I knew she was still there.

"I hope you find peace."

I hated her.

For Albie.

For Windley.

For Edius.

For all the strings she'd pulled, all the pain she'd caused.

But still—

"I hope you both do."

A beat of silence.

Then—

"Fuck you."

The last words from a bitter cupcake.

21
THESE NIGHTS

I feel it, captive ones—the end draws near.

I'm not sure I'm ready. Yet, in a way, I'm glad. Every ending births a beginning, and closing one great adventure means stepping into another.

The sun and moon knew the moment the Dracon fell.

And when I awoke—

I was under the blanket of night.

True night.

And it was so much bluer than I remembered.

I opened my eyes to the stars.

Winter was creeping, and the stars knew it. They burned white—searing and brilliant, large and small, strung together in quiet constellations. Luna's orb hung above it all, watching. Waiting.

Night felt different from dusk or dawn. It carried a knife-edge clarity. And for a time when most of the world slept, why did it feel so awake? Why did it feel like I could run forever?

I sat up.

A silhouette stood against the hedge wall—pitch-black, sword raised to the sky.

I knew that stance. I'd seen him like this before.

Only—oh, how things had changed.

"Getting a charge, Rafe?"

The sword dropped instantly.

And he turned—eyes gleaming with Luna's frost.

"Y-Your Majesty!" The magician rushed to my side, breathless and more energized than I'd ever seen him before. No longer angelic, yet somehow brighter.

"We didn't know if... We couldn't get the ring off." His gaze fell to my hand.

The ring—Ascian's, or technically Pip's—remained on my finger. Its stone pulsed with something shifting deep within, colors swirling, almost alive.

I would snuff it out.

But not yet. Two Spirites deserved to see it destroyed.

"We're back in the labyrinth?"

I scanned the clearing—the umbrella-leaf tree I'd grown days ago stood exactly where I'd left it.

"Yeah." Rafe cleared his throat. "The others are posted farther in. Windley figured it'd be...wiser not to keep you at arm's length while you were unconscious, so we set up a separate camp."

I blew out a breath. "Probably for the best."

Rafe's gaze lingered, faint concern furrowing his brow.

"What?" I asked, suddenly self-conscious. "Do I look that bad?"

"You look fine," he said—too quickly—then added, "Just checking you feel all right. You were down a while."

"How long is 'a while'?"

"Three days."

I lurched upright. "Three days?" I scanned our surroundings again, now with new understanding. "You carried me all this way?"

Rafe scratched at his temple. "Mostly the larger guy."

"Edius," I corrected. "You two are on a first-name basis by now, surely."

Rafe huffed. "Edius."

The name snagged my thoughts. Edius carried me...the whole way?

One corner of Rafe's mouth twitched. "Try keeping it under three nights next time."

"I usually limit myself to one at a stretch," I muttered, pulling a knife-sharp breath of night air—and feeling every mile that still lay ahead.

I would end this soon.

Exitium.

And now, I knew what had to be done about the Crown.

But first, I had a few things to take care of.

Rafe misread my hesitation.

"Why not keep it?" he suggested casually.

I tipped my head. "Keep it?"

Rafe rolled one shoulder, tugging at the strap of his weather-scarred cuirass until the leather creaked back into place. "The Crown," he said at last. "Wouldn't hurt to keep that kind of power in the queendom. And Beau's family figured out how to pass the echoes down, generation after generation— maybe you could do the same with the Crown."

"It's certainly an idea, Rafe, but one I must decline. It's not safe for power like this to exist in the physical realm. It should never have fallen in the first place. We'd all be better off if..."

My eyes drifted toward the heavens.

The answer was now clear.

But I didn't share it with Rafe just yet.

"If?" he pressed.

"Never mind. Why don't you get some sleep? I'll keep watch. Show me where the others are?"

Rafe didn't hide his suspicions, but he led me down the winding path to the first clearing.

And there they were.

Edius—strewn near a pretty girl wrapped in robes, suppressing the gentle glow of her dark skin. Gwen.

She was fuller than the first time I saw her. Her long lashes fluttered softly in sleep, her body no longer frail, her flesh vibrant and strong.

Her heart steady.

Edius's too—beating contentedly, though the amorous side remained clamped tight.

For now.

I smiled at them for only a moment before pressing a hand to my lips to smother a laugh.

Because a short distance away, at the base of a cherry tree—

Windley was curled up hugging it like a long-lost lover.

"Oh, geez."

But when I looked at Rafe—

There might've been the faintest twinkle in his eyes.

He rolled them anyway.

"Here." I willed plush, lush moss to grow beneath them, cushioning their sleep, and carefully set up a patch specifically for the temperamental magician. The cherry tree stretched taller, its branches widening to shelter them from Luna's glow.

Rafe settled away from the others but didn't remove his eyes from me. The wind was playful through his dark waves, tugging gently at the fabric of his tunic—mended and re-mended, worn through battle yet stitched with care.

"Your Majesty, I..."

The young knight second-guessed himself, but ultimately chose to finish.

"I'm glad you're back...Merrin."

The words came stiffly but honestly.

It was one of the very few times he ever dared to address me without a title. Warmth bloomed through my chest at the sound of it.

"I wasn't as worried as those two, but...the queendom would have suffered a great loss without you."

I bet Beau found it adorable—the way he scowled and flushed whenever forced to share emotion.

"Enough of that, Your Majesty."

He meant the goofy expression I was surely wearing.

I covered it. For his sake.

Instead—

"I'm glad to be back. This is far preferable to where I was... I need a favor, Rafe."

His shoulders snapped rigid.

I bit back a laugh. "I promise—it's nothing like last time."

He exhaled, leaning onto his elbows, gaze tilted to the moon. "Alright—name it."

"Next time you spend a 'sun day' with Soleil, take me along."

He frowned. "Why?"

"Because I have a few questions for her."

Rafe didn't press me further, though I felt the unspoken suspicion hanging in his silence. The night pressed closer, all quiet wind and silver-cast branches. Distant rustlings of unseen creatures blended seamlessly with the steady, rhythmic breathing of those asleep nearby—as though the labyrinth drew a deep breath, then finally exhaled.

Eventually, Rafe rolled over. And soon, he slept.

They all slept.

The fire dulled to embers, painting trunks in slanted, flickering light. Wind stirred leaves in a hush, rustling through labyrinthine archways like whispers through ancient bones. Above, the stars pulsed steady and bright, the season's first chill sharpening their glow.

I watched over them—fiercely protective, acutely aware of their vulnerability.

I'd carried responsibility before, but never like this.

A queen keeps layers between herself and her subjects.

Not here.

Not with these souls.

My people.

Under the drippings of night, beneath a sky preparing for winter, beneath a tree I had grown for us, surrounded by those who had gone the distance for my cause, who trusted my power to keep them safe—

I had never felt more worthy.

When you're a queen, you're taught to be served.

But only in serving others had I ever felt like a true queen.

I settled near Windley, though not so near as to let him feel my heat.

But Spirites had a very keen sense of smell.

Not more than a minute passed before he stirred.

Rolling onto a mattress of nature's best moss, he groaned. "Damn flowers. It's like she did this to torture me."

He cuddled up closer to the tree's trunk.

I giggled.

His eyes shot wide open.

"Majesty!"

"Shh!" I crouched forward, clamping a hand over his mouth before he woke the others. His lips were warm against my palm, his breath hot and exasperated.

He pulled my hand away, squinting through the dimness, brows furrowed. Then, as if confirming I was real, he slowly ran a palm down my arm, stopping at my wrist.

"You're awake," he said, barely daring to believe it.

I nodded, watching his expression shift—from relief to something softer, something unreadable beneath the familiar Windley smirk.

His eyes flicked past me toward the others, then back. And suddenly—without warning—he pounced.

I barely had time to brace before he tackled me, rolling us into a tangle of limbs and moss. He landed half atop me, breath unsteady, arms locking me in tight.

"I missed you," he exhaled against my hair.

I smiled into his shoulder. "It's been three days."

"Exactly. Do you know how long that is in Windley years?"

"How long?"

"Forever." His lips caressed the curve of my ear, voice heated and low. "And what's worse? I had to let Edmond carry you. The man got to wrap his arms around you and smell your hair for miles. Miles, Merr."

"Did he at least behave himself?"

"Tch." Windley pulled back, his gaze hooded, mouth all smug. "Didn't even nuzzle you. What a waste."

I rolled my eyes, but before I could respond, his nose skimmed my temple as he took a slow, deliberate breath.

"Goddess, I missed this," he murmured. "Missed you."

His teasing faltered, voice gone raw. He cleared his throat, squared his shoulders, then slapped on a grin—snatching up the swagger he'd dropped for a heartbeat.

I arched a brow. "Steady there, rogue?"

"Never better." His fingers trailed absently down my spine, an unconscious indulgence. "Just reeling from the tragedy of the last few days."

"What tragedy?"

He flopped onto his back with a theatrical groan. "Forced to sleep alone—like some thread-bare stable lad banished to the hayloft."

I clucked my tongue. "A calamity fit for the epic poets, truly."

"You jest, but it was awful."

I turned onto my side, propping my head up on my palm. "Well, your suffering is over. You can go back to sharing a bed with Rafe."

His hand found my waist, fingers pressing lightly at the small of my back. "*Rafe*, she says..."

The fire crackled nearby, cinders throbbing like breathing light, and the night carried the hush of a world in waiting. He nudged closer—not quite touching, but close enough that the air between us felt charged.

He pulled me in, wrapping me against him with slow deliberation, as if etching every detail into memory. His lips pressed to my forehead, lingering, his breath warm against my skin.

We were dirty from travel, our clothes frayed, our bodies worn.

And yet, here in this nowhere, I was as happy as any night we had spent together in the grand chambers of the queendoms.

So many nights out of bed when we shouldn't have been.

Drinking, talking, flirting.

Talking.

Flirting.

How long, I wondered, had I felt this way about him?

Far longer, I suspected, than I'd ever know.

"I love you, my queen."

"I love you, my devil."

He liked that one.

When he closed his eyes, he did so smirking.

Under the branches of the tree I'd grown for us, Windley's fingers threaded through mine—like he was stitching us together. I'd run my thumb across those defined, inviting knuckles countless times.

Now, as I traced the back of his hand again, his thumb paused on my own. A tiny scrape of metal met his skin. His grip cinched; his pulse lurched.

A sharp inhale. A slow-released breath.

Then—

"Oh my goddess, you're still wearing it?!" His eyes locked on the ring gleaming against the fire-glow.

I followed his stare to the swirling stone. "Oh—yes. I planned to destroy it."

"Uh, yeah—destroy it." He bolted upright. "Destroy it now."

"But I want you and Edius there for it," I insisted. "I reckon you'll both get closure seeing it done."

"Fine, fine." He waved me off—then, cupping his hand around his mouth, stage-whispered, "Psst, Ed! Wake up!"

"Windley!" I slapped a hand over his mouth.

He licked my palm in retaliation.

"E—ew!"

"Oh, darling, my saliva's well integrated with yours by now," he muttered, before calling out again, "Hey, berk! Wake up!"

It was all quite loud for a whisper.

"Stop!" I hissed back. "You'll wake Gwen! If you need this done right now, I'll wake Edius. Deal?"

But as I rose to do just that, he caught my hand.

"Wind?"

His face was half-hidden in the shadowy glow, thumb rubbing across my nails before pressing a knight's kiss to my knuckles. "I just want it gone," he murmured, voice graveled with sincerity.

There was something vulnerable in the way he held my hand, something that made his strength feel more desirable rather than less. His bare shoulders tensed as if bracing himself for battle, but his grip on me was nothing but gentle.

I dropped back down to kiss him, lingering a moment to breathe him in.

When I pulled away—his face was a mix of things.

All of them endearing.

"I understand," I whispered. "I don't find you irrational for wanting it. I'll wake Ed, we'll destroy the ring, and then we'll continue what we started, yes?"

A grin threatened his mouth. "I missed you. More than I can say."

I squeezed him once before rising to wake Edius, still sleeping nearby, next to his adopted sister.

I meant to rouse him with a light tap.

But the moment I knelt near, his senses beat me to it.

Edius stirred instantly, nostrils flaring, eyes slitting open like a panther catching a scent in the dark. "Mer...rín?" His voice was thick, tangled in sleep.

And then he moved.

Fast. Instinctual.

Like Windley before him, Edius pounced—dragging me close, folding me into his chest, fingers carding through my hair, tucking it feather-light away from my ear.

His breath was warm at my neck.

"E-Edius—"

Edius breathed into me. "Thank gods, you're back." That chest—broad, solid, safe—heaved against mine. "You had us worried."

Yes, it felt good to be held in his oversized arms.

Yes, it felt good when his mouth settled at the nape of my neck.

Edius was difficult to resist.

But I wasn't his.

I nudged him back, soft but sure.

"Ed?"

His fingers still fastened to my shoulders. "Sorry, Highness." The words came out raw, even as his hold stayed gentle. "Boundaries—I'm...learning." Yet he couldn't quite bring himself to let go. His eyes dipped away. "Everything feels different now," he muttered, mostly for his own benefit. "Got to work out what to do with that."

When he'd believed death was certain, he'd split the shell around his heart—and there was no forcing it shut again. Love had slipped free, hopelessly one-sided. And I was achingly aware that I'd let it happen.

The air between us pulsed—taut, heavy, waiting. His breath hitched. "Damn, you look beautiful. It's hard to even look at you." One hand remained on my shoulder, fingers tensed as if fighting the impulse to slide upward. "I'd kiss you right now if you weren't his." His voice was wrecked. "And then I'd hold you all night."

The look in his eyes was unbearable—gutting. A look I'd never wanted, one I'd spent weeks trying to outrun.

But the thing about love? It doesn't obey.

You can bargain with it, barricade against it, swear it off entirely—and it still goes where it pleases.

Love has no map. No logic. And love—

Love is merciless.

Beau was proof of that.

Rafe was proof of that.

Windley was proof of that.

And I? I was learning the lesson all over again.

"Shit." Edius wrenched away, dragging a hand down his face.

"Edi..." I breathed, grounding myself. "I don't want to hurt you."

His jaw hardened, unreadable. "That's not your burden."

Something tightened in my throat. "I never meant for this."

He looked away, collecting himself before his gaze came back—steady now, no apology in it. "Nor I."

Silence stretched, weighted but calm, until he added with quiet certainty, "And I'll own every second of it." A spark lit behind his eyes—unbreakable, unmoving, a vow rather than a plea.

Right on cue—

"You can kiss me, mate!"

Perfect timing. Windley's arm was already slung around Edius's neck. "Come on. One kiss from me's all it'll take to make you forget this human." Then his gaze slid to me, tone shifting into something almost worshipful. "This delectable... empathetic...soft-skinned human..."

And now they were both looking at me that way.

Windley swallowed hard, eyes slightly predatorial. "L-let's just take care of the ring, yeah? Deal with all this later?" Under his breath, he muttered, "That Crown makes you a goddess-damned magnet."

"The ring?" Edius finally asked, his words slower now, like they needed to settle into the shape of his mouth before leaving it.

I held up Ascian's ring, the stone shifting colors like something alive. "I'm going to destroy it. Windley insisted it be tonight, and we wanted you as witness."

Edius stole a glance at sleeping Gwen.

"Fine by me. Just let me—"

He reached out, grazing fingertips over her hand, feeding her a small pulse of Spirite power.

A quiet assurance. A tether.

It was warming, his care for her.

He caught me watching and flicked me a look of repose, as if simply my gaze offered comfort.

"She's really excited to meet you."

Oh. My. Heart.

And as I felt the affections pouring out of him, beating greater than that rock of his would allow...

That was the moment I knew what else I had to do.

A way to ensure Edius experienced a love like the one I shared with Windley.

But because my plan depended on the mercy of others, I kept it to myself.

For now.

On a raised platform of land, high above the silver-bathed labyrinth, I stood between two incubi, overlooking fields and coasts, with the coolest wind tossing our dirty hair and dirtier clothes.

And though moonlight had never before infiltrated the layers of my skin—tonight, I felt the touch of it.

In this setting, I held Ascian's ring against Luna's glow and looked one last time into the face of evil.

Curling my fingers around the cool metal, I knew what things lay beyond its portal.

With all that I was, I summoned Exitium's power, letting it crawl through my soul, my veins, down to my fingertips.

I clenched hard around the ring.

And when I opened my palm—

Dust whirled upward, ferried off on the radiant sigh of a goddess.

The Spirites reacted differently.

Windley doubled over, hands braced on his knees, breathing shakily.

Edius simply stared after the dust, gripping his opposite shoulder.

I let them anchor themselves before we departed.

Windley descended first, and I followed.

But when it was Edius's turn, he caught me by the back of my shirt and nodded for Windley to go ahead.

"Edi, it's best if we don't separate ourselves—"

"Thanks."

The word cut across mine—short, blunt, pure-Edius.

I blinked.

"For Gwen. For smoking Ascian. For putting up with me." He caught a pinch of my shirt between two fingers, gave it a brief tug, then let it fall. "That's it."

But it wasn't; the silence between us admitted as much. He raked a hand over the back of his neck, exhaled into the cold.

"I owe you. Any time you need an extra fist—or a wall to hide behind—I'm there. Day or night. Next week or fifty years on, doesn't matter."

Hands slid into pockets; his gaze drifted off to the dark.

"Okay. That's all."

Fifty years from now?

For those of predatorial descent, love was something of a curse.

By now, Windley had reached the base of the incline, watching us from below.

He stood cast in shadows, arms folded, mouth solemn.

But he wasn't jealous.

Because he knew what Edius had asked of me.

Because he knew I'd allowed it.

Because he knew the consequence of Pip dying in Edius's place.

And so, the look he carried...was one of sympathy.

"I'm going to fix this, Edi," I said quietly.

"Fix it?"

Moonlight made his lashes impossibly dark, outlined in silver, as he stared at me.

"Don't."

"...What?"

He exhaled, rubbing a palm over his chest.

"Don't get me wrong, highness, it hurts like hell, but..."

His pulse was erratic, pushing blood to every reach of him.

"Having—" He clenched his jaw. "Having something there feels nice. Being around you feels nice."

His heart was beating.

Beating.

"It's like you make me stronger and weaker at the same time."

His gaze searched mine as I fought not to search his back.

And that heart of his.

Beating.

Beating.

He swallowed tightly.

"Shit," he swore. "I just gotta say it, Merrín. It's like it's gonna fuckin' burst outta me if I don't."

"Edi—"

His eyes closed.

He drew in deeply.

"I..."

And then—

"I..."

But bit back that forbidden phrase, finishing instead—

"Like you. Enough to leave it at that. And I'm gonna do all I can to make sure you stay with the person you're meant to be with. I don't intend to fuck things up for you."

Just one of many well-intentioned people, all trying our best—I clung to the hope that at least some of Edius's attraction was magically induced.

That this would all be easier once I relinquished the Crown.

That the goddesses would come to believe, as I did, that people were capable of change.

But before that could happen...

I needed to visit Soleil.

22

BY THE LIGHT
OF THE SUN

With the labyrinth felled, we rode our stags north across fields dotted with brittle brush curling away from autumn's death. If Edius had planned to part ways with us after retrieving Gwen, his plans had changed.

"I'll stick around till your affairs are tied up and you're back home safely," he said. "As a bodyguard."

It was as good an excuse as any. We all knew I needed no protection, but I wouldn't have let him leave even if he'd wanted to—not until I was sure that heart of his was freed of me, not until Exitium was banished beyond the mortal realm. And even then...

"I don't know, Edi. Seems to me Gwen might like living in a castle," I said.

A face peeked over Edius's shoulder, gemstone shimmering like water under sunlight. "Really?!" Gwen's excitement was immediate. "Are there hidden passageways?"

I tapped my chin. "I know only of two. I'm sure there are more."

"There are more." Windley smirked, voice dripping

mischief. Of course, he would be the one to know hidden passages in a foreign queen's castle.

Then again, it was his home now, too. The parchment in my pocket was proof.

"I, uh..." Edius rubbed at the back of his neck. "I don't know if that's a good idea, dove."

Normally, I would've agreed.

But I had a plan. And if that plan failed, I would make another. And another. And another. I wouldn't let Edius's heart be chained to me forever.

Gwen's fingertip lit blue as a dragonfly landed there. All manner of creatures followed her—butterflies, fireflies, even things with more legs than I cared to count. Nature was drawn to her, so much so that Edius had to keep shaking off tagalongs whenever he carried her. Now, the stags bore that burden.

"But Edi! I don't want to go back to the light realm! And I don't want to go back south. And...I could help out. I bet they don't have a castle medic—not one like me, anyway."

Her eyes shimmered—truly shimmered—dancing blues and pearly whites and lavender to match the crystal on her forehead.

"My invitation isn't for you to come work, Gwen, but to be a lady of the court—though personally, I don't think I could stand it, and can understand if you'd prefer an occupation," I said.

"And I hear there's an opening or two in the queen's guard," Windley chimed. "What say you, Ed? I think we could tailor a uniform to fit those shoulders." He glanced at Edius's build. "Might take two uniforms, but we'll get there."

Edius flicked his eyes between us. "You know that's not a good idea."

"But if your heart were free of me?" I asked gently. "Then would you consider it?"

"I told you, I don't want you to—"

"I have a plan. A way for you to both keep it and lose it."

Windley's eyebrow arched with intrigue.

"'Course you do, you little mirefox," Edius muttered, mouth betraying the hope he tried to hide. "We'll see, Gwenny."

"Yay!" She hugged him tighter around the neck.

"Well, this is nice, isn't it?" Windley stretched in the saddle. "Not being chased for once? Not worrying about randomly leaking power and giving ourselves away to enemies —*Edmond*." He fake-coughed into his hand.

"Why are you coughing at him?" Rafe, trailing behind, finally piped in. "You're the most impulsive one here."

Windley feigned shock. "More impulsive than our lion-like queen?"

Rafe shifted his scowl toward me. "Er, sorry, Your Majesty."

"Rafe?!"

"Besides," Windley continued, "I wasn't coughing because he's impulsive; I was coughing because he used to be one of said enemies."

News to Gwen.

"G-Gwen!" I pivoted, desperate. "See those bushes over there? Those are crimson thorns. The needles have a numbing quality. Ground, they're useful in remedies for rashes, burns, and other shallow pains."

"Wow! You're a queen and an alchemist?" She was quite impressed for someone who'd never need medicine.

Behind us, Rafe and Windley were still bickering.

"Which I'm sure he loves being reminded of—" But Rafe suddenly stiffened, attention jerking skyward, where Soleil burned golden overhead. His face tensed.

"Sun day?" I guessed.

Ruefully, he nodded.

If I had it my way, it would be his last.

We made camp beneath a grove I'd grown for us. As Rafe and I prepared dinner and Windley mended a tear in Rafe's cloak, glowing, giggling Gwen busied herself plaiting Edius's shoulder-length hair into two long braids.

Windley took immediate interest. "Ooh, looking good, milady. Ever consider asking the queen to grow some flowers for you to tuck right in there?"

Edius swatted his hand away. "We're good."

"Another excellent idea, Sir Windley!" sang Gwen. "Queen Merrín?"

She didn't need to ask. The ground around her was already springing up with blooms that had no business opening during winter's first bite.

There were some aspects of the Crown I would miss.

I found Rafe staring into the painted horizon, where Soleil steadily crashed into the earth. "We should probably..." He trailed off, fingers flexing at his sides.

I tilted my head.

Then, without looking, he grabbed my hand in his gloved one. "I just want to make sure you're pulled in with me."

Never had I imagined Rafe taking my hand before all this. Never had I imagined gaining a brother.

"We're almost there," I murmured.

Soleil burned brighter with every step—redder, hotter, until it felt as if we were entering a dragon's mouth.

The twilight broke. And we stood upon a warm palm, high above a many-colored coast, surrounded by prism-hazed clouds. Soleil's voice blew through us like a summer wind. "Rafael?" Her presence was all-consuming, golden light spilling from her like a river. "Why have you brought the holder of the Crown to me?"

Rafe frowned. He didn't know the answer.

I stepped forward. "I asked him to do it. He had no part in what I'm about to say. Please, don't punish him."

Rafe tensed at my word choice. "Punish?"

Soleil lifted us higher until we were level with her face, lashes as long as swords. I had seen her before, yet still my breath caught.

"Hello, little royal," she said, her voice both fire and silk. "I wondered if you'd return. I haven't watched a hume so closely in many eons—your journey has been entertaining."

"My journey isn't over," I said. "I've learned the true purpose of the Crown—to banish the one whose name shouldn't be spoken in the mortal realm."

Forget that name. It's a grave better left untouched.

Her fire-bright eyes narrowed. "So, you wish to ask for my help."

"No," I said firmly. "I can accomplish it alone. What I need from you is...something adjacent."

"I do not comprehend."

I drew a steady breath. "I intend to destroy your body."

Rafe's head snapped toward me. "Your Majesty?"

Flames flared around Soleil's body. "You've come to threaten me?" she asked. "You mean to destroy my body as you destroyed my sister's?"

"I...do."

Rafe's hands found his weapon, but I didn't move. I met the sun goddess's gaze, unwavering.

This was the only way.

Soleil snapped her fingers. Sunbeams—golden counterparts to Luna's moonbeams—materialized from her skin, three spectral warriors forged of sunlight, featureless but lethal.

The moment they attacked, Rafe moved.

"This again?" he scoffed, striking without hesitation. His

frost sliced through the first sunbeam before it fully formed, the golden spectral body hissing into vapor.

But as the second surged toward me, his irritation dissolved into alarm. "Your Majesty!" he shouted, already slashing through it, expecting me to act.

I didn't.

Easily, I could've destroyed them. Just as easily, Soleil could've tipped us from her palm into the sea below.

This wasn't a battle. It was a test.

I let the last of the sunbeams seize my arms, its touch scalding, aura like peak summer. Rafe, defensive at my side, openly scowled.

"I'm fine, Rafe. Return your sword. There's no need for it."

But instead of obeying, he crouched low, watching as Soleil drew us closer to her radiant face.

"You do not intend to fight me," she said, voice like embers in a dying fire.

"No," I confirmed.

"Yet you intend to end me?"

"Yes," I said. "I will destroy your body—but I wish to do so with your permission. Only if I fail to convince you, will I resort to other measures."

Diplomacy had never failed me—at least, not with reasonable beings.

Soleil studied me, golden lashes casting sunlit shadows. "Very well. I will hear your petition."

She snapped her free hand, and the sunbeam holding me melted back into her palm.

Rafe was at my side in a flash, his glare cutting. "*What are you doing, Your Majesty?*" he muttered.

"What I have to."

And so, I revealed my plan.

To Rafe. To Soleil. To the setting sun.

I had little confidence going into this moment. Soleil could refuse. She could turn against me. She could erase me from existence before I had time to resist. But I had to believe that a being responsible for sunrises and warmth, who painted the world in gold, would stand against destruction's reign.

"I intend to banish the destroyer to the skies the way I banished the moon goddess," I told them.

Rafe's expression was unreadable, his amber eyes pools of calculation.

Soleil's voice rumbled like the shifting of tectonic plates. "The destroyer has no astral form. You cannot banish her to the skies, for she will consume everything in her path."

"I know," I said. "That's why I'll create one for her."

The Crown of the Wood had already proven capable of impossible feats. If it could create a soul, a beating heart, an eternal spirit—then surely, it could forge a celestial prison. A new astral body.

"The sun and moon are mighty," I continued, "but the soul is something beyond fathom. I will create a heavenly sphere for the destroyer. And I will banish her to it."

A ripple slithered through my body. *Exitium.* Writhing.

Vita flared in response, warmth unfurling through my limbs like a hand slipping into a glove.

Soleil remained silent.

"You mean to let the destroyer share the skies with my sister and me?" she finally asked.

"Yes."

"Then why must my body be destroyed?"

I drew a slow breath. "When I banished the moon goddess, she bled into the mortal realm, staining stretches of land in the north. I fear that where she failed, a goddess of destruction would succeed. If I banish the destroyer to the skies, I must ensure she stays there. She can have no ties to our world."

Soleil listened.

"I have lived with the destroyer inside me," I said. "I know the power of her corruption. She is an ender of stories, and if she remains, it's only a matter of time before ruin follows. She was meant to exist at the end of days—but that space is already occupied, and the cost of sending her there is too great."

The goddess's flames wavered, absorbing my words.

"I am imperfect—fallible," I admitted. "Self-interested, capable of harm. But I try to be fair, to be just, to weigh the good of the many. And, as though the stars themselves whispered it to me, I know what must be done: Exitium must be banished to the astral realm."

I spoke the forbidden name without hesitation. I didn't fear her. I didn't fear myself.

Soleil's flames flickered. "Even if the endless stars are a suitable prison, that does not explain why my physical form must be destroyed."

I gave a slow nod. "To strengthen the barrier between the astral and mortal realms. There can be no ties."

Her golden glow dimmed in thought. "My body is one of those ties."

"Yes."

Soleil's eyes, molten as a solar flare, settled on me. "And if I say no?"

"Then I'll move to other methods of negotiation."

Her massive hand tensed. "I wish to know them."

I swallowed. This was the part I'd hoped to avoid.

"I know I cannot simply destroy you," I said. "We need your protection for Rafe, should the moon goddess revoke her power again."

A pact-less conjurer is as ripe as the fertile grounds of spring.

"So," I continued, "I would threaten something else you hold dear."

Rafe tensed beside me, shoulders locked.

"My child," Soleil finished.

I bowed my head.

Rafe went stone-still, save for the slow rise and fall of his chest. He didn't appreciate my willingness to threaten his unborn child, no matter how empty the threat.

Soleil's voice was unreadable. "I have watched you, little one. I know you would not harm an innocent."

I swallowed. "I don't think I would...but you cannot be sure." I lifted my head. "I believe people are capable of change —both for better and for worse. If pressed, they're capable of horrific things. I have seen it. Souls don't start dark, but they can be tainted. I am just as susceptible."

Soleil's palm relaxed. "Well, then. I am glad it will not come to that."

"Wait, what?" Rafe's voice cracked with surprise.

Soleil shimmered like liquid gold. "I have had my fill of the hearts of men. My final wish is already granted. I will watch my child from the skies. And I will aid in protecting the races I swore to oversee."

Deep calm settled over me. "Thank you, Goddess."

And I knelt.

Rafe stared, unblinking. A queen kneeling before a goddess.

"But before it is done," Soleil said softly as dawn, "I wish to feel mortality one last time. I wish for a final night with the conjurer."

You really have to wonder what Rafe was doing to these women.

I turned to the magician. "That's up to him."

Rafe huffed, already returning his sword to its sheath.

As Soleil lifted him into her grasp, I set to my own task.

Gathering sand from the wind, I molded it into a small, compact capsule, carefully pouring into it Exitium's destructive essence. I'd never deliberately shaped the goddess's power into a solid form before, yet intuition guided my hands—subtle whispers from every shadowy enchantment I'd encountered, every lesson Vita had offered, guiding me through each careful movement. Sweat pooled at my brow, the labor draining my final reserves, until at last, my limbs trembled with exhaustion.

When done, I held up the capsule, shadows swirling ominously inside.

"When you're ready, return the conjurer to where you took us from," I said, voice strained but steady. "Then consume this."

Soleil plucked the capsule gently from my palm. "Very well."

The world around me shimmered, light fading, heat dissipating.

"And, Goddess?" I called.

"Yes, little one?"

"I swear your child will be cared for. I will protect them. I will love them as my own."

Soleil's glow faltered briefly. "Her," she corrected.

The light collapsed.

I was back in the mortal world. The moon was high, gleaming over a fire where two Spirites waited anxiously. Overhead, Luna burned brightly, as if showing off for all the world.

I sat beside the fire and waited. And waited.

And just as the moon began to sink and the sun threatened to rise—

The earth trembled.

A blast rang across the heavens.

The sound of a goddess's body shattering.

23

RELINQUISHING
THE CROWN

Tere is a time between autumn and winter when the
air takes on a keen edge, murmuring of things to
come. The greens grow brittle, curling inward,
bracing for the inevitable frost.

It was under such skies that I wandered away from the
others, into a nameless wood, and called upon the goddess
sleeping within my heart.

Vita's warmth unfurled through me. *"Yes, Merrin?"*

"I see you're no longer ignoring me," I noted, fingertips
drifting across the rough bark of a dying tree.

*"To ignore is to refuse to notice something, little royal—and I
have always noticed you."*

"Then why did you refuse to speak?"

*"Because the greatest of life's fortuities come to pass when
one is unobserved. That is when humes look inward, when
flowers bloom, when tides shift. I was not ignoring you—I was
allowing you to flourish."*

I exhaled. *Flourish* was one way to describe it. *Struggle* was
another.

I sank my fingers into the cool earth, feeling the steady, pulsing heartbeat of the land. "You've heard my plan," I said in a leaf-rustle undertone. "Do you approve?"

"I heard it before you even spoke it aloud, but your plan is missing a detail. When you deliver the destroyer to the skies, what will you do with me?"

I smiled inwardly, pressing a hand to my chest. "You'll remain here, seeded into the earth as the mother of our world."

"And the Crown?"

"Will form a new barrier between the heavens and the earth."

Vita grew silent, the wind licking idly at my ears.

"Is that as it should be?" I asked, hesitant.

"When the destroyer fell, the Crown was created to bind her, and so it did. Creation and destruction are opposing forces; to keep balance, I, too, was bound. With the destroyer expelled, I shall be free to watch over the mortal realm."

"And Soleil will watch over the skies—with Luna, I hope." I paused, wind threading softly through my hair. "You had to know I wouldn't willingly sacrifice the Spirites to banish Exitium. Was this the alternative you intended for me to find?"

"There were countless possibilities yet unwritten on your pages. This is not a bad one. But are you certain you wish to relinquish such immense power, Merrin? It goes against your very blood."

"Beyond a shadow," I said immediately. "There is such a thing as too much power. The Nemophile's Crown is too much. I'm ready to be rid of it. I intend to set my plan into motion at dawn."

"And the favor you wish in return?"

She knew me too well.

I clutched my chest tightly. "When you're freed from the Crown, you'll have abilities you lack now, correct?"

"*It is as you say.*"

"Then I do have a request. I know you never promised me anything, but I hope you'll grant this in exchange for banishing Exitium." I released a slow breath, gazing deeply into the shadowed woods. "I know you've felt it, Vita—their love for me. And I know you've seen their merit."

"*The beastlings,*" she confirmed.

"Yes. They weren't born your children, yet you allowed them life because you recognized, as I do, that children often diverge from their parents' whims. We change, moment by moment, in ways deeper than we realize."

My pulse hitched; I gathered my thoughts like loose reins. "Pip said Spirites were given the capacity for love merely to relate to your other children. But they deserve more than that. You've witnessed their sacrifice, devotion, and fierce will to protect. They may be untamed, but they're loyal. They deserve to love freely—to move on if their love is unrequited."

My voice dwindled to a plea. "So, when you're no longer bound to the Crown—please, Vita—unlock the Spirite hearts. Allow them to love more than once. This is my greatest wish."

A dawn-gold warmth spread through me like the first touch of sunrise. "*Is this what you truly desire, Merrin?*"

"Yes."

"*Even more than children of your own?*"

I admit I did hesitate.

I hadn't considered that possibility. A world where I could bear a child with Windley—a tangible future—would indeed be beautiful. Yet...

I felt a daughter's love for Albie without knowing if he was truly my father. I felt a sister's love for Beau, though we shared no blood. Family surrounded me, though none were born of my flesh.

Family wasn't defined by blood.

"A child needn't be born of me to be mine," I whispered tenderly. "Perhaps they'll never bear my name, perhaps they'll never wear a crown—but that doesn't mean I cannot raise them as my own. Countless children are without mothers. I'd never deny them the love of a childless mother."

Vita's warmth surged with gentle approval.

"Then heed my warning, Merrin. This change occurs at a foundational level. To untether one beastling is to untether them all. Should I grant your wish, all beastlings will experience love as humes do—including your destined one. Are you certain this is your wish?"

My heart stuttered, pausing for a single beat. I imagined the security of knowing Windley would always love me, that his heart would remain mine alone.

Yet—

"Yes," I answered swiftly, firmly. "I don't want a forced love. Even if it means risking losing him someday, I'd rather he have the freedom to choose. A love like that is worth any risk."

Windley and I had crossed lifetimes to find each other. Of all souls in the void, his had reached strongest toward mine. He was shadow to my light, shore to my sea, the sweetest piece in a chocolatier's box.

We were meant for each other.

I wasn't wrong.

"Very well," Vita consented, a soft laugh weaving through her words. *"The moment you release me shall be the moment your wish is granted."*

Relief shivered through me.

It meant Edius would one day be free.

Not immediately. Not soon. But someday, his heart would move on.

He wouldn't die unrequited.

A tightness I'd carried deep in my chest finally loosened, unraveling with slow relief. "Thank you, Vita."

"You've done well, Merrin. I always knew you would be the one to use the Crown for its true purpose."

Her warmth lingered, a comforting presence as I returned to camp, drawn toward the watchful glow of firelight. Across the flames, Edius's affectionate gaze found mine. For once, I didn't turn away in shame.

I smiled at him—truly smiled—because soon, his love would no longer be a curse.

Windley's arm wrapped around me, his fingers lazily tracing patterns along my shoulder. Nearby, Rafe knelt beside Gwen, patiently showing her how to quarter carrots, his movements cautious, deliberate.

Practice, I thought warmly.

Not for war.

But for fatherhood.

"When the moon shines gold?" Gwen's eyes widened in awe. "You hold a party for it?"

"The gilded lunar festival," hummed Windley, amusement coloring his tone. "Guess I'll get out of guard duty this year, eh? Have fun, chap."

"You most certainly will not!" I scolded with mock authority before breaking into a grin. "I'll need someone to accompany me, now that..."

My grin faltered as two pendants nestled beneath my cloak circled together in ways they shouldn't. Windley caught the fade in my voice and rested his chin atop my head. "We'll organize a sendoff for him once we're back in the Crag, yeah? And it had better be grand—Sir Albie knew absolutely everyone."

Across the fire, Edius's expression darkened, as it always did when Albie was mentioned. Gwen tilted her scarf-covered head slightly, sharp eyes flitting from Edius to Windley to me. Perceptive little thing.

"It will be a celebration of his life," I said fondly. "With mead. After all, a knight's greatest honor is to fall protecting his queen."

Rafe caught my eye briefly before slipping his gaze away.

No, I wasn't healed. Perhaps I never truly would be. Grief wasn't something you outran. But I was healing, and today at least, memories of Albie brought comfort rather than despair.

"What's your favorite food, milady?" Windley asked Gwen, deftly steering us back toward lighter topics.

"I'm partial to raspberries," she replied eagerly. "Or rather —raspberry-flavored anything, really."

"Excellent choice," he purred, absently rubbing the back of my hand against his cheek. "I'm sure there'll be raspberry-flavored tarts or other such nonsense at next year's lunar festival—assuming you'll still be around, that is."

Edius shot him a disdainful glance.

Not much longer, I thought.

Not much longer until his heart would be free to roam.

That night, I lay awake through the darkness, listening to the hushed crackle of flames, with Windley's warmth steady beside me. He'd guessed, without me having to say it, that this would be my final night donning the Crown of the Wood.

"Do you think you'll miss it?" he murmured, lips grazing my neck in sultry, intentional kisses.

I nearly said no, but that felt too abrupt. And really, when I thought about it—"A bit. I'll miss creating something from nothing. Perhaps I'll take up art. I paint like a drunken goose, but I could squabble about with a brush and see what happens."

His mouth trailed indulgently along my shoulder. "Well, if you need a model..."

"Let me guess—you're eager to get undressed?"

"Who said anything about undressing? I didn't mean a nude model, lewd queen."

The glint in his eyes said otherwise.

"And you?" I asked, my words soft as midnight air. "Will you miss it—having your girlfriend bonded to a goddess?"

"What, being unable to touch you without spiraling into a frenzy?" His fingers followed deliberately up my thighs. "Not. At. All. As I've told you before, I'd rather savor you properly— have some semblance of control. I fear I've lost my suave factor."

"Suave factor?" I meant it sarcastically, but it came out breathless, distracted by his hands poised dangerously at my hips. "One must first possess something in order to lose it."

His teeth flashed tight and predatory. "Careful. I still have a world of secrets, queenie. Ways to punish you. Ways to make you *beg*."

And I would come to know them all. In time.

We camped near an unnamed forest at the queendom's outskirts, where familiar stars glittered in the velvety night. Windley and I whispered and teased as the others slept, fire embers drifting toward the sky like sleepy fireflies.

I watched their slow ascent, patiently awaiting dawn.

And then it arrived—the first tender strokes of orange washing across the distant horizon. My skin prickled, inspiration swelling in my chest as daylight crept into the world.

"Alright," I whispered to Windley. "It's time."

I left him by the dying fire and stepped toward the rising sun, drawing crisp morning air into my lungs, bare feet chilled by dew-dampened grass. Each step resonated, rippling through existence as I carried the Crown of the Wood—the

Nemophile's Crown—with its invisible threads binding destruction to my mortal will.

Within my chest, Vita's warmth swirled like a glowing tide, Exitium's dark presence clawing restlessly at the edges of my awareness.

"All humes are bred from destruction. All things are made to be destroyed." Exitium's fallen voice slithered through me, cold and seductive, as I stood before the dawn. *"I've felt your blood-lust, Merrin. You crave power, and you'll find none greater than mine."*

"You're right—I do crave power," I said, my voice echoing with defiance. "But I crave it only so I can protect—even if that means protecting others from myself. Yours is not the power I want, Exitium. I reject it, and I reject you."

My fingers curled into white-knuckled fists, and I fixed my gaze on the horizon. Drawing the deepest breath I could, I sensed the reliable thrum of life beneath me, resonating through my bones. I let my mind wander far beyond, summoning images of Luna, Soleil, and the innumerable stars whose cosmic luminance had always sparked my wonder.

Then, I willed that vision into reality.

Windley shouted a warning behind me as a gale ripped outward from where I stood, toppling small trees and flinging loose earth in a swirling storm. Vita's energy cascaded through my veins like liquid starlight, and in front of me, matter began to coalesce: a colossal, onyx-hued orb, hovering just above the ground, reflecting the moonlight in ominous gleams. Castle-sized, it loomed with both grandeur and threat.

"Lion queen?! What in the hell is—"

But I shut my eyes, withdrawing into a space that felt like springtime dawn—a realm where the air held a subtle shimmer and the scent of fresh buds. I passed my fingertips through drifting motes of light until I found the diadem upon my head.

Lifting it free, I gazed at the crown's gemstones, blazing on one side like crystalline ice, and on the other like polished coal: a testament to the duality of creation and destruction.

The Nemophile's Crown.

Its weight settled heavily in my palms. So much power. So much possibility. And I was ready to let it go.

But there was just one problem.

"Vita?" I turned the crown slowly in my hands.

"Yes, Merrin?"

"How...do I actually do this?" I meant literally. "Breaking it won't help—it was broken before, and last time, I cast half of it away with Exitium."

"Observe the gemstones set into the prongs," Vita patiently instructed.

Two largest stones lay at its center—one radiant, one shadowy.

"To remove the stones is to sever our bonds."

Simple enough. "And after removal?"

"The Crown of the Wood will diminish swiftly. Act quickly to place us where you must, then cast the empty crown skyward. Feel it—in marrow and muscle. Desire it fully, and it shall be."

It was only then that the full weight of relinquishing the Crown struck me.

"Merrin? Your breath has been still too long," Vita said susurrantly.

"These are our last moments together, aren't they?"

Warmth—stronger and gentler than ever before—spread through me. *"No, little royal. Just as I am with you now, I will remain with you wherever you tread. You may not always understand my words, but you'll find my voice in crashing waves, whispering winds, in earth beneath your feet, and in every breath you take."*

But...that wasn't quite the same, was it?

Or perhaps it was.

Maybe there was love and life in all creation, if only one had ears to hear it clearly. Perhaps I'd simply been fortunate enough to truly listen.

Eyes moist, I returned to the mortal world, gem-less crown again atop my head, a lightstone in one hand and a darkstone in the other. Invisible yet tangible, creation and destruction strained eagerly in my grip.

I stepped toward the hovering mass, pressing my palm into its glassy surface and carving out a cavity with destructive force.

The invisible stone in my hand felt impossibly heavy.

There was a moment when my fingers refused to release it. A flash of weakness when I considered just what I was giving up.

Feel it—in marrow and muscle. Desire it fully, and it shall be.

But I knew, deep in my heart, the echoes were a burden. Exitium was a burden. And this world had no place for her.

With unsteady fingers, I set the stone into the cavity I'd created—mindful, as though placing a cracked egg—then sealed the opening as I withdrew my arm.

Immediately, I felt lighter, like releasing a breath I hadn't realized had long grown stale. It was startling how accustomed I'd become to the shadowy weight of Exitium staining my soul.

Vita's stone still clasped firmly in my palm, I willed the globe upward, larger, and higher it rose—expanding as it climbed. Like a great shard of obsidian mined from the darkest cavern, it glittered defiantly in the sunlight, ascending beyond Soleil, swelling until it loomed as vast as a city.

Vitality.

Mine was fading quickly, so I drew from the grass around my ankles, pulling energy from dying stalks until they browned and withered. Reaching farther still, I borrowed from the trees at my back, ushering them into an early winter slumber. They would live, but their leaves curled and greens faded as I gathered strength, determined to seal Exitium's fate.

Everyone else had roused by now, rattled by the surge of power that had collapsed the tent and doused the fire. I continued feeding the orb—Exitium's new astral cage—drawing life from beneath my feet, from deep roots and delicate stems, funneling the earth's heartbeat into the dark mass above.

Emerald radiance burst from my feet and raced to the far horizon—the lush hue of first creation. Grass bent low in wide, rippling rings as Vita's power rolled across the field. Overhead, the onyx sphere fattened, then began its slow ascent.

The air quaked. A hollow, canyon-deep rumble shook my bones—as though Exitium were clawing at the walls of her new cage. One last, thunderous pulse buckled the sky, made my heart falter.

Then came silence.

From the ground the sphere seemed to dwindle—not withering, but racing beyond mortal reach. Once past the rim of our realm it flashed like a newborn star, smaller than Soleil or Luna, a dark bruise on the noon-blue sky. Night would swallow it; day would reveal it again, a mute warning of the ruin sealed inside.

Legends would sprout around it, I was sure. Tales would swirl to explain the eerie new celestial body, because we few witnesses would never divulge its true purpose: a prison for a primordial ruin.

It was fascinating, really, how myths began.

With Exitium exiled to that distant darkness, I sank to my knees, still crowned by emerald light, and pressed my palms to the living earth. I was ready to sow the greatest seed of life. Yet my fingers hovered, and a familiar pang lanced through me—an ache that stung under my skin and gathered tears in the corners of my eyes.

"Vita?"

"*I am here, Merrin.*"

"I..." Words failed me, caught on the lump swelling in my throat.

A bell-like laugh swirled around me. "*Why do you despair, little royal? You have achieved our purpose. This sorrow is unnecessary.*"

I stared at my dirt-covered hand, refusing to let go of Vita's gemstone. "I don't want to lose someone else I hold dear," I choked out.

"*You have nothing to fear,*" Vita murmured tenderly. "*I will be with you until the end of your days. You have the strength. Let go.*"

I felt weak.

"*Let go, Merrin.*"

I felt small.

"*Let go.*"

Then, through the radiant jade of creation's glow, another voice came—wrinkled, gruff, achingly familiar:

"It's okay, My Queen."

A wizened hand slipped over mine, and the wiry tickle of a mustache pressed against my forehead.

"Just because you can't see someone doesn't mean they ain't there."

"A-Albie?!" My heart lurched. The brilliance flared, too intense, too overwhelming, and when it receded, I found myself alone. My palm lay open, Vita's gemstone gone, buried deep beneath the earth.

"*With you, steadfast daughter of the wood, my roots are content.*"

Slowly, shakily, I rose, wiping tears against my shoulder, my fingertips still trembling from the touch I was certain I'd felt. Gone were the powerful presences that had become a part of me, yet their light lingered inside.

My light remained.

I reached upward, removing a crown no one else could see, and with the last remnant of my Nemophilist's power, cast it skyward. I willed it to shatter and spread, forming an invisible veil to separate heaven from earth—an unbreachable barrier keeping the darkness forever at bay.

Emerald brilliance pulsed beneath me, weaving outward through a million roots. Restored fully, the goddess Vita flowed into seed and stem, returning herself to the very world she'd created.

Our task was complete.

Exitium was expelled.

And as I swayed on unsteady feet, vitality drained, I turned just in time to witness two figures collapse to the ground behind me.

Those born of predatory lineage clutched their chests, eyes wide, as the invisible chains binding their hearts finally fell away.

24

WILL YOU?

"See, now this—this is *so* much better."

At the edge of the Scarlet Wood, Windley was holding my hand and stroking my arm, admiring the feel of my skin now that it no longer hummed with divine energy—save for the faint traces naturally carried by royal blood.

It had been a day and a night since I'd released the Crown, and Ruckus had done a commendable job carrying me while I recovered my strength. Truly commendable—for he was the best boy.

Apparently, I'd always had a soft spot for the naughty ones. Speaking of which—

"Touch her, Ed. See how it feels." Windley offered up the hand he'd taken captive, then paused halfway. "Er, if that's all right with you, Merr?"

It was more than all right.

I was eager to see if Edius's feelings had shifted during the ride.

With cautious steps, like someone approaching a rabbit

caught in a trap, Edius moved closer, gently placing a fingertip against the plush of my cheek.

He frowned. "She still feels good."

"Well, yes, she's always felt good, but this is much more manageable." Windley swatted Ed's hand away, replacing it with both of his, squishing my cheeks between them.

"I am a queen, I'll have you know."

Both men erupted into snorts, my words thoroughly distorted by my squished face.

Even Rafe released a quiet chuckle from atop his stag, where he'd taken a turn holding a sleeping Gwen securely in his arms. He quickly cleared his throat when my stare turned lupine.

I elbowed intrusive Windley away. "Out of my way, pinkie."

"Aw, it's pink again?" he asked, straining unsuccessfully to glance upward. He muttered to himself, "Why's it always pink?"

In truth, it was green—but that could remain my little secret.

The wistful rustling of leaves surrounded us, whispers from a forest painted stark white and crimson flame. I stepped toward Edius, placing my palm softly against his chest. Beneath my hand, his heartbeat quickened—not from magic, but from something infinitely more human.

"Do you feel different, Edi?"

His gaze, ancient yet vulnerable, captured mine. "Different, highness?"

"About me?"

His eyes dropped slightly, voice roughening. "I still like you, if that's what you're asking."

Not quite the answer I'd hoped for.

I stepped closer, slipping my arms around his waist and

resting my head against his chest. I waited, knowing Edius wouldn't be able to resist drawing me nearer—it was a cruel experiment, perhaps, but necessary.

As expected, his arms enfolded me in a fierce, protective embrace, his voice dipping low. "What's this about, Merrín? I'm always happy to hold you, but your boyfriend's right there."

Yet his hand coasted up my back, settling as he melted beneath the familiar comfort.

"So damn good," he murmured into my hair.

Warmth. Safety. Protection.

Whoever captured his heart next would be incredibly lucky.

"Concentrate, Edi. Beyond how it feels physically. When you hold me now, do your feelings seem...different?"

His breath faltered against me, restraint evident in every tense muscle. "It...does feel different."

Carefully, he eased back to see my face clearly, his brow creased with confusion. "What'd you do?"

Relief flooded me.

Thank goddess. Yes, *that* goddess.

"What?" Windley's curious face suddenly appeared between us. "What's it feel like, Ed?"

Edi rubbed thoughtfully at his chest. "Before, it stretched forever—endless, unchangeable. But now it feels...closer. Like it's finally allowed to shift."

Windley scrunched his nose. "'Allowed to shift?' What the fuck does that mean? Let me try."

Without waiting for permission, Windley swept me up, pressing me playfully against his chest. He dipped his face into my neck, teeth grazing my skin. "Yup, still delicious."

"W-Windley, focus."

He let out a quiet, rueful huff, closed his eyes, and after a pause, shrugged. "I don't feel any different, darling."

Sweet relief washed through me again, milder this time. I cupped his cheek, words meant for his ears alone. "I asked Vita to break the Spirite curse altogether—every heart unchained. That means the ties holding *your* heart, and Edi's, to mine are gone. You're free to love more than once now."

Windley jerked away in immediate panic. "What? Merrin, why would you do that?"

I offered a comforting chuckle at his desperation. "Just because you can love more than once doesn't mean you will. Humans can love many times, but I've only loved once."

Windley opened his mouth, ready to protest again, but another quiet voice interrupted him.

"Me too." Rafe stood calm, his expression quietly certain. "I've only loved once, too."

Windley visibly deflated, his panic giving way to understanding. "Well, good. Because I don't want anyone else either —ever."

My fingertips brushed his chin, tilting his gaze up to mine. "We'll care for it together—this wild thing we've grown."

Because even monsters deserved nurturing.

Edius watched quietly, thoughtful and subdued.

I returned to him with careful grace. "Do you understand, Edi? I may be your first love, but I won't be your last. Your heart will heal, and someday, someone else will claim it—and it won't hurt this badly again."

Wind rustled the fiery branches above, showering us with vibrant leaves. Edius looked stricken, disbelief raw in his gaze. "You...did that for me?" he asked, the words rasping out low and rough. "You could've had anything, and you chose this—for me?"

"It wasn't just for you," I replied, my words wrapped in quiet earnestness. "But you inspired it. And I hope now you'll consider our proposal to come to the queenlands. The Crag could use a knight like you. Our family has space for you and Gwen, whenever you're ready."

Edius swallowed, turning his head so his hair veiled his expression. "I reckon...we could manage a visit."

"At least," Windley added warmly, looping an affectionate arm around him.

My hand settled welcomingly on Edius's shoulder. "Even if it's only ever visits, you'll always belong with us, Edi. You're family now."

He cleared his throat, still not quite meeting my gaze. "Thanks, highness. For, uh—everything. Especially for letting me ambush you back in those woods."

That quiet admission carried the weight of every unspoken sentiment. For Edius, it was more than enough.

And though it's been many, many years since those days—and though Edius has come and gone and come again—the Queendom of the Crag remains, and will always remain, his home.

At the edge of the wood, we turned toward the coast—most of us, anyway. Rafe dismounted, easing the sleeping Gwen into Edius's waiting arms before offering me his deepest bow.

"Have a good visit, Rafe," I murmured, lungs already tightening. "And give Beau my love. When you return, it shall be to retrieve your release papers, yes?"

I hadn't meant for it to happen, but the tears slipped free anyway.

"Y-Your Majesty?" Rafe stammered—a rare slip. "Geez, Merrin, I'll be back in a week."

"I know!" I turned away, briefly burying my face into my cloak. "But I'm thinking about after. We'll hardly see you at all!"

"You hardly saw me before," he pointed out dryly.

True enough. He'd done everything possible to avoid the throne room.

"Treat Queen Beau right, chap," Windley chimed cheerfully. "Remember to let her have the good side of the bed."

Rafe rolled his eyes extravagantly. "I don't need relationship advice from you."

Windley's grin only widened. "Eh, you'll be back for tips soon enough—once you're ready to spice things up."

Rafe swatted him away—something he'd done many times and would surely do many more. But as the grumpy magician remounted his stag, drawing around his shoulders the cloak of a queendom that was no longer his, his expression softened. "I meant what I said in the labyrinth, Your Majesty. I hope you consider it."

It would be a shame. Your people like you, and...the Crag would mourn your leaving.

"Thank you, Rafe. I'll keep your advice close."

In truth, my decision had already been made, after carefully considering his words.

"Oh, hell," he sighed upon catching sight of my watery eyes again. "Your Majesty, I'll see you in a week."

"Tootles, chap!" Windley sang, wiggling his fingers.

Rafe exchanged a tired nod with Edius—a bond born of shared annoyance, destined to bloom into grudging warmth. Windley and I had that effect on people.

As hoofbeats faded westward, the three of us turned toward

a home I both missed and dreaded, a place where my heart had fractured between duty and desire.

"Oi, Ed," Windley broke the silence, "mind if the queen and I step away a minute before we head out?"

Ed adjusted Gwen with careful ease against his chest. "Long as you don't run off with her. I don't know anyone else up here, and I don't have a map. If you're gonna fuck, make it fast."

He still wore his braids.

Windley pawed playfully at him. "Ah, come now—I'm not the sort foolish enough to run off with a *queen*."

Precisely the sort he was.

Before anyone could argue otherwise, Windley looped his arm through mine and whisked me off into a wood we'd walked many times before—though never with my veins humming quite like this.

To find myself alone with a predator—a loving, supportive, devastatingly seductive predator—was a swoon-worthy sensation indeed.

Windley spoke not a word as he led me deeper, feet crunching pleasantly over brittle, auburn leaves. He scanned the trees with thoughtful precision.

"What are you looking for, Wind?" I finally asked, my curiosity overwhelming me.

Still silent, he stopped abruptly, positioning me carefully between two pale, peeling trunks. He stepped back, studied me with narrowed eyes, then shook his head and moved me along again. He repeated the process a second time, then a third.

By the fourth attempt, my patience snapped.

"What exactly are you doing, Windley? Are you trying to get us lost? Do you even know how to return to the others?"

"Of course I do," he replied breezily. "They're back that way—I can smell them." He gestured vaguely behind us, then guided me in a completely different direction. Perhaps he really did intend to steal me away.

I would remember it clearly...

Every detail etched itself into my memory: the woody scent of the forest, the brittle snap beneath our feet, the sharp, fresh bite of autumn air, and the overhead sky, gray and heavy as smoke.

We were filthy—my hair tangled with twigs and scattered leaves, Windley's pants torn, his face sun- and wind-burnt.

It was on the sixth attempt at positioning me that his expression transformed. This time, when he stepped back to study me, a wild, victorious grin lit his face—so bright I turned instinctively to see what had caught his eye.

It was breathtaking: fiery branches framed against pale trunks, vibrant and defiant against the muted sky. If he'd been searching for the forest's most romantic vista, he'd found it.

When I turned back, Windley was already down on one knee.

Not the kneel of a knight bound by duty, but something deeper—unguarded, heartfelt. Vulnerable. Hopeful.

Waiting.

"It wasn't finished the last time I asked," he began, his voice carrying a dusk-warm resonance, hair shimmering scarlet like the surrounding trees, eyes glinting emerald in the muted daylight.

Balanced between two fingers was a small wooden ring.

"I've been working on it forever," he admitted, words rough-edged yet tempered-warm. "It's from that tree—the one you blighted back in the Emerald Wood. I knew it hurt you to do it, so I thought perhaps we could give the wood a new life. Oh—but don't worry, it's not blighted. I took it from a branch that had already fallen." He paused, swallowing nervously, before continuing. "I...made this for you, Merr, and—"

I laid a hand against my heart, breath caught. "Windley—"

"Wait, darling," he broke in, a plea shining in his eyes. "Let me finish properly, alright? Even if you say no, I need to ask you like this."

I nodded, unable to speak.

"I'm not a clean man, Queen Merrin," he went on, his words gaining steady weight, "but you've never once made me feel unworthy. You were my first friend in the realms—the first to see worth in me until I could see it myself. You're fierce, fearless, endlessly generous, and you make me reach for the better version of who I could be. Loving you has been the simplest, surest thing I've ever done."

He blew out a quick breath, a hushed, nervous laugh slipping after it.

"I love you more than I know how to say, Merr. The day you told me you loved me back—I replay it every night. After feeling your heart in my hands, I never want to let it go. I understand the limits: you can't marry me in the royal chapel, I can't give you heirs, and this may be madness to even ask. But I have to. Loving your best friend—and being loved by them— might be the greatest magic there is."

It truly was.

"I'll never stand between you and your crown," he promised, a tender ache in his smile. "I won't make you choose me over your queendom. Hide me, parade me, love me only when we're far from court—whatever keeps your burdens light. Just...don't stop loving me. Bound heart or free, you're inked into my veins."

He drew a breath, held out the ring.

"So, queenie—" a nervous laugh escaped—"I'm braced for a no, but I have to ask: will you marry me, Merrin?"

Madness? Perhaps.

But I had always believed our world was vast enough for impossible dreams.

The answer spilled out, bright and certain. "Yes, Windley—I'll marry you. But only if it's for real."

"I-I... What?" His hair flashed a jubilant fuchsia—irrefutable proof of his shock. "Say that again, queenie—just to be sure I heard right?"

"I said yes, Windley," I laughed joyously. "I'll marry you, and it will count in every way possible."

He stared up at me, face slack with the sweetest disbelief.

"But I'm not giving up my crown," I added firmly, "nor will I hide you away. I love and respect my people, so they deserve to choose. I will tell them the truth of my heart, and they may take me as I am—or name another ruler."

"Merrin, that's—"

"I love you," I interrupted, my voice clear, steady, resolute. "And I would give up everything to have you. So what will you do about it?"

What indeed?

Under that gray autumn sky, amidst trees of flame and frost, he swept me into his arms and kissed me ardently—deeply—and somewhere in that heated embrace, the wooden ring found its way home upon my finger, exactly where it belonged.

25

ALL THE COLORS

This place was beautiful.

The waves glittered like gemstones beneath a sapphire sky, clear enough to glimpse the crystalline coral dotting the shallows and shaped by the gentle tides. The Crystal Sea. Albie's homeland. A place he'd always wanted to show me.

I stood at the water's edge, breathing in the sweet scent of spring air. Funny, wasn't it? How each season tasted a little different. This spring had thawed swiftly, following a winter that was far too busy.

"Here you go, my queen."

Windley rose from the sand, pants cuffed at his calves, shirt fluttering loosely in the breeze, hair a dazzling shade of blue. He placed something delicate in my palm—a cluster of coral, weathered and softened by the waves—before resting his elbow atop my shoulder, a habit he seemed to favor more by the day.

"Goddess, it's pretty here. Just look at those clouds, Merr! Damned if they don't show every color."

He was right. The sky boasted every color, reminding me of Soleil's ethereal domain, of those sunsets I'd always loved—and of Windley's ever-changing hair.

"Thank you for humoring me, Windley. I know it was a long journey."

"Eh, where the queen wants to honeymoon, the queen honeymoons." He dipped lower, scrutinizing me with a sparkle in his eyes. "But are you certain you're holding up okay? I know you worried about how it might feel being here."

I drew a hand to the pendant at my chest. "Just because you can't see someone doesn't mean they aren't with you." I let the words drift, soft as the waves. "I feel him here. And it isn't a bad thing."

Windley sniffed theatrically. "That's unsettling. Are you telling me Sir Albie sees everything I do to you behind closed doors? Because I'm certain he wouldn't approve of that. Or *that*. Or that other thing—"

I silenced him with a kiss—my charming, irrepressible rogue of a husband.

Smiling against my lips, he traced a finger along the pendant at my throat, then down to the matching one resting against his own chest—the one I'd given him on our wedding day.

"I've made up my mind, once and for all," I told him.

He jolted in surprise. "You have?"

"I don't want to know."

He groaned in mock distress. "Really? I thought you said you *did* want to know. Do you realize how hard it'll be to carry this secret around?"

"I imagine it won't be hard at all. You, my love, are an excellent keeper of secrets."

"Flattery will get you everywhere, little minx." He flicked

my nose playfully. "Fine. But if you ever change your mind, you know where to find me."

But I wouldn't change my mind. I'd never know for sure if Albie was my father by blood, but he was my father in every way that mattered. And that was enough.

A breeze stirred softly, spinning tiny flecks of sand around us.

"You know—" Windley leaned his elbow against my shoulder again. "I don't think it's normal to bring your friends on a honeymoon." He cast a glance over his shoulder to where Beau relaxed beneath an umbrella beside her newest magical guard, and where Edius helped Gwen construct an increasingly ambitious sandcastle. "Especially when said friends are about to pop."

True, Beau was looking particularly round these days.

"Come now, I'm more than happy to share our holiday. They've been through plenty too."

Windley sighed. "I suppose I should be glad they let you out at all. The court's demand for you has only grown since we returned."

"That tends to happen when a queen vanishes for weeks on end. Mother Poppy still checks my chambers nightly."

"I know." Windley pouted theatrically. "Wakes me every fucking time." He tightened his grip around my shoulders. "Perhaps we should just keep heading north, give them all a proper scare." His voice dropped to a teasing whisper. "I've thought about it often—stealing you away someplace no one could ever find you. Claiming you as my own..." His lips brushed warmly against my ear. "No one ever has to know."

But he knew me better than that.

"Kidding." He released me with another dramatic sigh. "You did, after all, explicitly forbid me from stealing you in our wedding vows. Do you realize how difficult that was for me? Goes against every instinct I have."

A giggle drifted over from Beau's umbrella.

"Yeah, yeah, laugh it up, Queen Beau," Windley called back with a playful scowl. Under his breath, he muttered, "You won't be laughing when I steal the queen for real."

And truly, he wore the gleam of a devil.

Nearby, Gwen laughed brightly, settled happily into her new role as the castle medic. And Edius? He was smiling. Freely, unguardedly, without hesitation. How it warmed my heart.

When he caught me watching, something flickered briefly across his face—a shadow of pain, a lingering thread of love not yet fully faded. But I believed, deeply, that it would fade. And indeed, it vanished quickly, replaced by his signature smirk.

"Got something in your hair, Merrín!" he shouted, cupping hands around his mouth.

"Excuse *you*," Windley shot back. "It's a mane." He reached into my curls, plucked out a long black feather, then straightened abruptly in alarm. "A widowbird?!" He spun frantically, scanning the skies. "Where the hell is it? I swear to goddess, if one of those damned things followed us here—"

I smirked. "Psh. An incubus afraid of a measly bird?" I poked him squarely in the forehead. "What's that phrase you always use? Dull in the wits?"

Windley's scowl deepened. "Those creatures are demons," he grumbled, eyes still warily sweeping the sky. Then he narrowed his gaze suspiciously at me. "Wait. You didn't sneak that feather here from home, did you? Goddess, Merr, did you plant it just to mess with me?"

Of course I hadn't. But I wasn't about to admit that.

Laughter and gentle bickering carried us through most of the day, and when nightfall settled, I stood quietly at the shore, embraced by the cool kiss of an awakened breeze, watching starlight shimmer across the crystal waves.

And I felt happy.

I was lucky to have lived the life I had. Lucky to have loved as fiercely as I had.

Surrounded by memories—of those still with me, and those gone but never forgotten.

EPILOGUE: WITH ALL MY LOVE

One of the greatest lessons I learned during my time as the Nemophilist is that friendship can be found in the least likely of places. The lines between villain and hero, friend and foe, rival and ally—they're rarely as straight as we think. There is merit to be found in even the darkest of places, and sometimes, light and warmth are hidden behind only the thinnest of shrouds.

You may not believe me, but to this day, Sestilia remains one of my closest friends. I visit her each year on her birthday, though no longer as Queen of the Cove—you didn't think we'd let someone like her keep her throne, did you? Fear had ruled the Cove for too long, but fear is a weak tether on its own, and with the right nudges—some external, some internal—those chains loosened. The people did not resist when the time came, and to our surprise, neither did she. Perhaps she had been waiting for someone to finally tell her it was time to let go. And truly, losing her title was for her own good. Her healing could only begin once she was freed from the chains that held her there.

As it turns out, that kind, beloved sister of hers, the one

whose untimely demise left a queendom grieving? Not so kind. But, like so many stories, that one isn't mine to tell.

And then there's Flora. Beautiful, warm, honey-voiced Flora. Hard to believe I ever thought of her as a threat. There is no kinder soul than lovely Meraflora's. If you're wondering, yes—she's visited the northlands more than once. And Edius? Well, let's just say he visits her quite often.

As for Windley and me, we went on to adopt a swarm of ill-mannered children—two of whom you've already met—and the castle of the Crag became known as a place of laughter and life. None of our children would bear a crown, and I was glad for it. They were free to forge their own fates, and really, there's no shortage of royals to take my place when I go.

Perhaps fate had always intended it this way—perhaps I'd always been meant to be the one to turn the tide. The Spirites call it "wyrdbound"—as though destiny itself pulls two souls together, intertwining their paths forever. If that's true, then my wyrdbound one found me in a tenderhearted beastling who'd been trying to steal me from day one—and, in the end, I was all too willing to be stolen.

The years passed, and though Windley's heart was unchained, it never wavered. Love, I've come to understand, matures, evolves, and deepens—much like we do. For Windley and me, our joy was abundant, and our days were long.

And always, in the distant sky, the obsidian orb hung—a reminder of battles fought, promises kept, and the darkness we overcame.

But if I'm being honest, that orb would see more action before the end of my life, though that journey would not be mine to take. Rather, it would fall to a pair of twin girls—one born with the power of the sun, the other with the power of the moon—who would rise to fulfill a prophecy none of us yet knew.

But that story, while quite interesting, isn't one for me to tell either.

And we're nearly out of time.

So—what did you think? Have I kept all my promises? Are there mysteries left unsolved? I'm sure there must be one or two. But, like most of you, I'm only human.

I'm grateful to have spent this time with you, to have had a reason to put it all down into words. Stories are best told by firelight, and even better told to willing ears—pointed or not.

So, thank you, captive ones, for listening. For getting to know me. For letting me bare my saga.

This Saga of the Crown.

It is so very important to share the stories that shape us.

I, the Great and Mighty Merrin—an of-the-people, for-the-people type, or so I try to be—wish you many adventures of your own, friendships that are full, and a love that enflames your soul.

With all my love,

Merrin